BLUSH

"You must believe me when I tell you that I love you, Sarah, and would do nothing to hurt you. I love your fire, your drive, and your stubborn determination. If you'd just let down that wall you keep up between us, I'd be able to show you."

"Don't try to get around me by speaking of love at a time like this, Bryan Carson," Sarah fumed, barely able to maintain her anger at his unexpected confession. "How can I ever trust the man who took over my company? You ask too much of me, Bryan."

"Sarah, look at me," he said, taking her fragile shoulders in his strong hands. "Won't you ever let me come near you? How long do you plan to keep me away?" His fingers turned her face up to his as he searched her eyes for an answer.

"Bryan, I . . ."

He did not wait for her to finish. His mouth closed over hers in a deep penetrating kiss.

ENJOY THESE SPECIAL
ARABESQUE HOLIDAY ROMANCES

HOLIDAY CHEER   (0-7860-0210-7, $4.99)
by Rochelle Alers, Angela Benson,
and Shirley Hailstock

A MOTHER'S LOVE   (0-7860-0269-7, $4.99)
by Francine Craft, Bette Ford,
and Mildred Riley

SPIRIT OF THE SEASON   (0-7860-0077-5, $4.99)
by Donna Hill, Francis Ray,
and Margie Walker

A VALENTINE KISS   (0-7860-0237-9, $4.99)
by Carla Fredd, Brenda Jackson,
and Felicia Mason

BLUSH

Courtni Wright

Pinnacle Books
Kensington Publishing Corp.

http://www.pinnaclebooks.com

To my father with love and appreciation.

Chapter One

"I won't do it!" Sarah Tillings fumed to her assistant, Holly, as she stood at the window with her back to downtown Dallas. "I won't work for that man. Tillings Industries is my company. My father and mother built it and managed it. The company is mine now, and I won't do it. That's all there is to it." She fell into the soft leather of the chair behind her desk. Her red lips puckered into a pout. Her usually gold eyes smoldered a threatening amber. Every nerve of her trim body tightened in anticipation of battle. Her soft brown skin flushed with anger. It had been her father's desk. Now, it would be *his* if he wanted that, too. As controlling partner owning fifty-one percent of the cosmetics company, he, Bryan Carson, could have anything he wanted. Sarah wondered what that would include and how long before she felt the sting of his demands.

"Sarah, you have no choice. You tried to fight him, but he won. You tried to get everyone you knew to rally behind you. You played every trick in the financial and corporate book. He had more leverage, more money, and stronger backers. The fight is over. He played better than you. It's time you faced facts,'' Holly counseled.

''I wonder if my being a woman had anything to do with it. Would he have been so quick to take over a man's company? I bet a man could have secured the last-minute financing I needed until the new fragrance could be announced,'' Sarah snorted contemptuously. She knew how some investors and bankers still felt about a woman running a major company. They still thought that a woman's place was in the house, not the board room.

Holly shook her head sadly. She had been Sarah's assistant for the last five years, ever since she had inherited the company when her father died. Before coming to work for Sarah, Holly had been her college roommate. They were best friends, although quite different. She was not as strikingly beautiful as Sarah. She did not have Sarah's sparkling gold eyes, accented by coal-black lashes, curled dark-brown shoulder-length hair, and soft reddish-brown skin, but her warm brown skin tones and large deep-brown eyes perfectly complemented her trim runner's figure. Unlike Sarah, whose temper often flared and whose comments had a tendency to be biting, she possessed a quick mind that easily grasped figures and marketing concepts and a gentle wit that made everyone feel comfortable around her. They had had such great times together in college. They loved to take ski trips together or travel to the beach. Sometimes they had even accompanied Sarah's parents to exotic spots like Morocco or Turkey, where they had spent hours shopping in bazaars and trying on jewelry.

Of course, all of that had stopped when her finances had taken a turn for the worse after her parents' death in a car crash. When Sarah offered her a job as her special assistant, she quickly accepted. The offer had not been charity. Sarah knew that Holly's skills would be helpful at Tillings, and she looked forward to having her best friend with her again. Sarah had hoped that they could relive the old days. But the requirements of their jobs had kept both of them too busy for play time to return to their lives.

Seeing Sarah so distressed, Holly only wished she had the ability to help her, now that she was in need. She understood Sarah's pain, but she knew the reality, too. Sarah was out as the controlling force behind Tillings Industries, and *he* was in.

Holly knew there was nothing Sarah could do but accept the fact that things were going to be different from now on. She needed to get on with life and the running of Tillings Industries as best she could when Bryan Carson took over. With any luck at all, he might leave the day-to-day operation to her and concentrate on the financial end of the business. Better still, he might be an absentee partner and leave everything to her. She would have to wait and see. Today's meeting should answer all of her questions.

All of Dallas had whispered about and speculated on the future of Tillings Industries, the prominent black-owned cosmetics and perfume company, ever since the death of Sarah's mother Grace from cancer. She and Martin had worked hand-in-hand to create the great empire. When her father became too grief-stricken to run the company, the sympathic muttering turned to cries of discontent. Martin fell into a deep depression when she was no longer there to advise him. It was almost as if his right arm had been severed. His drive and energy vanished. She had given him a focus. Together, they had built an empire. He often failed to report to work, leaving the running of Tillings to the department managers: capable men, but lacking in the big-picture vision necessary to sustain a thriving company. He lost interest in everything and, for a while, everyone. Mostly, he sat and stared out the window of his magnificent office. He would not take comfort in anything he had created. He appeared not to notice even when Sarah tried to cheer him with stories of her adventures. He could not shake the toll that Grace's death had levied on his mind and spirit.

As he slowly recovered, he found himself in the arms of

another woman, the former Mildred Banning, whose charms distracted him from the business. The voices became loud with anger and said that she had bewitched him with her beauty and her exciting ways. Martin and Grace had known her from their fun-loving countryclub days. He had played golf on a regular basis with her husband. She had dined regularly at their home. She had appeared to be almost as involved in her husband's business as Grace had been in Tillings. She had attended fashion shows and worked on charitable causes with Grace. He thought that when the lovely widow extended her hand to the lonely widower she would be another Grace, and that she would love the company as much as he did. She appeared kind, loving, interested in his troubles and in Tillings. She listened as he talked for hours about Grace and the plans they shared to make the company into a bright future for Sarah. She consoled him when his spirits hit rock bottom. Her presence buoyed him up and, after a while, made him feel alive again. Although she never suggested that he return to the management of the firm, she did coax him back into the world of the living, through fabulous vacations, and parties populated by the most interesting and exciting of people.

Always a home-loving man, Martin found himself in a whirlwind of excitement. They danced away the night in Dallas's fabulous clubs, on the Riviera, and in Monte Carlo. They bought opening-night tickets for plays in New York and in London. They dined by candlelight in Paris and San Francisco. They sunned and swam in Acapulco and Portofino. He purchased the jet and employed a pilot to fly them everywhere they wanted to go. He tore through the countryside in a red Ferrari with Mildred at his side.

A conservative, fashionable dresser, he listened to Mildred's advice on clothing, and added more color and flash to his wardrobe. He became a devout wearer of Armani. He bought a diamond pinkie ring and a studded money clip. He wore rakish hats tipped over one eye and carried a gold-handled cane. He became someone his friends and business associates did not recognize. Gradually, they stopped inviting him to their social functions because they thought he would be bored with their simple pleasures. He was cut off from everyone who had once known Grace and him. He traveled only in Mildred's world.

He became self-possessed and interested in no one but the glamorous and exciting Mildred and the life of excitement she gave him. Martin would listen to none of his closest advisors, who suggested that he turn over the reins of the Tillings empire to Sarah. He still saw her as a child, even though she was certainly well-prepared to step into his shoes. Mildred said that the company could run itself until he finally wanted to settle down again. She said the company did not need Sarah's help to stay afloat. She even suggested that Sarah might attempt to lock him out when he did try to return. She hated Sarah's beauty and brains, and was jealous of the love Martin had for her. She put as much distance between them as possible.

At first Martin resisted this final change to his life. He missed the companionship of his only daughter, their long conversations, and their dreams. Mildred convinced him that Sarah only pulled him down. She was a reminder of the old life, the days of hard work and long hours, the months of planning and worry before the announcement of a new product. Sarah and Tillings Industries had made him an old man before his time. Mildred had restored his youth and carefree living. So, after a while, the lure of the parties, the excitement of the theater and its lively people, the smell of the money-laden gambling tables and the horse races, and the pleasurable feeling of being admired by a woman as alive and vivacious as Mildred made him forget even his devotion to Sarah. She became part of his old life, along with Tillings and his hazy memories of Grace and hard work.

And then, one day while on a trip to Rio, he married Mildred. With that final step, the downward spiral was complete. His closest advisors had seen the rapid downturn of the Tillings empire, but Sarah had refused to face what was happening under her father's lack-luster management. She wanted to believe that everything was the same as it had been when her mother was alive and Martin was still vital and interested in more than having a good time. She blamed the changes on her new step-mother rather than on her father. There was nothing Sarah could have done even if she had been able to speak with him. Mildred had all but poisoned his mind against her and the company, claiming that both held him back and kept him from enjoying life. After all, he had given most of his adult life to building an empire. Surely he deserved a break. The company, his daughter, and Grace had drained him of his energy and manhood. Mildred had allowed him to be the kind of risk-taking daredevil that all men dream of being, but few are brave enough to become.

Martin forgot the dream he had shared with Grace of leaving a legacy for Sarah so that she would never encounter the glass ceiling faced by other women, or the discrimination in the work force that foiled the plans for success of so many African-American people. Gone was the plan of passing on the reins of a financially healthy Tillings Industries to her. In his new frame of mind, he forgot that no one argued with the color of money and that it was the greatest leveler and the supreme equalizer. He was too busy spending it to remember the time when he had none. He lost sight of the fact that money, position, and power are essential for an African-American woman. He did not remember the years of building that base. Without any one of the three, Sarah would be at the mercy of bigotry and prejudice. He took everything, except the pursuit of fun, for granted.

When he died and Sarah took the helm, Dallas gave her a chance to revive the business. She sought help from everyone she could. She borrowed from all possible sources and brought out new products as fast as the plant could manufacture them.

But nothing worked to stop the downward spiral her father had set in motion. Finally, time worked against her. Everyone knew what Sarah refused to accept. A takeover was inevitable.

The Board of Directors met for weeks before deciding to accept Bryan Carson's offer to purchase controlling interest. Since its creation more than thirty years ago, no outsider had governed Tillings. Her parents' dream had been for her to inherit a thriving company that would make her financially secure and independent all her life. Even when they decided to trade it on the New York Stock Exchange, they worked hard to keep the intimate feel in the business, the family touch. Everyone said Tillings Industries felt just like home. From the upper level management on the thirtieth floor to the mail room on the ground floor, everyone was happy.

But now the future of the company rested in a deal that left a bad taste in everyone's mouth. No other choice existed but to sell fifty-one percent of the company if it were to recover and become prosperous once more. Anything else would not give them enough financial leverage to satisfy the stock market, to save the financial ratings, or to open new avenues of much-needed cash flow. Tillings Industries needed Byran Carson's money. She was forced to eat her pride, but she did not like it.

Martin's death in a fiery crash during a car race five years ago had left Sarah with a crippled company and unbelievable debt. She worked hard to undo the years of damage, but every success brought new failure as she discovered more areas of her father's neglect. No department had been spared his inattention.

Sarah and many of her executive-level officers had been very worried when she could not fend off the take-over. What would the new partner bring to Tillings Industries? Would Sarah's role in her father's company diminish? Would the ''glass ceiling'' imposed on women at other companies become a reality at Tillings, too? Would she carry a title as the Tillings' heir, but have none of the responsibility for the operation of the company? What would this new partner want to change? What would he take away? Would Tillings have the family feel of Martin's day? It had always been, until recently, a profitable, multi-million dollar enterprise that cared about its employees. Would that level of concern continue?

So many questions. Today, some of the answers would be forthcoming. Bryan Carson was due to arrive at 10:00 for his first day at the helm of Tillings Industries.

"What would my father say if he knew? I should have seen the take-over coming. I've failed him, and I've failed this company. We were ripe for it. Here we sat, a once-profitable, long-established company, in trouble and under the leadership of a young black female. I should have done anything to save it. But, no, I was too busy being Madam Executive to read the fine print. So much for the value of my high-priced MBA," she groaned, hiding her face in her hands. She would not let herself cry. She would never stop if she started.

"You're being too hard on yourself. You simply ran out of places to turn. That's all. Remember, you didn't put Tillings Industries in this mess . . . your father did," Holly added softly. She knew the mention of her father's weakness as a manager was a tender point of discussion with Sarah, who blamed his failures on Mildred.

"That's small consolation at a time like this. Besides, it wasn't entirely his fault. That wife of his certainly did her part to ruin us. I still should have been able to stop this takeover, even if Daddy couldn't manage his wife. I've had five years to turn around our finances. I just could never get ahead. There was always one more area that needed attention, one more repair. We simply were not financially sound enough to support all that needed to be done to make Tillings Industries successful once again."

Sarah looked around the mahogany-paneled office. Every inch of this company had her father and mother's stamp on it. They had designed the concentric circle pattern in the soft mauve carpet, flown to South America to select the mahogany for the paneling, and worked with the decorator to match the fabrics and leathers on every sofa and chair that filled the thirty-story office tower complex. They had even hand picked the gold faucets in the bathroom. No detail had been too small. No expense had been spared. At the grand opening of the building, her parents had made sure that flowers filled every office, lobby, and elevator. Gifts of fragrance samples were handed out at the door by perfumed men and women in elegant evening clothes.

Stroking Sarah's dark-brown shoulder-length hair, Holly advised, ''Your father would be proud of you. You couldn't foresee the take-over. You did everything you could, short of selling yourself. You know he wouldn't have wanted you to do that. He wouldn't have wanted you to sacrifice your principles, even for his beloved company. You know how he felt about honor and integrity. Even after Mildred's influence, he held those principles even higher than his love of Tillings. You have to hold on to what you have left of your legacy. Remember, you're still a partner. Bryan Carson may have controlling interest, but he doesn't own Tillings Industries alone, you know.''

Slamming her fist on the desk, Sarah, walked to the window, saying, ''I should have done anything, including selling myself to that man, to keep him from gaining control. I know that Daddy had strong principles, but he would have and probably did sell himself many times to keep us solvent when my mother and the dream were alive. At the very least I should have begged my stepmother to help me keep Bryan Carson out of the business. But it all happened too fast, and she wouldn't have helped me anyway. She'd like to see the company bought out lock, stock, and barrel. That would drive the value of her stock sky high. She'd sell out in a heartbeat for the right price. You know, that's what worries me the most. What if he finds out that we're really not one big happy family here? What if he finds out that Mildred would sell me into slavery if she thought she could rid herself of the Tillings Industries connection forever? We'll have to keep him buried in the stories of the good old days and not let him learn about the here and now.''

''I don't think that's possible. The newspaper painted him as a pretty savvy guy. But we can try,'' Holly interjected. In the years they had worked together, Holly's level head and sound judgment had helped Sarah over many rough times. Sarah confided in her assistant about everything . . . personal and professional. There were no secrets between these two best friends.

Sarah barely heard Holly's comment as she thought about all her father's questionable business relationships, disguised under layers of paint, soft leather upholstery, crystal stemware, and congenial dinner parties. She wondered if Bryan Carson had uncovered all of them when he researched the company. She remembered stories she had heard over the years about some of her father's business connections. She was sure that more than one of them had been quite unsavory. Her mother had not welcomed some of them into their home. He said that all business had its layer of grime and odor, even the cosmetics industry.

She thought that her father had a penchant for attracting people of questionable character. Take her stepmother, Mildred, for instance. Mildred was from one of the best families in Dallas. She knew how to entertain everyone from the nobility to gardeners. Her parents often admired her business sense, as well as her feel for style, but wondered if she ever showed any true warmth without first calculating the return from her effort. She was so unlike Sarah's gentle mother, who always placed the needs of others before her own. The loneliness and despair after Grace's death were the only things that could have driven him to Mildred's arms—that and the adventures she promised.

Sarah looked out the window at the sprawling town below. From the thirtieth floor on this clear day, she could see the whole town spread before her. At one time, when her father had first supervised the construction of this building and had moved into the penthouse suite, he had had influence over all he could see from this same window. One way or the other, it had all belonged to him. He knew all the right politicians and the most accessible bankers. He was invited to the best parties at the most highly respected homes and country clubs. For a black business man, he did pretty well for himself. No doors were closed to him.

Peering out at her city, Sarah remembered a story from her childhood; her father had told it to her one day during the happy times when her mother was still alive. She was home from college on winter break. The three of them had been sitting in their living room. He stood beside the roaring fire with a glass of red wine in his hand. Her mother sat on the sofa next to her. He spoke about the time, when she was about five years old, that they had been invited to the Rolling Hills Country Club by Jason Parson, the town's most respected banker and her father's friend. Her parents were millionaires many times over by then, but her father was still nervous about the way they might be treated at the white country club. People could be so cold, so condescending, so inhospitable, and downright mean. Still, he could not turn down the invitation. Martin knew they would talk about him behind his back. He could not stop the gossip. He simply worried about what they would say to his face—what they would say to his daughter. He did not want her feelings hurt by either their words or their actions.

He should not have worried. The red carpet had been rolled out for them. From the moment they drove up in his BMW, the service had been superior. Someone always stood by to hold doors and pull out chairs. The waiters even shook open their napkins and placed them on their laps. Everyone was extremely welcoming. When Jason offered Martin's name for membership, he was accepted without question on Jason's recommendation.

Her father beamed with pride at his wife when he told Sarah
that her mother had looked especially beautiful that night. She
had spent the day at the beauty salon having a manicure and
a facial, and she looked like a million dollars. Her raven-black
hair hugged her head in a fashionably short cut that showed
off her diamond earrings to perfection. Her earth-tone blush
brought out the natural red in her skin. He had never been more
proud of his wife and business partner. Looking past her at
Sarah, her father knew that she would be as beautiful as her
mother one day. She already had the same long slender pecan-
colored legs and regal carriage. But her eyes were his . . .
disarming gold eyes fringed with coal-black lashes. Yes, many
hearts would be broken by his daughter, Martin had thought,
taking his place between the two beauties and propelling them
toward the private dining room, where Jason stood, smiling his
warmest welcome.

Her father told her that, despite his original worries, the
evening had been a big success. The black velvet of Grace's
cocktail dress had clung just right to her every curve. The
diamonds in her ears had sparkled—just enough to show that
his wealth was real, but not too much to be ostentatious. He
said that every man had envied him not only his good fortune
and his wealth but the beauty and charm of his wife. He had
beamed with pride as he told Sarah that everyone had fallen
in love with her as she waltzed in her black patent leather shoes
while standing on his feet. Her three-tiered apricot dress with
its many crinolines had whispered with every step. Her fat,
dark brown curls had bounced each time she turned her head.
Her youthful enjoyment of the anecdotes endlessly shared by
the old men at the table had won her a place in their hearts.
And, as the crowning glory of the evening, over cigars in the
Madison drawing room, Jason had given him the deed to the
Tillings Tower, a massive structure on prime Dallas land.

Brushing quick tears from her eyes, Sarah said aloud to
his portrait, hanging over the mantle, "You wouldn't think

everything was so grand, now, Daddy. I've ruined it all. But I'm not licked yet. I will not give up without one last fight. Bryan Carson may have bought controlling interest in the company, but he has not bought me. I will get it back, somehow. You'll have to be there with me, Holly. I won't be able to do it alone. Fighting both Bryan Carson and Mildred would be too difficult without you at my side.''

"We've been friends for a long time, Sarah. You bailed me out when I had no future ahead of me. We stuck together during some pretty crazy stunts at school and some wild adventures since graduation. We'll survive this mess. Don't worry. If there's a fight, you can count on me to be right with you,'' Holly answered.

Holly watched Sarah straighten her thin shoulders as she turned toward her desk. Her gold eyes glinted with a frightening fire. The red silk suit accentuated every curve as she marched determinedly to her office door. She was every bit the corporate gladiator ready to do battle.

Sarah grabbed up her attaché case from the chair and headed out the door for the walk to the board room. Holly did not like the look of determination that hung on the corners of Sarah's red lips. She had seen it before when Mildred had tried to force Sarah to sell the company at her father's death. Mildred had an income from the stocks that her father had issued in both her name and Sarah's, but she was no real threat. She could not sell them without Sarah's approval. Yet Sarah had a suspicion that Mildred independently owned several lots, as did most of the prominent citizens of Dallas. Still, Sarah did not think she posed any threat, but she knew that Bryan Carson did.

"Give him hell, Sarah!'' Holly called after her.

Without a backward look, Sarah waved her well-manicured hand high over her head and continued her walk down the hall to the board room. She was ready for whatever Bryan Carson had to offer.

Holly could tell from the way Sarah held her shoulders, the

tilt of her head, and the rat-a-tat-tat of her heels on the floor, that Sarah was ready for a fight—a fight that would start in the board room in ten minutes. Where it would end, she did not know, and was afraid to guess. She hoped that the corporate world, Dallas, and Wall Street were ready for this new Sarah Tillings.

Chapter Two

The board room sat at the opposite end of the floor from her office. Her father had had it designed that way deliberately. He said he wanted to walk past his executive offices before every meeting to get a fresh feel for the life of his company. As Sarah walked down the hall like Joan of Arc preparing to face a foe, she felt tension in the air. Every door was open. Anxiety flowed from every office. Inside, everyone waited. The meeting with Bryan Carson would decide their futures, too. Would they pass the day making corporate decisions concerning the buying, marketing, packaging, and retailing of cosmetics, or would they spend it packing personal belongings into cardboard boxes that they would carry home at the end of the day? Their futures rested on the shoulders of this tall, thin young woman of barely thirty. It was a heavy load. They waited to see if she could carry it.

"Good morning, John. Good morning, Mary," Sarah called and waved as she passed the office of the Senior Vice President of Finance. John Fraser stood at his secretary's desk, coffee cup in hand. This was already his fifth, and it was not even 10:00 yet.

"Morning, Sarah," he replied. She had a task before her, all right. Shaking his head, John wished there were something he could do to help. He knew that he had armed her well with all the figures she needed, but she had to do this alone. She now carried his figures in the black Gucci attaché swinging loosely from her left hand. What she had to do, she would. She was Martin Tillings's daughter.

The takeover had not really surprised him. He had known the condition in which Martin Tillings had left the company's finances. He had expected someone like Bryan Carson to gain control through an infusion of much-needed cash and sound managerial judgment. Yet he was confident that Sarah would find a way to regain control. Her father had fought many attempts to unseat him, and won, and Martin's blood coursed through her veins. He would join her in the board room in just a few minutes. If she needed any help, he would be there for her, as he had been for the last five years. He had stood behind her father in the past. He would not desert her now.

Sarah reached the end of the hall. Pausing for a moment with her hand on the gold handle of the board room door, she squared her shoulders again and adjusted the jacket of her red silk suit. She had worn it for the effect it created. A warrior should always wear her best armor into battle. This suit fit her perfectly, from its lightly padded shoulders, to the crisscross double closure that hugged the curves of her ample figure, to the hem that stopped exactly two inches above her knees. Even the gold buttons—that matched the color of her eyes—rested at her waist with the purpose of drawing attention to its twenty-four inches. She was ready.

Opening the door, Sarah surveyed the assembled company. Her legal counsel, Patrick Alexander, occupied his usual seat directly across from the door. He looked up and smiled as she entered. Across from him, with his back to the door, was Jason

Parson, her father's long-time friend and trusted financial advisor and banker. Jason turned as he heard the clicking of Sarah's heels on the highly polished oak floor. His eyes were red-rimmed. Poor man had probably spent a sleepless night.

Taking her small hand in his, Jason led Sarah to her seat at the head of the long mahogany table. Her father's portrait hung on the wall over the mantle behind her. His deep gold eyes smiled down on her as Sarah slid into the thick, wine-colored leather, giving him a slight nod of acknowledgment. Opening her attaché case, she spread the contents of her folders in front of her.

Sarah looked across the table at the empty seat. Bryan Carson and his entourage had not yet arrived. Two places were set up for his assistants, one on either side of him. At least they were equally weighted, man for man.

Crossing her legs, Sarah glanced at the clock over the door. The meeting should have started five minutes ago. She was not accustomed to being kept waiting, and she did not like it. Was Bryan Carson trying to unnerve her by pulling a stunt like this? Was this the way he played the game, to get the better of his opponents? Keep them on edge and distracted, then lower the boom on them? Or did he simply have problems with punctuality?

She folded her hands in her lap. If this was a ploy of his, it would not work on her. She would not let him get the best of her. She would not let him gain the upper hand. She would give the appearance of having waited patiently. She would ignore his tardiness and unprofessional behavior when he finally decided to grace the board room with his presence. She felt a surge of anger filling the pit of her stomach. She would have to work hard to control her facial expression.

Sarah had never formally met Bryan Carson. She had seen plenty of photographs of him in the business sections of the paper—on the society pages, too, if she remembered correctly. Once in a while, she would see him at a social function she attended, but she had never really spoken with him. Jason Parson had pointed him out to her as a business associate of her father and mother. She recollected seeing him pictured with one pretty woman after another on his arm as he flitted from one social function to another. He was certainly an unlikely business tycoon, but the long list of his acquisitions over the last few years said he knew what he was doing.

She, on the other hand, preferred to stay home and take care of business. There was always work to occupy her leisure hours, including fragrances to test, advertising to approve, and product names to consider. She had precious little time for a social life and never made the society page's gossip section.

When she could sit still no longer, Sarah walked to the window and looked down at the tiny cars below. Tapping her foot in irritation, she made up her mind that she would give him five more minutes . . . until fifteen past the hour. Then she would return to her office and the work piling up on her desk. She could not afford the luxury of spending a morning waiting for him.

As she made her way back to her place at the table, the door suddenly swung open. In the doorway stood Bryan Carson. His massive shoulders filled the space, blocking out all but the tops of the heads of the two assistants behind him. Smiling his most charming society-page smile from one ear to the other, he advanced toward her with his hand outstretched.

Sarah's hands froze on the clasp of her attaché case as she gazed into his steel-gray eyes. She had expected him to exude power—but not this. She had not prepared herself to come face to face with his wide chest and handsome face. She had willed herself to envision him as balding, despite the flattering photographs in the paper. After all, at forty-five, he was considerably older than she. She had hoped for some sign of age or, certainly, lost virility. Yet, he possessed a full head of curly black hair over his mahogany forehead.

She watched as he advanced toward her, his outstretched

hand a rapier heading for her heart. Involuntarily, she extended hers to him. He clasped her cold fingers in his oversized hot hand. Then he imprisoned it with the left. The warmth of his fingers on her wrist made her shiver, despite the anger that burned within her. Damn, he was handsome! He was much better-looking in person than in the photographs Holly had spread out on her desk. She had not been prepared for the physical impact he would have on her.

Bryan Carson's gray eyes caressed Sarah Tillings's face. He lingered on her fiery gold eyes, then slid to her Tillings "Passion Red" lips. Was the flame that burned within those eyes in contrast to the cold little hand that he held prisoner in his own, he wondered? Was there a warm heart beneath that red suit? Would she ever drop the defenses that the stiffness of her shoulders told him she had carefully placed between them? He made up his mind to find out everything about Sarah Tillings that had not already been scorched into his memory over the last twelve years. She had been a test of his endurance since she was eighteen. She did not know that he had waited for her to develop into the woman he knew she would one day become. Martin and Grace had groomed her for more than a life as an ornament; she had been trained to lead. And he had been hand-picked by her father to be her partner, a position he had waited to assume until the time was right. Now was that moment. Yet he had to be careful not to scare her away with his true intentions. He preferred for now that she think of him as the playboy tycoon the newspaper articles painted him to be. There would be time later to reveal the truth. For the time being, he would play the part.

His eyes continued their leisurely journey from Sarah's shoulders to her ample breasts to the tiny waist and luscious hips. Did fire burn under that red silk suit? Was he looking at the tip of the iceberg, with the center lying hidden below?

He was well aware of her father's reputation for preferring passionate women. That was what had led him to fall in love with and marry Grace, and later to fall for Mildred. Did his daughter possess his same passionate tastes? He knew instantly that he would make it his business to find out.

Sarah shuddered again. This insolent man was looking at her in a way no other man had dared. He had the nerve to stand there in her father's board room—no, in her board room—and undress her with his eyes. Her temper flared as he lazily smiled into her upturned face. He had kept her waiting for fifteen minutes, and now he was playing Prince Charming. Who did he think he was? He might own fifty-one percent of Tillings Industries, but she owned the other forty-nine percent. She would not be treated this way, not by him or by anyone. She had never allowed such liberties and was not about to start now with this interloper.

Extracting her hand from his with a sharp jerk, Sarah controlled the anger welling in her breast and calmly made the introductions. Wrenching his eyes from her face, Bryan greeted Jason Parson and Patrick Alexander. Then he turned and introduced his own staff. As Sarah indicated his seat at the other end of the table, he sauntered in the direction she pointed. Her anger flared with every step, as the essence of him filled the room. The man did not even carry his own briefcase; his assistant had that task. From what she could see, these two—his legal counsel and his assistant—were used to following two paces behind him. The eyes of his assistant, Crystal March, followed him with an expression of total adoration. Sarah wondered if she were that in touch with his personal needs, as well. She wondered if he expected the same treatment from her. Fat chance! But today was no time for idle thoughts. There was a battle to be won.

Without taking her eyes from him, Sarah reopened her files and cleared her throat. She was ready to give the performance of her life. She would fight this arrogant, self-assured man for control of her company. Two percentage points would not stop her.

"Mr. Carson, I am so happy you could take time out from your busy schedule for this meeting. It is important that all players understand the rules after a take-over. The executive staff needs clear direction to insure smooth transitions and continued financial success," Sarah began, barely holding back the anger in her voice. Her hands lay clenched on top of the files she had brought with her. She could still feel the warmth of his fingers on hers. She tried hard not to think about the reaction they caused in her. She had important work to do that required her full attention.

"Miss Tillings, I've been looking forward to this meeting since the papers were finalized. Nothing could have kept me away. Now that I've had the opportunity to look over the plant and sample, first hand, some of the fragrances, I'm even more certain that I've made the right decision. Our staff has been most helpful in showing me around," Bryan Carson responded, without shifting his eyes from her mouth. He could easily see that her sensuality had heightened over the years. He desperately wanted to take her into his arms and kiss her angry mouth.

"Am I to understand, Mr. Carson, that you arrived late to our meeting because you took it upon yourself to visit the plant unannounced? Why wasn't I informed? I would have gladly given you a personal tour of the facilities myself." She seethed at the reference to her staff as "our" by this interloper, this Johnny-come-lately, this newcomer. He might be frighteningly appealing, but she would not tolerate his rudeness.

"Please excuse my presumption, but I prefer to see new acquisitions without the help of management. That way I get the true feel of the place, not just what others think I should know," he added, matching the formality of her tone. He carefully controlled the smile that flickered at the corners of his mouth. He struggled to suppress the memory of the bikini-clad eighteen-year-old he had met many years ago.

Lacing her fingers together until the knuckles turned white, Sarah responded, "You can rest assured, Mr. Carson, that nothing would have been withheld from you by me or by any member of my staff. Tillings Industries is a proud company, as our corporate profile shows. Our manufacturing facility is the best in the business, quite state-of-the-art. We have nothing to hide."

"Wonderful. Then I'll look forward to a more personal tour from you soon," he said, gazing at her bust line. Sarah understood immediately. He thought she was part of the package and an acquisition, too. She would have to work at reducing the size of this man's oversized ego.

Sarah could feel flames dart across her cheeks. The nerve of him, looking at her that way! She was not some little flirt or showgirl he had picked up as the day's entertainment. She was his partner and his equal. What made him think he could wear such a smug expression? She almost snapped at him, but decided instead to remain cool, even though a fire raged within her. She would not sink to his level. This man had made it clear what he thought of her. She would see to it that she never let him suspect that she found him even the slightest bit attractive. He would never know that the aroma of his cologne mixed with the smell of soap and manliness made it difficult for her to breathe. This was war!

"Well, then, Mr. Carson, shall we go over the figures? Perhaps discuss our expectations for a successful working arrangement?"

"The first order of business, Sarah, is for us to stop using our surnames. We'll be working together as partners. Second, I need to see my office. I have calls to make. This isn't the only company I manage, you know. I cannot be far from a telephone. I've been out of touch too long already this morning. Any other discussion can wait until a need arises."

Sarah could feel the anger that consumed her body change from hot rage at his arrogance to cold dread in a matter of seconds. Did he intend to handle day-to-day operations of Till-ings Industries? The terms of the agreement had led her to believe that she would still be at its helm. Should she ask for clarification, and possibly be considered weak, giving him the chance to pounce, or wait until another opportunity afforded itself? She did not like uncertainties. With this man she was anything but sure of the ground on which she stood.

"We were unclear as to the size office you intended to occupy. I haven't moved my things from the president's office as yet. Exactly how often do you plan to be here? The terms of our agreement were unclear. As the primary partner, you're entitled to the larger office, of course."

"I thought my attorney had made that perfectly clear. I apologize for any confusion. I'll be calling Tillings Industries my home base from now on. All of my other responsibilities will be run from here. As to the size of the office, that's immaterial. I don't want to put you to any inconvenience, since it might tend to start our relationship on the wrong foot. You stay where you are in your father's office. I don't intend to try to fill his shoes, and my feet are much too large for your shoes. The fit would be much too tight. I'll be content with the empty one next door to this board room. As far as I'm concerned, it's business as usual, with as little interruption as possible. I'll leave the operation of Tillings in your capable hands."

Sarah was not sure whether she should be relieved or angry. He sounded sincere in his respect for her father's reputation, but the comment about the size of her shoes and her capable hands was almost sarcastic. She would file this away for later. Too much was happening too fast. At least she would not have to leave her father's office. Losing control of Tillings had been bad enough, but moving to another office would have caused unbearable sorrow.

"I'll show you to your office. Your assistant can arrange to have your boxes moved from the hallway," Sarah said, rising from her seat and closing her attaché with a decisive click.

Turning toward him she asked, "Ready? Shall we adjourn this meeting until we both have time to read through the list of expectations compiled by the other? I've been away from the operation of Tillings too long, also."

A cat-like smile flickered at the corners of his mouth. He was ready for whatever combat this strong, beautiful woman had to offer. Bryan knew that he would have to be careful with this one. If he came on too hard and fast, he would scare her away. He was not a man who admitted defeat gracefully; he never played to lose. He had laid his plans too carefully to retreat now. Too many years of planning and waiting had led him to this day.

His hand brushed hers as he reached for the doorknob. The sparks surged along his arm and farther south. Yes, he did not want to lose his one. He had waited twelve years, and not for the company, either. He wanted Sarah Tillings.

Bryan remembered the first time he had met Sarah, although it was all too clear to him that she had no memory of the afternoon. Why should she; she had been eighteen and had just finished her freshman year in college. Her mind was elsewhere as she sat under the umbrella beside the country-club pool. Her father had proudly introduced her around, and then excused himself to make some phone calls. Sarah had contentedly settled with a book in a lounge chair. She had been totally unaware of the impression she had made on all the men. The string bikini she had worn had shown off her maturing figure perfectly.

But Bryan had been very aware of her. She was too young for a man of thirty-three, and much too innocent about the ways of the world—corporate and otherwise. One day she would be just the right age. By then, the difference in their ages would be forgotten. He burned the memory of her long, brown legs, firm buttocks, small waist, and full eager breasts into his mind for the future. When she was older, they would meet again. The years of waiting and their pasts would be forgotten, with only the future on their minds. Until then, he would follow her every move through the society pages with as much interest as he had tracked Martin Tillings's business ventures.

After all, Martin and Grace had arranged for him to meet Sarah. Although they knew that she was much too young to consider marriage now, they wanted to make sure that the right man would be standing in the wings when the time came for her to settle down and take control of Tillings Industries. With a man like Bryan at her side, Sarah would benefit by the experience of his years in business and the confidence of his connections in the financial world. They thought of it as an arranged marriage and the merger of two fortunes and well-established families. Bryan, after seeing the eighteen-year-old Sarah, thought of it as a golden opportunity.

So, with Martin and Grace's help, he kept a scrapbook of clippings and letters from her parents that highlighted the events of her life. He knew of her accomplishments in college, graduating Magna Cum Laude from her undergraduate studies, and with honors in her masters work. He often wondered why Martin kept her out of the business and suggested that he might consider giving her a position with responsibility to test her mettle. Martin had replied that her studies took priority and that there would be time enough for her to devote herself to the company.

In time, as he occasionally saw her at social functions when in Dallas, he began to feel true affection for her. He dated other women, but they never seemed to compare with the smiling, confident Sarah who smiled up at him from the papers, or who danced past him at Dallas's best parties. When he heard that Tillings Industries was in financial difficulty and in danger of being taken over in a hostile merger, Bryan knew he had to do something, not only to save the famous company, but also to help the woman he had grown to love. He was prepared for her rejection of both his assistance and his affection, but he would have to try to prove himself worthy of her confidence and love.

Well, Sarah had certainly matured well, Bryan thought as he followed her down the hall to his new office. The kick pleat in her close-fitting red skirt flared with each step, revealing the same shapely legs he remembered. This time they did not exit a string bikini but were wrapped in the sheerest of stockings. Panty hose probably; there were no telltale garter bumps. Sarah was a new woman: no clumsy garter belts for her. At least not during the day, Bryan thought with a smile. He stored that thought away for later, too. He would buy her one if she did not already have a collection of them in her lingerie drawer.

Sarah stepped aside as they reached his office. Moving past her, his arm nearly brushed against her firm breasts. "Control yourself, old boy," he thought. "You've waited this long; don't spoil it now. Take your time. This one is worth waiting for a little while longer. Give her a chance to get to know you. Anything you do now would be misunderstood as part of the take-over process. That's not the way you want this to go. You want her to come to you of her own accord."

Listening to his own advice, Bryan nodded his head and extended his hand. "Sarah, I'm looking forward to a very profitable and enjoyable association with Tillings Industries. I know we'll settle into a team the likes of which the corporate world has never seen," he said, closing his fingers around hers. This time her hand was warm, probably from the anger that burned in those incredible gold eyes.

"Thank you, Bryan, I'm looking forward to our mutual success," she replied, matching the pressure of his fingers with her own. It would not do to show even the slightest physical weakness to this man.

With that, Sarah left him at the door to his new office and walked the length of the long hall to her own. Feeling his eyes on her buttocks, Sarah realized that this hall would not be long enough to suit her. Maybe he had allowed her to keep her office in an effort to create harmony, but he was still here in her father's company. A truce had not been called. The war was still on.

Safely behind her office door, Sarah breathed freely for the first time since Bryan had arrived fifteen minutes late for their ten o'clock sharp meeting. In the seclusion of her office, she was able to analyze her reactions more clearly. The nerve of him to have kept her waiting like that, as if her work were secondary to his. He had gall taking himself on a tour of *her* plant. So what if he owned fifty-one percent. Someone new should act a little new, her mother always said. Learn the surroundings first, get the lay of the land, and then act familiar and change things. Obviously, Bryan Carson had never heard those words of wisdom.

And the way he looked at her—as if she were the profit-and-loss section of the annual report. Examining every curve that way! Who did he think he was, anyway? He had bought controlling interest in the company, but she had not been part of the incentive package!

Still, she could not deny even to herself that there was more chemistry between them than she had ever felt with any man. The touch of his hand had made her tremble and go jelly-kneed. On more than one occasion, she had been glad to have been sitting down. She was sure her father was glowering at her from his portrait on the board room wall behind her the whole time. He was probably chiding her for being so taken in by a pair of extremely broad shoulders, a wide chest, and muscular thighs barely contained by an expensive, perfectly tailored suit. She alternated between being angry at Bryan for his power over her and furious with herself for her own weakness. How could she expect to wrestle control of Tillings Industries away from him if she melted every time she looked into his steel-gray eyes?

"Buck up, girl!! Get a hold of yourself. Martin and Grace Tillings's daughter would not act like a silly schoolgirl," Sarah chided herself angrily, looking at the view from the penthouse of Tillings Tower. The panorama always had a calming affect on her.

Sarah had never allowed any man to sweep her off her feet. She would not start now, when so much was at stake. Okay, so he was the most handsome man she had ever met. He was the most self-assured and self-absorbed she had ever encountered in her lifetime, too. He was everything she had always said she would never find attractive, despite his six-foot-five inch, well-muscled frame. He was cocky, arrogant, and so damned handsome she imagined herself running to his office and throwing herself at him.

Sarah shook herself and pressed the intercom button connecting her office to Holly's. She had to plan the next move. She could not afford, financially or emotionally, to be caught off guard by Bryan Carson. She had to stay one step ahead of him, at all cost.

"Holly, could you come here, please? We have some work to do. Call John Fraser and Patrick Alexander and tell them I want to meet with them in half an hour. Oh, yes, and bring the personal file on Bryan Carson," she said to her friend. There was work to be done, and Holly was the one person she could count on to help her.

Chapter Three

Sarah had always looked forward to board meetings. She liked sitting in her father's chair with his hand-picked advisors around her. She enjoyed the closeness they shared as they discussed the success and problems that were part of the daily operation of a large company.

Today, however, was different. Since Bryan Carson had arrived, she had begun to loathe the weekly sessions. She resented his presence. He had no right sitting across from her, looking at her and her people, smiling at her with that air of superiority he wore so well. He did not belong in her father's company, in her company, in the shadow of the portrait of her father that smiled down on them every week.

Sarah steeled herself against another session . . . another hour of sitting across from his smiling face. Even in her distaste for him, she had to admit that he was painfully handsome. That lock of hair that always fell across his forehead drew her to him. She wanted desperately to push it back into place among the other black curls.

She shook herself to stop this foolish reverie. How could she ever think with any desire about the man who had taken over her father's company and threatened to deny her of her heritage and legacy? Her father had left Tillings Industries to her. Still, she hoped that she did not betray herself and her feelings. She did not want to give him any incorrect perceptions.

Bryan had not removed her from the presidency, as she had expected, yet she felt that he was holding back, being polite, until the right time to strike. She was not sure when that would be. He might be waiting until after the announcement of the new fragrance to assume the helm of the restored Tillings. She would watch him carefully. She did not want to be caught off guard.

Taking her customary seat at the head of the long mahogany table, Sarah checked the clock. Ten o'clock on the dot. Everyone was ready for the meeting to start, except Bryan. Memories of their first board meeting flashed through her mind. He had been late that day, too. Since then, he had managed to arrive more or less on time. He would stride confidently past her to his seat at the opposite end of the table. Along the way, he would stop to chat briefly with John Fraser, the Senior Vice President of Finance, or Patrick Alexander, the company's legal counsel. His tag-along assistant, Crystal, would follow at a respectable distance in his looming shadow.

Today, just as he did every week, Bryan appeared at the board room door just as Sarah had called the meeting to order. Instead of interrupting the flow of her opening remarks, as he usually did, he pulled up one of the extra chairs that lined the paneled walls and sat down next to her. The heat radiating from his body almost caused her to lose the train of her thought. The nearness of him was unnerving. She had to struggle to keep her mind on what she intended to say as she watched him cross his well-muscled legs.

Adjusting the crease of his trousers, Bryan sat back in his chair and gave Sarah his undivided attention. He had deliberately arrived late this time, and selected a seat next to her. He had grown tired of sitting opposite her. He wanted the closeness of her smooth skin, not the hard cold stare of her gold eyes. He also wanted to see if his presence would have the same effect on her as hers did on him. Every time he was near her, he felt his groin tighten into an embarrassing bulge that belied his thoughts.

He was tired of this game of keep-away they had played since his arrival. He wanted to take her in his arms, but was afraid that she would think he wanted to control her as he did her company. One moment she looked as if she wanted to be in his arms, to share his warmth, to give herself to him as much as he wanted to be part of her. The next she wore an expression of extreme indifference. He had decided to take matters into his own hands. Today, after the others left the board room, he would make his move.

Bryan's nearness made it difficult for Sarah to concentrate on the agenda she had so carefully prepared. It almost took her breath away. She felt the current of electricity that passed from his hands, quietly folded on the table, to hers, without his even touching her. She grew warm from the heat that was transmitted from his relaxed body to her tense one. She squirmed in her seat in an effort to escape his power. Everywhere she moved, it followed. His presence seemed to fill the immense room, making it feel small and confining.

Slowly, he eased his muscular leg closer and closer until it touched hers. Her body tensed as his warmth transferred itself to her body. She immediately sat upright and tightened her grip on her pencil. Her fingers lost their color with the effort. Yet her voice remained controlled; no quivers or thickening gave away her reactions. Quickly, she moved her leg away, without giving him a sideways look. She fought against the emotions that filled and confused her. She could not possibly find this usurper of companies attractive. She had promised herself that she would keep her distance and keep him in his place, at least until she knew him better.

Sarah took a deep breath as the burning spot on her leg cooled from the distance she placed between them. She struggled to regain her composure, all the while hoping that no one in the board room had noticed her flustered state. Just when her breathing had returned to normal, the pressure from Bryan's knee returned to burn a spot of pleasure in hers. This time she could feel her cheeks coloring as her insides grew warm and liquid. Her womanly parts burned even more than her knee from the nearness of him. Part of her wanted to brush his leg away, but the other part would not let her.

"Damn the man for being able to do this to me! He's trying to make a fool of me in front of everyone. Well, I won't let him," she thought angrily.

Sarah sat still. Despite her irritation with him, she struggled to keep her treasonous emotions and the pleasurable pain in her groin from showing in her face. Carefully, she looked around the room to see if anyone had noticed her predicament. Since Holly was not looking at her strangely, she decided she had succeeded in masking her feelings. Even Bryan's adoring, madly infatuated assistant Crystal was not looking at her.

Glancing at her out of the corner of his eye, Bryan saw the look of anger that quickly flickered across Sarah's beautiful face, to be replaced by an expression of total indifference. He doubted that he looked as well composed. He knew that his insides were on fire. He was sure everyone in the room knew that if the meeting did not adjourn soon he would rip the gold silk suit with matching blouse and buttons from her body and take her on this uncomfortable-looking table.

To his relief, Sarah reached the last topic on her agenda. She opened the floor to unscheduled topics of discussion and received none; she adjourned the meeting. She reminded every-one that they would reconvene next Monday, and thanked them

for coming. Instead of rising immediately, she slowly and carefully gathered her papers and laid them inside her attaché case.

Bryan could not have risen, if he had wanted to, without
exposing his thoughts to everyone in the room. The lump in
his pants was huge, painful, and very noticeable. He waited
until the others had left to reach over and cover her small hand
with his. Immediately he could feel the trembling of her fingers
as she struggled briefly to free herself.

Turning angry yellow eyes on him, Sarah demanded, "What
gives you the idea that you can take such liberties with me?
What makes you think you can make under-the-table advances
to me in front of my entire management team? Just who do
you think you are? Do you think that owning controlling interest
in Tillings Industries gives you the right to impose yourself on
me?"

Bryan tightened his grip on her small hand with the "Passion
Red" nails that matched her lipstick. He quietly looked into
her furious face. Underneath the fury was something else that
struggled to free itself. He realized that her anger was not really
directed at him, but at herself, for whatever it was she fought
against feeling.

"Sarah," he began. "I've waited all this time for you to
accept me. I couldn't wait any longer for you to reach out to
me, to want me as much as I want you. I've watched you
struggle with your feelings, and I understand your conflict."

"What could you possibly know about the way I'm feeling?"
she shot back, pulling her hand from his. "You don't even
know me. We've worked together for a few short weeks. You
certainly have some nerve assuming you know me. You've
made an even bigger mistake in assuming that this move on
me would be the way to show me whatever interest you feel
for me. You're pushy and arrogant. Those are two qualities I
find especially irritating in a man. Just because you're used to
women throwing themselves at you, don't think I'll act the
same way. I'm not some simple-minded female who finds you

irresistible. I'm Sarah Tillings, the president of the company and the daughter of Martin and Grace Tillings. Don't you ever forget that. I got along just fine before you came here and will gladly do it again.''

Bryan smiled at the sparks that flew from her. She was everything he had hoped she would be and more. He had been afraid that Martin might have spoiled his only daughter in his desire to make her happy. He was glad to see that she was spirited and independent. He had experienced too many clinging vines in his lifetime, and had hoped that she would not be one of them.

Standing at his place, Bryan smiled down at her and said, "I'm glad to see you have fire in your veins. You spend so much time covering your emotions, I was afraid ice water ran through your system.

"Yes, I'm pushy when I want something or someone. I pushed until I was in the position to take over Tillings, not as a possession, but to save something that once belonged to a man I've admired all my life. Although you never knew it, your parents and I were old friends. In many ways, they were my mentors. You don't remember, but I met you years ago, when you were eighteen, and you've been on my mind ever since. I'm pushing now to show the woman I've wanted for a long time that we're right for each other. You think the success of the new fragrance will enable you to buy me out and send me away. You might be right but, until then, I'll continue to batter away at your defenses until they drop and you let me into your life.''

With great difficulty Sarah rose to her feet. Her legs felt like quivering globs of gelatin from the nearness of him and from the anger that pulled at the fiber of her being. Her head swam from the myriad emotions that tumbled around inside. Her arms ached to wrap themselves around him while her hands itched to slap the smile from his handsome face.

"I could never take you into my life, Bryan. You have tried

to force me out of my father's company. I'll never forget that.
I know your money has kept Tillings afloat, but I'm not ready
to admit that I couldn't have done it without you. If I could
only have talked the banks and other investors into giving me
a little more time, they would have seen the financial success
of the new fragrance. They became impatient and would not
wait. Because of them, you were able to move in. I'll never
forgive you for that . . . never.''

With difficulty, and a note of indignation in her voice, she
continued, ''Tillings Industries is my company. My father and
mother built it. I know there were troubles under his management but it wasn't anything that I couldn't handle with time.
The investors acted too quickly because I'm a woman. You
hopped in with what I believe were mixed motives of greed
and concern. You have what you wanted, but I'm not part of
the deal, regardless of the admiration you felt for my father or
what you think you feel for me. There's no way that I'll ever
see you as anything other than an interloper, no matter how
hard you try, or how much you do to save my company. There's
simply too much rough water between us.''

Bryan wanted to take this strong, proud woman into his arms
and comfort her. He could see the anguish that tormented her,
and he regretted causing her any further pain. For her part,
Sarah needed to cling to her loyal thoughts about her father
and her failed plans to save his company; she was not ready
to admit that either had failed her. At the same time, she wanted
to reach out to him for the emotional stability she had missed
since her mother died and Martin abandoned her and the company after marrying Mildred.

''Sarah,'' he began as he reached for her.

''No, don't, Bryan,'' she interrupted, pushing away his outstretched hands. ''For the good of our working relationship,
you must keep your distance. I appreciate your devotion to the
memory of my parents and your professed but oddly displayed,
affection for me. However, at this time, I can give you no

encouragement. We are business partners and nothing else. To think that more might be possible would be presumptuous on your part. I ask you to refrain from making any further demands on my life.'' She would not drop the wall between them, not yet. She had to maintain the distance that was between them until she could sort out her emotions. But, first, she had a perfume to sell and a company to buy back.

He saw the distrust in her eyes as she hastily stepped backward to avoid his touch. The heel of her pump caught in the thick pile of the deep gold carpet and threw her off balance. Bryan made a mad grab for her wildly flailing hands and pulled her forward in time to keep her from falling backward. He wrapped his arms around her until she regained her footing. Her small yet voluptuous body was warm against his. The smell of her perfume was intoxicating. His manhood reacted immediately to the nearness of her. Reluctantly, he released her and stepped away.

Looking up into his eyes with her arms crossed protectively over her chest, Sarah muttered, ''It looks as if you're always saving me from a fall.''

''I'm always happy to help a lady in distress,'' he joked, with a slight bow that brought his face even with hers.

Sarah felt his breath on her cheeks for a fleeting instant before finding herself once again in his arms. She was not sure just how it had happened and did not care. All that mattered at this moment was that she was in Bryan's arms, pressed against his solid body, where she felt safe and cared for. Deep within her, in a place where secrets are kept, she knew she would always be safe with him around to watch over her and Tillings Industries.

Bryan's lips immediately began to explore the angles and hollows of her face. When he had finished memorizing every curve, he kissed her eyelids and ears before moving to her throat and the mounds of her breasts. Sarah felt weak at the knees and quite lightheaded as she clung to him. A warm liquid sensation welled in the pit of her stomach and spread to the region between her shapely legs. Slowly, his hands caressed her shoulders and back. As she writhed under the tantalizing pressure, he moved downward to massage the small of her back and her buttocks before crushing her into his throbbing manhood. She gasped when she felt it pushing hard and hot against her thigh, even through the fabric of the clothing that separated them.

Without her bidding, her hands caressed his shoulders and back, pulling him ever closer. Her tongue darted around his, making Bryan moan with desire. Then her fingers slid downward across his flat hard stomach to hesitantly stroke the bulge that threatened to push through the fabric of his black pinstripe Armani suit. He groaned louder and pressed himself against her exploring fingers. Growing bold from her ability to bring him pleasure, Sarah increased the speed of the circular pattern her fingers drew on his hard organ.

"Sarah, I've waited so long," he muttered hoarsely into her hair, in a whisper she barely heard. His hands pushed up the fabric of her suit and fondled her buttocks through her thin flesh-tone panty hose. He wanted her more than he had wanted any of the other women who had filled his bed, but never his heart. He had waited all these years for the eighteen-year-old girl to grow into this beguiling, almost thirty-year-old, woman. Finally, she was his.

Sarah did not stop to think about the meaning of his words as she stood wrapped in his arms. She was hot and cold, burning and freezing all at the same time. No man had ever made her feel this way. None of the young black Dallas men of society had ever held her with such authority. No one had ever made her want to forget her position as the president of Tillings Industries, the way Bryan did. Never had she been so close to losing control of her reason and allowing her passions to take control of her actions. It was almost as if Bryan Carson had control of her mind, as well as her body, as he brought her close to delirium with his hands and lips.

Then, suddenly, something snapped inside Sarah at the very thought of the power he exerted over her. Suddenly her mind began to clear from the fog of passion. She was again able to think rationally, without her desire for him getting in the way of reason. Questions flew around in her head as quickly as reason had flown out. What did he mean when he said he had waited a long time for her? They had been strangers until he took over her company. Nothing had existed between them until then. Things were getting out of hand and moving much too fast. Was this Bryan's way of gaining more power over Tillings? Did he plan to seduce her and make her fall in love with him, only to take the presidency of her company away from her? Was she destined to become just another much-photographed and talked-about pretty woman on his arm?

"Bryan, stop this instant," she said, pushing away from his hungry hands and mouth. "I am not one of the perks of your fifty-one percent ownership."

As she spoke, Sarah rearranged her clothing and quieted the emotions that raged within her. She knew that if she had not stopped him at that moment, she never would have had the strength or desire to push him away. Even now, as she stood within fingertip distance of him, she had difficulty maintaining her resolve. She had felt so good in his arms, better than she had ever felt with any of the other men she had known, who had often been threatened by her money, power, and position as the head of a company. For once she had met a man whose own sense of self was strong enough not to be challenged by hers. She needed and wanted him so much that it was almost impossible not to throw herself into his arms. She looked into the expression of confusion that flickered through the lingering passion that clouded his steel-gray eyes and reddened his perfectly shaped lips.

Yet she could not forget that she was Sarah Tillings, the president of Tillings Industries.

Bryan thrust his clinched fists deep within his pockets. From the expression on his face, she could tell that he was struggling to control the flames that still burned in his groin. He spoke from his wounded pride, and with something else that she could not recognize, as he said, "You're absolutely right, Sarah. It was unforgivable of me to be so taken by your charms that I would even think of compromising you. My regrettable actions have shown that it is quite dangerous for me to sit near you during our meetings. From now on, I will refrain from joining you at this end of the table. It's safer for both of us that way. However, I was of the impression that you were freely giving yourself and your kisses to me. If I have been mistaken, I apologize. I think it's best that I excuse myself and return to my office. Good morning, Sarah."

Squaring his shoulders, Bryan sauntered to the board room door. Turning the handle, he left her standing, flushed and flustered, at the table.

Sarah had barely enough energy left in her legs to carry her to the edge of the board room table, where she slumped in a pile of gold silk. The taste of his kisses lingered in her mouth and the touch of his fingers burned her skin. Reaching for the agenda notes that she had used to conduct this morning's business, she fanned her face to reduce the heat that flamed there, before anyone could find her in this state.

As composure returned, something Bryan had said flashed through her mind. At the height of passion she had not paid much attention to his mutterings, but now she wondered what he'd meant when he'd said, "I've waited so long." He had waited so long for what? They had known each other for a relatively short amount of time. Surely he did not consider a few weeks to be a long time.

Wracking her still-frazzled memory, she tried to remember any other occasion at which she might have met Bryan. There

were many social events in Dallas, ranging from Texas barbe-
cues to formal galas. She did not remember ever seeing him
at any of them. She knew she had never met him at a cosmetic
manufacturers' conference. Until he bought controlling interest
in Tillings Industries, cosmetics meant perfume and aftershave
to him.

Tapping a well-manicured nail on the mahogany table, she
thought back over the dinners her father had hosted when he
was the president of Tillings. Running her mind's eye over all
the faces, she could not find Bryan among any of the crowds
of people who had flocked to her father's house or the club,
always too eager to attend a Tillings affair.

Suddenly a spark of memory kindled. Somewhere in the
forgotten recesses of her mind, she held a vague memory of
having been introduced to Bryan when she was in college. She
could not remember where or exactly when, but she could
dimly place him through the fog of years. To her teenaged
mind, he was one of her father's friends, an old man. After all,
he would have been around thirty-five when she was eighteen.
He would have been older than she was now. To a young girl,
Bryan would have been ancient and hardly worth noticing. She
remembered her parents talking about him, too, almost as if
they wanted her to take special note of his accomplishments.
Every time he bought out another company or escorted another
beauty to a theatrical opening night, they pointed out the article
about him. They praised his ability to take a struggling company
and turn it into a profitable one, as if they wanted her to find
his activities admirable.

Sarah remembered, too, developing a sort of crush on him.
Every time he acquired a new company, her parents clipped
the article and showed it to her. Her father kept an ever-
expanding folder of them in his file cabinet. She had heard so
much about him and seen his photograph in the papers so often
that she had found herself overlooking the age difference and
concentrating on his successes, both personal and financial. He

was athletic-looking, with a slim build and a full head of hair that tumbled in loose curls over his forehead. At times, she even found herself measuring other men by his standards.

"Oh, well," Sarah muttered to herself while collecting her meeting notes, "whoever he was and whatever he might have meant, he's here now. I'll have to be more careful when I'm around him. I can't have this happen every time he touches me. Damn the man for being so attractive and sexy. I wish I didn't find him so appealing. It's strange that I feel so safe with someone I've known for such a short time. As soon as I introduce the new fragrance and it starts to sell, I'm going to do all I can to get him out of Tillings. After he's gone, I'll have the time to figure out how I feel about him and why. Until then, I can't afford to drop my guard."

Walking to the door, Sarah paused for a moment and looked around the room. Her father's portrait smiled down at her. With a quick shudder, she closed the door behind her, knowing that the board room would never look the same again.

Bryan sat behind his desk, thinking about what had transpired between them and about what had almost happened. He had been carried away by her beauty and his love for her. He had never planned to press so hard, to urge so intensely, to want her so desperately. He knew it was too early to let her know how he felt. He was afraid that this slip in his composure might have scared her away. He could not afford another incident like this one.

Stretching his tall, muscular frame, Bryan spoke aloud to his silent office, "I'll be more careful next time. Now that I know she's drawn to me, too, it will be easier for me to take my time. I just hope Sarah doesn't keep me waiting too much longer. I've already waited twelve years for her to grow into a woman. Loving her doesn't make it any easier, because every time I see her I want to take her into my arms. Well, Martin and Grace, I hope you're happy. You wanted me to love and protect her, and now look at me. I bought a company that produces perfume to save it for a woman who pretends to want nothing to do with me. What a mess this is!''

Now that the pressure in his groin had subsided, Bryan could return to his work. As long as he kept his mind busy, he might be able to get through the rest of the day without thinking of Sarah. He would have to learn patience, which was not one of his strong suits.

Chapter Four

In the weeks that followed, Sarah and Holly spent almost every minute together as they scanned the financial statements, personal anecdotes, newspaper articles, and photographs they had compiled looking for signs of weakness in the facade of Bryan Carson. So far, all they had uncovered was that he liked women—and not any particular one. They could uncover nothing to indicate that there was a special woman in his life. He dated many of them, and seldom the same one twice. The reports showed that his finances, both personal and professional, were in perfect order. Every company he owned turned sizable profits every year. His skillful management had put even the weakest on the road to recovery. Sarah reluctantly agreed that there was no doubting his abilities, his insights, and his talents. From what she could tell, his personal life was in the same impeccable order. Not even the slightest hint of scandal was associated with his name.

Sarah and Holly became exasperated. This man was too good to be true. All their efforts had turned up nothing. Actually, as much as Sarah hated to admit it, all the facts showed that Bryan Carson was just what Tillings needed. A nagging thought crept around the fringes of her mind. Bryan Carson might actually be better for Tillings Industries than her father had been, toward the end, after her mother's death and his remarriage to Mildred had dulled his senses. Bryan was much like her father had been, before grief and folly changed him. He had her father's drive, his ambition, and his ability to scope out a situation and quickly devise a solution to the problem. As much as she hated to admit it, Bryan had her father's charm, too. He certainly was as handsome as Martin Tillings. His red-brown skin shone with health. Exercise had toned his body, and that belied his age. He certainly did not look forty-five years old. And he certainly possessed a certain magnetism.

Sarah thrust these thoughts from her mind. There was no comparing him to her father. She could not and would not be that disloyal. She would not allow herself to join the other women in Tillings Tower in lusting after Bryan Carson. She would not think that he could be good for Tillings Industries.

After all, the company was only experiencing temporary setbacks and would have survived without his meddling. She had hired the best people, and was on the right track to success after her father's neglect. Bryan Carson had stepped in too soon. In another month or two the company would have been financially sound again. The new fragrance would be a sure-fire hit. She did not need Bryan Carson or anyone else to save her from the vultures that had circled overhead. She could take care of herself and Tillings.

She refused to think that maybe he was exactly what she needed in her life, too. She had been too busy with the company to need male companionship for anything other than escorts to social events, or so she had told herself. She had pushed away many suitors. They simply did not live up to her expectations for a partner. Only in moments of deepest loneliness did Sarah admit that she was afraid to allow herself to depend on someone else. She had watched her father suffer when her mother died; his whole world went with her. She knew his marriage with her stepmother, Mildred, had never really satisfied him. She did not want to be in a loveless relationship. She preferred to be alone, with only Tillings Industries for company than to share her life with someone she really did not want.

Still, on quiet evenings, when the fire roared in the fireplace, or on Sunday mornings when Dallas was at last still, she longed to feel the pressure of someone's hand on hers. She would love to wake up to a special someone's sleep-smoothed face. She relished the thought of being able to cross her big queen-sized bed to snuggle against his broad chest and feel his maleness harden at the nearness of her. In the still of the morning, she often dreamed of moving her body in rhythm with his, of sliding her legs around his waist, and of matching her thrusts to his until their bodies glistened with perspiration and sleep was a distant memory. She longed to lie spent but happy in his arms, with the responsibilities of Tillings forgotten. Somehow, Sarah thought she would never know this happiness. She made Tillings her life and pushed these painfully sweet thoughts far from her mind.

Her past relationships had fizzled before they really got started. The men had always felt threatened by her devotion to the company. Even her childhood friend, Frank, had not been able to stand up against the pull of Tillings on her time. Their engagement had ended almost as soon as the announcement appeared in the paper. Some said that she had broken his heart so badly that he had never been able to settle down with any one woman after loving Sarah. Sometimes when she caught him looking at her, she thought that maybe it was true. That is, until he fell for Holly. Now they were only best friends. They shared so many of the same interests, such as dancing, watching old movies, listening to the opera, and going to baseball games. He even enjoyed roller skating. Their relationship was perfect, except for one thing . . . her love for Tillings. With

Bryan, she felt that he would understand her need to care for the company, and stand by her side while she did. Together, they would be the perfect corporate couple, just as her parents had been.

Until now, she had been successful in avoiding entanglements in either her business or her personal life. However, Bryan Carson had entered her life and threatened the security of her carefully constructed world.

Sarah and Holly had been sitting with their heads together for hours when the door suddenly burst open and Bryan Carson walked in unannounced. "Hello, ladies," he roared as his broad shoulders filled the doorway. Sarah took a deep breath as Holly rose to leave.

"Don't go, Holly. I just stopped by to see if Sarah could take a break for lunch on such a bright, beautiful Friday. Maybe she could finally give me that personal tour of the plant she promised me. You're welcome to join us, if you'd like," he said, leaning against the door frame, his arms folded across his chest. He seemed to take amusement in finding the two women together. He smiled from one ear to the other, showing perfectly straight teeth.

"No, thanks, Bryan. I have more than enough to do here. Thanks for the offer," Holly responded, easing the papers back into the files and picking up her coffee cup. Although she was learning to trust him, she still did not care for the man any more than Sarah did. She made it a personal rule never to break bread with someone she did not like. She certainly did not intend to ruin her lunch by sharing it with him.

Bryan's eyes never left Sarah's face as he stepped aside to let Holly pass through the door. It was clear that Holly was unimportant to him. Her simple beauty paled in comparison to Sarah's vibrancy. Why settle for less when you can have more, he always thought. Besides, he was in Dallas because of Sarah Tillings. She drew him to her as a moth follows a beacon of light.

Matching him stare for stare, Sarah thought, sarcastically, "I wonder how anyone could have such a perfect smile. His parents must have paid a huge orthodontist's bill when he was a child. No one was ever born with choppers like that. They certainly fit his perfect image. Immaculately tailored silk suit, unwrinkled handkerchief linen shirt, and spit-polished soft kid-leather shoes. Bet he never even sweats—in any physical exercise." She returned his smile through clenched teeth.

"I'll be right with you, Bryan. I'll meet you at your office as soon as I tidy up a bit. I'll ask my secretary to phone ahead to Duke's for reservations. She'll give the plant manager notice of our arrival, too, since I don't usually pop up unannounced. Besides, I want you to experience the latest Tillings fragrance, and Edward Morris will need a little time to prepare. He's the main chemist on the project, you know," she said, without taking her eyes from his. She forced her eyes to sparkle engagingly into his expectant face. Two could play this game, she decided.

Sarah would not let Bryan Carson unnerve her again, regardless of the depth of the dimples on either side of his mouth and the endlessly deep cleft in his chin. With a little effort, she might even become immune to that runaway curly lock of hair that fell gently over his forehead. Maybe it would stop reminding her of a little boy just up from his nap with his head all tousled from sleep. Bryan's hair had the same disheveled look in every photograph in Holly's personal folder on him. Part of his calculated personal charm, no doubt. He was certainly the right mixture of sophistication and boyishness. He had obviously planned his appearance as part of a well-tailored package designed to snare every available woman. Sarah wanted her body language to tell him that she would not fall into his net.

"All right, but don't take too long. I'm starving. I hope Duke's serves good food. I haven't eaten since lunch yesterday,'' Bryan replied, easing himself from the door and closing it gently behind him.

Sarah dropped into her chair. The effort of maintaining her cool had been great, and she was beat. Slumping in her chair, she wondered if the reference to the missed meal was designed to impress her, maybe even lead her to think his hands and mind were too full of Dallas beauties to consider stopping for food. She doubted she would be able to eat a bit with him watching every move she made. His eyes penetrated not only through her clothes, which had long since ceased to exist under his gaze, but to her very being. She felt them caress her, delve into her thoughts, try to possess her. He was a dangerous man. Anyone with that much power was not to be trusted. She would have to be careful around him. More careful than she had originally thought. It would be too easy to allow herself to fall prey to his charms, to become his prize, to allow him to possess her as he had taken control of Tillings Industries. She had to step carefully and show him that she was not part of the spoils of the take-over war. If only he were not so damnably handsome. She hoped that a pimple would sprout on his divinely chiseled face before she met him for lunch.

Picking up her telephone with trembling hands, Sarah called Edward Morris's number herself. The task would help calm her nerves, and give her a focus other than Bryan Carson for her thoughts. He answered on the second ring. ''Edward,'' she said, ''this is Sarah Tillings. I'd like to stop by your lab around 2:00, if that's okay. I'll be bringing the new partner, Bryan Carson, with me. I want him to sample the new fragrance. Maybe you could give a discussion of the perfume-making process. I hope our visit won't interfere too much; I know you're on a tight schedule.''

The voice on the other end responded, ''No problem, Ms. Tillings. I'll have everything ready. See you at 2:00.''

Replacing the receiver, Sarah straightened her shoulders and smoothed the wrinkles from her skirt. If only Bryan were as easy to deal with as Edward Morris. Her life would be a piece of cake. But then Bryan would not be the tycoon he was if he were mild-mannered like Edward.

Walking to the door, Sarah glanced over her shoulder at her father's portrait hanging over the fireplace. He had been such a handsome man and a kind person. Everyone said he died too early. She was grateful to have known him for as long as she did. He had been a wonderful father—loving, gentle, kind, caring, encouraging. It was he who had encouraged Sarah to major in business and earn an MBA. He was not necessarily preparing her to follow in his footsteps; he wanted her to follow her heart. Her heart had always been with Tillings Industries ever since she was a little girl sitting beside him at his desk.

Sarah gazed into those gold eyes and that warm smile. She missed him terribly, even after five years. She often wondered what he would do when facing similar problems or opportunities. He had prepared her well, much better than the MBA did, for the practical running of Tillings Industries. She knew every fragrance by heart, every component of every powder, and the marketing strategy for every product. Tillings was in her heart, all right, in her very soul and in every fiber of her being. She was Tillings and the company was her.

"Well, Daddy, I'm off to lunch for round two with the enemy. I'm not really expecting to win, not yet. I'm hoping for another draw. I have to figure out his weaknesses first. I don't think Bryan's what he appears to be. I think there's more to Bryan Carson than meets the eye. He's too practiced, too polished, and too perfect. I think it's all an act. I have to find out what he's hiding. Then I'll strike. You know, Daddy, you prepared me for many battles in industry, but you never told me that I'd find myself attracted to the opponent. I guess that's one of the lessons I had to learn for myself. Anyway, nothing's going to stop me, not even his gray eyes and that irresistible lock of hair."

She closed the door and headed for combat, with a confident air she did not feel.

Sarah was not the only one struggling with her thoughts. Bryan Carson could not push Sarah from his mind as he returned to his office. He had known many impressive women in his time. Some had great physical beauty. Others had tremendous power that made them attractive. Never had he known a woman who possessed both the cool savvy of business and the fantastic beauty of Sarah Tillings. Shaking his head, Bryan thought that he had never dreamed that the beautiful teenager he had met years ago would turn into this stunning corporate head. He had underestimated his opponent, something he never did. He would have to be careful, tread softly, and learn her weaknesses. He could not afford to let her see his. It was much too early for her to know that he had been in love with her since that first meeting twelve years ago.

Sure, there had been many women since then, but none who meant anything to him. He had even allowed his name to be linked personally with some of them. That was all part of the carefully planned publicity that accompanied his image. It was all carefully orchestrated to make him appear even more desirable, and to make everyone think that he was not only an accomplished businessman, but a ladies' man as well.

Every time he had posed for a photo with a beautiful woman on his arm, he had thought of Sarah. He had watched her from afar since she was eighteen. His personal file on her contained every clipping Martin and Grace had sent him. He hoped her file on him was as extensive. He was counting on it as his cover to throw her off guard. He had gone to great lengths to insure that his attraction for her was carefully hidden until he was ready to show her his true self. He did not want to arm her defenses.

Still, it would be hard, keeping his composure. He badly wanted to take her into his arms and to feel the softness of her cheek against his. He needed to smell the scent of her hair, to caress the small of her back, and to feel her press her willing body to his. This would be the most difficult deception of his life. Yet he would continue the charade, for as long as it took for him to win her confidence in his ability to manage Tillings Industries. He had to save the company from the disaster he knew loomed on the horizon. Until he could put a face on the shadow he saw lurking in the halls of Tillings, his true self and intentions would remain hidden. He decided that it would be better for her to distrust him while he waited for the cyclone he knew was building.

"Miss Tillings is here to take you to lunch, Mr. Carson." His secretary's voice interrupted his thoughts.

Calling on all his resolve, Bryan opened the door and stepped out. The next test of his strength awaited him. He would have to maintain his composure in the limousine ride to the restaurant. With Sarah sitting that close to him, he would have to fight the temptation to take her into his arms.

The long apricot stretch limousine glided through traffic on the way to Duke's. Sarah and Bryan sat in total silence. Each one felt the electrical charges that filled the confined space. Sarah glanced fleetingly in Bryan's direction, to find him studying a map of Dallas. He was trying to familiarize himself with his new home. Probably memorizing the locations of the best restaurants, she thought. He would need new haunts to which he could escort his usual bevy of females, she mused sarcastically. Well, he would find plenty to do in this town. Besides the fabulous restaurants, night clubs, and theaters, the city boasted immaculately maintained country clubs. Ownership of Tillings automatically gave him membership in Rolling Hills Country Club. It was the same club in which Jason Parson had introduced her father to Dallas society many years ago. The Tillings family was a staple at every function there. Her stepmother was especially well known. She never missed the opportunity to meet and greet the rich and famous of Dallas.

Sarah's mother died when she was eighteen, the same year

Bryan first met Sarah. In many ways, that had been a turning point in her life. Her mother had been the pillar of, not only black Dallas society, but the Tillings family and empire, as well. When she died, Martin changed. Jason Parson and John Fraser ran the company while he hid away, spending six months in total seclusion before quickly, and without fanfare, marrying Mildred. Even after he returned with his new wife, Martin never really devoted his attention to the business. His mind was elsewhere.

After about a year of the hectic life he led with Mildred, his health began to fail. Jason and John kept Wall Street from finding out, until Sarah finished her graduate studies. But, by then, much of the financial damage had been done. They did not have Martin Tillings's head for fragrance selection and marketing. Sarah inherited a company that was on very shaky ground. The bottom continued to slide from under Tillings Industries until finally Bryan Carson stepped in.

Out of the corner of his eye, Bryan could see her staring out the window. He glimpsed the perfection of her shapely legs and the perkiness of her profile. Her skirt eased up to display the pecan-colored loveliness of her calves and thighs. Briefly he allowed his imagination to picture the pleasures that lay beyond. He wondered if her hostility and coldness toward him were because he owned fifty-one percent of the business, or because of the publicity with which he had so skillfully filled his life.

Lunch at Duke's was one of the highlights of the business day in Dallas. Everyone who was anyone ate there. It was a place for making connections and deals. White table linen, crisply folded napkins, and fresh bouquets of carnations, gladiolas, and roses adorned every table. Crystal sparkled in the sunlight streaming in from the windows. Silver gleamed beside the carefully selected china emblazoned with the red "D" for Duke's.

Sarah gazed out the window as she tried to compose her thoughts. The limousine ride had been difficult. His presence had been too real. Although she sat squeezed against the door, as far from Bryan as possible, she could not avoid the warmth of his body and the piercing gaze of his eyes. She could still feel his energy radiating through her body. His presence had filled the car, as it now filled the restaurant. He was everywhere at once. There was no avoiding the magnetism of the man.

She was not alone in feeling the undeniable pull he generated. An audible gasp had filled the dining room when he entered. All of the women had stopped their conversation to gaze appreciatively as he walked by their tables. Their forks had rested untouched on their plates as their eyes turned to watch the sway of his massive shoulders and narrow hips.

The waiter had left them alone after taking their orders. She could not remember what she had selected; not that it mattered. She did not know how she would eat anything when the waiter brought their lunches.

Sarah looked up to find his gaze fixed on her face. He had been watching her the whole time. She could feel her cheeks color and her hands go cold. How long had he been studying her? What had he been thinking? She did not enjoy feeling like a treasured fish in an aquarium, yet she could not look away.

Bryan was the first to break the tension that held them transfixed. "Tell me about Dr. Morris. What sort of work does he do in that lab of his? How long has he been working on the fragrance he'll show me?" he asked, his voice thick with desire.

Grateful for the opportunity to talk about Tillings Industries' research and development arm, Sarah launched into a full description of the award-winning chemist whose new fragrance was destined to take the cosmetics industry by storm. Dr. Morris had joined the firm not long after she had become its president. His creations in cosmetics made him one of the most sought-after men in the field. The *Wall Street Journal* touted the addition of his talents as a major step to strengthening Tillings's penetration into the cosmetics market. He had lived up to his reputation and then some.

Everyone expected the new fragrance, to be announced next month, to pull Tillings Industries out in front of the other major houses. Sarah had stalled the take-over as long as she could, hoping that Dr. Morris would finish the project early and make the take-over threat a bad dream. When it looked as if the latest setback would keep her dream from becoming a reality, she had no choice but to give in. Still, she held high hopes that she would be able to remove Bryan Carson from the management of Tillings as soon as the fragrance became a household word and the money began to flow again.

Bryan listened closely to every word that fell from her lips. That woman could sell water to a cactus, he thought. She had the most beautifully defined, sensuous lips he had ever seen. He longed to pull her into his arms and taste their promises. He stared enviously at the pink tongue that darted between them.

He watched as Sarah's tongue darted between her lips, licking off the tiny spot of whipped cream remaining from the Boston cream pie. He wondered which was sweeter, the cream or her kiss. The pink tip of her tongue called up visions that were difficult for him to deny. He hardly heard her mention that they were overdue at the plant; she signed the check and rose from her chair. With difficulty, Bryan shook himself from this reverie before his thoughts embarrassed him.

Taking her elbow, Bryan guided Sarah from Duke's. The electricity jumped from her body to his fingers. He felt his fingertips tingle as he lightly touched the warm silk of her suit. He saw her eyelids momentarily flutter closed at his touch. Was she feeling the charge, too, or was it simply the glare of the sun streaming into the window that caused her to blink and look away?

Returning to the car, Sarah breathed a sigh of relief. One hurdle was crossed. Now on to the lab. She settled into the warm leather of the limousine seat and let the gentle hum of the engine caress her body. Perhaps it was the martini with lunch, but Sarah did not feel as threatened by Bryan. He was still a formidable foe, but the softness of his eyes and his touch told her that under his tough business exterior lay a man who had experienced much. She wondered if she would ever have the chance to get to know him. She knew the danger of allowing herself to cross the line between business and pleasure—especially with a powerfully attractive man like Bryan.

The plant stood only a few blocks from Duke's. Dr. Morris waited at the receptionist's desk so he could escort them to the lab when they climbed out the limousine. Chemical stains, ketchup, and mustard spotted his white lab coat. His hair was a disheveled wispy brown. His eyes peered nearsightedly over the top of his glasses. His tie contained similar spots and soup spills. His hands were dry and hard, sure and confident. Here stood a man whose main purpose in life was the chemical composition of money-making fragrance formulas. Everything else was secondary.

They walked the one flight of stairs down to Dr. Morris's lab with him in the lead. As the primary chemist, he could have had any laboratory space in the complex. Instead, he had chosen one in the bowels of the facility. He said that he would avoid the distraction of socializing with the other chemists if he removed himself from everyone. His only demand had been carte blanche privileges to order anything needed for his research. As a result, his lab was the best equipped in the cosmetics industry.

As Dr. Morris threw open the door, Bryan stepped aside to let Sarah enter. Bryan's errant thoughts were cut short by Dr. Morris's voice. He found it particularly difficult to concentrate on the details of fragrance development with the warmth of Sarah's shoulder only a few inches from his. Her particular womanly aroma filled his nostrils, blocking out all other thoughts or sensations. She did not appear to know he was in the room. Dr. Morris controlled her interest totally, or so he thought. He did not know that she struggled with her own emotions and the nearness of him.

She returned her attention to Dr. Morris. He had completed the explanation of the production of fragrances and was pouring samples of his latest creation onto testers for them to sample. First he handed them pure scent and then the essence mixed with alcohol, which was the final product.

Dr. Morris watched as Sarah and Bryan exchanged looks of approval. "Tillings Passion," as the fragrance was tentatively called, exceeded their wildest dreams. It was smooth, with an underlying hint of spice and something else, something elusive and distant, yet provocative, lurked beneath the surface. Already Sarah could see the dollars flowing into the company as women lined up at perfume counters across the country and around the world.

" 'Tillings Passion' will never do as a name," Bryan proclaimed. "What other choices has the name-selection committee suggested?"

Sarah replied, "So far that's the only one that appealed to everyone. It market-tested well with the trial group. Any suggestions you'd like to offer would be appreciated, however. Unless another is offered, we'll go with that one."

"I have a suggestion, all right. Let's call it 'Sarah.' I looked through the product names we've used so far. None of them shows a personal touch, a connection with a real woman, and the president of the company."

"I'm flattered, but I really must ask why you thought of using my name. It's really rather ordinary and sort of plain."

"There is a wholesome quality to the name Sarah, but there's something behind it, something elusive, just as there is something that escapes labeling behind this fragrance. When I think of women named Sarah, I imagine gentle strength, teamed with a comforting quality and a sense of self. At the same time, I can't help but remember the surprise every woman I've ever known with that name has offered. Sarahs are never what they appear to be on the surface. There's always something underneath that remains a mystery until they decide to share it. That's what I detect in this perfume, too. Something lies in wait until the right time," Bryan spoke more to her than to Dr. Morris, who controlled his urge to smile and discreetly looked away. It was obvious that a tension existed between these two. Maybe even a chemical reaction that they both were trying to fight.

Her cheeks blazed as Sarah responded, "We can test that suggestion, too. If it flies, great. I wouldn't mind having my name on a Tillings fragrance, especially not one that has the promise of financial success that this one has."

Turning to Dr. Morris, she said, "Thank you for the chemistry lesson. We'd best leave you to your work and head back to the office. We appreciate your giving up this time on such short notice."

Bryan extended his hand to the all-knowing chemist, who shook it energetically. He knew everything was in good hands with Dr. Morris. He also knew that the name "Sarah" would stick. The company needed the success and so did Sarah. He could tell from the twinkle in Dr. Morris's eyes that he had an ally.

Chapter Five

The return trip to Tillings Tower was long and slow. Early rush-hour traffic blocked the streets, although it was only 3:30. The heat of the summer day made the air in the limousine warm, despite the air-conditioning. Sarah had removed her suit jacket. The sight of the rise and fall of her full breasts under the cream and red striped silk blouse held Bryan's attention. He could not help but notice that Sarah did not sit squeezed into the corner of the back seat this time. The sea of leather that had separated them had disappeared. She sat directly in the center of her portion of the seat, with her hand resting on the cushion between them. She was so still that Bryan wondered if the heat had lulled her to sleep.

Sarah could feel his eyes caressing her body. She deliberately allowed the inspection, refusing to move or don her jacket. It was too hot and the sun was too bright. The afternoon had been too long and the strain of the day had been too great. She was far too attracted to him to turn away. Besides, she almost wished he would take her waiting hand in his. As the limousine crept forward at a snail's pace in the slow traffic, she wondered if she would stop him if he did. She doubted that she would have the energy or desire to pull away.

As the limousine pulled up to Tillings Tower, she realized that the moment had passed. Yet, Sarah could still feel the tension as they rode up in the crowded elevator to the penthouse floor, thirty-three stories above. She could feel Bryan's chest against her back as she took her place in front of him. His warm breath fluttered against the back of her neck.

Each floor brought relief from the crowding. Still, Bryan did not move and neither did Sarah. Was it a challenge, or a test of will? Who would be the first to put space between them?

As the door closed on the thirtieth floor, Bryan's hands came to rest on Sarah's shoulders. The warmth burned through her sweaty blouse and into her sticky flesh. Her face flared red, and her breath caught in her throat as he turned her around. She stood face to face with him. She could not turn away. She did not want to break his hold on her.

Gently, Bryan eased his fingers under her chin and lifted her face to his. For a long moment, their eyes locked. Then his began their journey to her upturned lips. Along the way, he memorized every hollow in her cheeks, the shading of her skin, and the slope of her jaw line.

His lips traced the pattern made by his eyes. He slowly kissed the curve of her upturned nose and her high cheekbones. His lips rested in the hollow of her soft brown cheeks and tickled the tiny hairs that grew there. Then he softly and gently brushed his lips in a slow, tantalizing whisper leading to her lips. He kissed first one corner and then the other before moving to his target. There his lips pressed against hers with a force that made Sarah's knees go weak. Their warmth seared into hers, holding her prisoner. Just when she felt herself beyond hope of resisting him, Bryan eased his tongue between her lips, making swift darting movements that sent sparks of passionate desire through her body.

All the while, Bryan's hands slowly caressed her shoulders and the small of her back, making small circles that sent surges of desire running through her body. Then they made their way to rest on the full roundness of her hips and buttocks. They pressed her against the hard maleness of him as he moved his hips against hers. She could feel the heat of her passion matching his. She wanted this man as she had never wanted another.

Sarah leaned against Bryan and clung to his neck. A small gasp followed by a groan from deep within her escaped from her parted lips. She had no will to resist him, and no desire to make him stop. She needed to feel the warmth of his embrace as it enfolded her. She wanted the fire and painful ecstasy his lips and darting tongue forced to bubble up from an unknown well within her. She needed to know that her own desire was matched by his. Her mind swam with thoughts, feelings, and emotions, she tossed on a sea of violent emotions. Memories of lonely evenings and empty Sunday mornings flew from her head as she moved her body against his.

Suddenly, reality invaded the security of his arms. What was she doing? This man was the enemy. He owned fifty-one percent of her father's company, and now he was trying to gain control of her. Worse, she was letting him. She was giving herself to him.

Angry at herself, Sarah pushed away from Bryan with all the strength she could muster. No, she would not surrender to him. She would not forget that she was Martin Tillings's daughter. Bryan Carson might have bought control of Tillings Industries temporarily, but he would not gain control of her for even a minute longer. She did not want anyone on her staff to think that she was having an affair with him to regain control of Tillings. Besides, there was always the possibility that the relationship would not work. He might leave her and go off to conquer yet another company and another woman, or she might end it once she had her company back. She did not want anyone to think that she used people the way her stepmother did.

"But I don't understand," Bryan stammered, trying to rees-tablish the lost moment. He had feared that she would retreat from him again. He remembered the lonely expanse of leather between them in the limousine. He did not want it to return. She felt too right in his arms.

"Oh, no; you don't. You think you can buy control of my father's company from under my nose, and then walk in here and run my life, too. As soon as my new perfume hits the market, I'm going to buy you out of Tillings Industries and my life forever. I don't know what came over me. It must have been the heat. I assure you this will never happen again," she said between angrily clenched teeth.

Sarah's sharp words helped Bryan to regain his composure. Thrusting his left hand deep within his pocket in an attempt to control the rising anger that was causing his passion to cool, he said, "I'm sorry to have misread the effects of heat exhaus-tion as a sign of your softening feelings toward me. Believe me, I never would have taken you in my arms if I had thought that you did not feel the same way, too. I'm not a man who needs to force himself on women."

Sarah felt the sting of his last words. She remembered the photographs and articles in the folder she kept locked in her desk drawer. Holly had clipped every one she could find about Bryan. It had not been a difficult task. His face filled the pages of every society paper in the United States. Everywhere he went, photographers waited to snap Bryan's picture. The images flooded through her mind. She saw beautiful women of every possible nationality and race poised on his arm. Women wearing ball gowns and mink. Women dressed in tennis skirts and sweat bands. Women astride horses. Women rallying the crowd at political dinners. Women profiling at film, music, and theatrical award shows. He was never alone. No, Bryan did not need to force himself on her. There were plenty of willing women waiting for him. A man with his tremendous good looks and great wealth never had to work to attract attention. It simply came to him, and the women with it.

As if in response to his word, the elevator door opened on the penthouse floor. Sarah spun around to face it. Her heels clicked furiously on the wooden floor as she marched toward her office. She left Bryan gazing after her and wondering if she would ever be in his arms again.

Sarah stormed into her assistant's office and slammed the door shut. Holly looked up from her paperwork. Sarah never came to her office unannounced, and certainly not in this emotional state. Not once in their long eleven-year friendship had Holly seen her so upset. She could not imagine what could be disturbing her.

"What's wrong?" she asked, putting down her pen and going to her friend's side.

"Bryan Carson, that's what wrong. That man is impossible. First he takes over my company, then he arrives late to our first board meeting and keeps me waiting fifteen minutes for him as if I have nothing better to do while he makes an unannounced visit to the laboratory. As if that were not enough, he continues to arrive at every Monday board meeting a few minutes late, making a grand entrance after I've already called the meeting to order. He makes me so mad I could just scream. He's arrogant, rude, opinionated, and impossible.

"Plus: he has started hitting on me. Sure, I find him attractive. That lock of hair on his forehead is a magnet for women, and he knows it. Just now on the elevator, he kissed me after flirting with me all afternoon at Duke's. Okay, so I kissed him back, but he took me by surprise. There wasn't anything else I could do. Anyway, I doubt he heard a word Dr. Morris said in the lab, because he kept lightly touching his shoulder against me.

"But what gives him the right to think he can take such liberties? I've done nothing to make him think that I'm the least bit interested in him. He has got to go. Tillings Tower isn't big enough for both of us. He fills every space and overflows into other people's. He's everywhere. He's in my office after he's left, in my dreams, in all my thoughts. It's just ridiculous," Sarah stormed, pacing angrily around the office. Holly stood and watched her with the tiniest trace of a smile flickering at the corners of her mouth. She knew better than to try to comfort her right now. Nothing she could say would make Sarah feel any better. Besides, she had begun to realize something that Sarah still denied to herself.

Holly had not, initially, been too fond of Bryan Carson either. He had taken over the company just when it looked as if Sarah would be about to solve their financial problems alone. Yet she had to admit that he had helped Tillings much more that he had hurt it. It was not simply the infusion of cash, but also his business sense and clear vision, that had helped put the financial picture into better focus. He knew how to invest and how to cut back without jeopardizing salaries or personnel. Many nights when everyone else had left for the day, she passed his office door to find him hard at work. He had a way of making contacts with the right people to make opportunities to showcase the product line come alive. His secretary said he was always on the telephone with possible investors. She finally had to admit to herself that he was a decent man.

More than that, she understood something that Sarah did not. Sarah was in love with Bryan and would not allow herself to face the facts. Holly had seen the way Sarah looked at him across the boardroom table when she thought he was not looking. She had heard the change in the tone of Sarah's voice when she spoke to him. She had seen the wistful expression that filled her eyes when she thought she was alone. Sarah would not admit it, even to herself, but she had it bad.

"Take it easy, Sarah. Start at the beginning and explain to me what happened. You're raving, and I can't understand a thing you're saying," Holly interjected among the muttered words of irritation that spewed from her friend like water from a broken pipe.

"I can't calm down. I've never been so angry with anyone. I wasn't even this angry when that creepy guy kissed me in front of everyone when I was a teenager. Bryan Carson has to go. That's all there is to it. If we weren't equal partners, this would be sexual harassment. I just can't believe the gall of the man!"

"What did he do? Start at the beginning and tell me everything," Holly prompted, trying to settle Sarah's rattled nerves. She sat on the edge of her desk and watched as Sarah's wild pacing slowed and then stopped on the mauve-and-navy-spotted carpet.

Standing with her hands tightly clenched at her side, Sarah took a deep breath. She spoke as calmly as her wound-up nerves would allow as she recounted the day's activities. Wrapping up, she said, "He held me so closely that the smell of his aftershave and cologne transferred to my skin and clothes. I can still smell it. It has covered over my own perfume.

"I didn't know what to do. Fortunately, we were alone. I don't know what I would have done if he had grabbed me like that in a crowded elevator in front of other people. At first I resisted, but I was so hot and tired from being with him and from the midday Dallas heat that I didn't have much strength. Besides, he's one terrific kisser. I couldn't help but respond a little bit. I'd have to be dead not to, but that doesn't mean that I wanted him to do it.

"Finally, I managed to push away and make him stop. I tried to give both of us a courteous out—you know, save his ego a little. Instead of accepting my peace offering, Bryan commented that he certainly did not need to throw himself at me, since more than enough women flocked to him. Can you believe that? First he insults me by grabbing me, and then he adds to it by mentioning other conquests. He must have forgotten that I'm his partner, not some society babe to be paraded from one party to the other. That man is not to be believed!''

Holly interrupted, ''Are you all right? He didn't hurt you, did he?'' She had noticed that Sarah had calmed down considerably as she spoke. Her breathing had returned to normal and her eyes did not flash as dangerously. When she had first burst into the room, they had been a dangerous, cold gold. Holly had never seen anyone's eyes that color before.

''No, I'm fine. I'm just angry, that's all. He even told me that women throw themselves at him. I guess that was supposed to make me feel that he was doing me a favor by paying attention to me. He must have been in the mood to take pity on the corporate president who was too busy working to date. That man certainly has nerve enough for three men. Wouldn't you have been angry if Frank had treated you that way?'' she answered, sitting on the edge of the nearest chair. She looked as if she would hop up at any minute.

''Well, to tell the truth, Sarah, I had been watching Frank for almost a year before he noticed me. You know he was in and out of a few marriages. Anyway, when he wasn't marrying or divorcing, he was waiting for you to see him as something other than a friend. It wasn't until he decided that you never would that he looked at me. But by then I had to keep myself from jumping on the man. I would have liked for him to have acted the way Bryan did, truth be told,'' she answered. Holly had never mentioned her long interest in Frank to Sarah before. Tillings had taken all of their energy. Now seemed as good a time as any.

''For that long? You should have said something. I would have had a talk with him sooner than I did if I had known how you felt about him. Anyway, it all worked out for the best. You two are happily together now. You make a good couple. I wouldn't be surprised if you got married one of these days. My problem is a little different. I don't like the man. I'll admit that I'm attracted to him—who wouldn't be—but I'm certainly not in love with him.''

"Really?" Holly asked cautiously, while playing with a paper clip.

"Of course, I'm not. Have you forgotten that he's the enemy?''

"Have *you* forgotten is more to the point.''

Sarah eased back in the chair. Suddenly a deep sadness descended over her face. "Oh, Holly, I can't believe this has happened to me. I'm not sure what it is about him that gets to me, but sometimes, like today, I find it hard to remember that he is the enemy. You know, I burst into his office unannounced yesterday and found him on a call to Morton Price, the big advertising executive who wouldn't give me the time of day because he said we were small potatoes to a company the size of his. Bryan was chatting with him about Tillings in a very casual tone. By the time he hung up, Prince had agreed to be our ad man. Can you believe it? And, only last week, Jason told me that Bryan made a huge personal contribution to the hospital fund. He just moved here, and he's already doing more for the community than most people who have lived here all their lives. You know how badly the hospital needs that new wing.''

"It's when I find out things like that that I just want to hold him, to kiss the dimples at the corners of his mouth, and to melt into him. I don't know what to do. I've never felt this way before. I'm sure the feeling will pass, but right now I alternate between feeling awful and ecstatic. But I can't allow myself to care about him, and I won't. He bought out my father's company and left me with less than majority ownership. I can't forgive him for that, ever. I don't care how much better life has been around here since he came or how much more free time I have now that he's carrying some of the load. I just can't allow myself to feel anything but sexual attraction to him, and even that I shouldn't feel.''

"Don't be too hard on yourself. You certainly can't help it if you find him attractive. There's not much you can do, either, if you find yourself in love with him."

"That will never happen. I don't care how much Jason likes him, or how much Bryan has done for Tillings; I won't fall in love with him. I'll just have to stay away from him until I never think about him anymore. That's all. I have far too much to do with running this company to take time out for love."

"Stronger women than you have fallen to Cupid's arrow. Remember Cleopatra?" Holly commented, returning to her desk.

With that, Sarah looked into Holly's skeptical eyes and walked calmly to the door. Turning around, she added, "You'll see. Even if I should momentarily slip in my resolve, Bryan will never know."

Holly whispered to the closed door, "I'm afraid this time it's you who will see. There are some things in life, Sarah, that you just can't control. Love is one of them."

Shaking his head, Bryan returned to his office and closed the door. He had promised himself after the incident in the board room that he would go slowly and not force himself on Sarah until she was ready to accept and trust him. Now, because of his lack of patience and the tension of spending the day with her, he had rushed her again and probably spoiled everything. Now he would have to start over and build her trust again. His parting words about other women had not helped, either. He saw the pained expression fill her eyes as soon as the words filled the space between them.

He gathered his messages but decided against returning any of the calls. They would wait until Monday. He had plans for the evening. Even though he was tired of the deception, he knew he had to continue the facade of being the eligible bachelor. After today's elevator ride, the charade would take on a

new twist. He wanted to show Sarah that she could not hide
from her feelings toward him. A little jealousy was just what
he needed to win her over. He knew that her reaction to him
had not been caused by the sun. She had clung to him, too,
but her pride and vanity had come between them.

Well, he had known it would not be easy to win this golden-
eyed beauty, this daughter of Martin Tillings. He had come to
Tillings Industries prepared to fight to get her. He knew that
convincing her that he had only the best interests of her company
at heart would be difficult, at best. Everyone in the industry
knew her reputation for being a hard-hearted business woman.
She had proven herself over the last five years as a force to be
reckoned with. She had gained the respect of every man and
woman in the cosmetics industry when she had brought out
three new fragrances and two new powders in the same year.
Her approach was aggressive. She was a fighter.

After months of working here, he could still feel the tension
fill the board room every time he entered. He could feel the
darts of resentment shoot from her golden eyes as she sat
across from him every Monday morning. The senior officers
had learned to accept him, but Sarah still did not totally trust
him. After this elevator ride, he wondered if she ever would.

Well, he had come prepared to fight. To fight the banks to
keep Tillings Industries alive. To fight the predators who still
waited, hoping that even Bryan Carson would not be able to
heal the ailing company. He had prepared himself to fight Sarah,
too. Slowly, she had learned to respect his business sense and
his devotion to Tillings. She knew that all his other companies
were second to this one in his affection, although she had not
guessed the reason. Still, she did not trust him personally.
Maybe she never would. Yet he was not prepared to stop now.
This weekend was just the beginning.

Chapter Six

Sarah was not in the habit of attending many social functions. She had never had the time, with the management of Tillings Industries so important in her life. Knowing Bryan's reputation for escorting beautiful women, she had quickly accepted the invitation to attend this weekend's charity ball. She had heard that he would be tonight's guest of honor and honorary chairman of the gala event. She could not resist the opportunity to show him that she did not need him, professionally or socially. With even greater determination, she wanted him to know that their relationship must and would remain strictly business. She would not be overcome by the heat of the moment again, especially not after today's luncheon and elevator ride.

The steaming water splashed off her body as Sarah slathered herself with the shower gel from the perfume line that just today had been named for her. The idea had appeal. Customers certainly liked to buy products with immediate name recognition. Other houses named products after their owners, chemists, and celebrities—why not hers?

As she showered, she hummed the tune from the old movie, *South Pacific*. She worked hard to scrub Bryan out of her hair, but it would take more than shampoo and a song. He certainly managed to get under her skin often enough, Sarah thought. It was not simply his fabulously handsome face, gray eyes, and mahogany skin, although they certainly helped. The way he walked, the sound of his voice, and the tilt of his head all made her burn with desire. These past few months had been horrible. She could not deny the feeling of desire that swept over her every time she looked at him, heard his voice, smelled his cologne, or watched him walk but, despite all that, she was not ready to trust him. His actions in the board room and the elevator had convinced her that he would own her, too, if she let down her guard long enough.

Try as she might, she could do nothing to remove him from her mind. Bryan was with her every minute of every day. No matter how hard she scrubbed her skin tonight, Sarah could not remove the feel of his hands on her body and the pressure of his kiss on her lips. No toothpaste in the world could erase the sweetness of the taste of his tongue.

She toweled off angrily. "Damn him!" she said aloud to the steamy bathroom. "Why did he have to come here? Couldn't he have ridden his great black charger and worn his fabulously fitted armor into some other company to save it? Why Tillings? Couldn't he have found some other damsel in distress to save? Surely there was some other company that needed his help. Why mine?"

Sarah wiped the mist from her gold-framed bathroom mirror and gazed at her reflection. She could see the changes the months of sharing Tillings Industries with Bryan had caused. She could not deny that some of the worry lines had softened. The furrow in her brow was not as deep. Having him there to share the financial worries had lifted the burden from her shoulders. Actually, Bryan had totally taken over the money end of Tillings, leaving her free to handle the production and marketing that were her strengths. True, he gave regular weekly reports as to the fitness of the company, but he never really shared any concerns about cash flow with her. He skillfully managed everything he touched. It was almost like having her father at the helm again.

Before Bryan entered her life, Sarah had always been able to seek refuge in this condo where she had spent her happiest years with her parents. Now, her thoughts of him went everywhere with her. Still, she loved to close the door after a hard day at the office, throw off her shoes and stockings, and walk barefoot through the thick carpet and over the colorful Turkish rugs. Her parents had bought them on one of their vacations when she was a child. With few exceptions, she had kept everything as it had been before her mother's death. Grace had selected the heavy mahogany furniture, the gleaming crystal chandeliers, the exquisite oil paintings, and the fabulous tapestry upholstery. Her sense of style had directed the selection of every accessory. Her father and Mildred had never lived here together, preferring instead a cold mansion on the outskirts of town. After graduate school, Sarah had returned and made it her home again.

Sitting at her dressing table in the large bedroom with its four-poster bed, Sarah dusted her face with a new evening powder, containing sparkles of gold for a healthy glow, that Tillings had just introduced on the market. Not bad, she thought, examining her profile under the low lighting of her bedroom. Easing her red satin gown up over her breasts, Sarah again caught the relaxed expression on her face and the gentle slope of her shoulders.

"No, it's not the same at all," she thought as she dabbed some perfume on her pulse points—the hollow of her throat, her wrists, behind her knees, and between her breasts. "I'm not impressed that he only assumed the title of chief executive officer and graciously allowed me to remain the president. I'm not as trusting and easily won over as Holly and Frank. They think Bryan only wants what's good for Tillings. I'm not convinced that he's that unselfish.''

She clipped her mother's diamond earrings to her ears, and snapped off the light before walking down the circular staircase. Catching her reflection in the foyer mirror, Sarah smiled. Looking back at her was a beautiful woman, the color of fresh roasted pecans, decked out in her finest. The red satin gown accentuated every curve. Her upswept hair revealed cascading diamond earrings that glittered at her ears. Red satin slippers with rhinestone-encrusted toes and heels sparkled on her feet. Bryan would find her hard to resist tonight as she twirled around the dance floor on another man's arm. Giving her hair a final pat, she walked to the living room. Her escort waited.

The grand ballroom at the Grand Palace Hotel glowed with the lights from the many sparkling chandeliers that hung overhead from the high ceiling. The wealthiest of Dallas society floated across the dance floor and visited from table to table, chatting about investment, futures, horse races, divorces, marriages, and scandals. Everyone who was anyone in Dallas glittered here. This was the main social event of the season. The only acceptable excuses for not attending were illness, death, or travel out of the country.

Sarah and Frank Rogers stood in the archway, looking over the throng of perfectly coifed women and splendidly attired men. Her hand rested lightly on his arm. They had been friends since they were children playing in the sandbox together. Now that he was dating Holly and their old romantic tensions were long behind them, their friendship was closer than ever. Holly had not objected when Sarah suggested that she would invite him to the gala tonight, knowing that she did not need the complication of having to make small talk. Besides, Frank and Holly both needed time to sort out some problems.

Frank had recently divorced his fourth wife. After five years of drifting apart, they had decided to call it quits. He did not regret the decision, and his relationship with Holly was most satisfying. He just needed time to clear his head and to sort things out and to be sure that he was not rushing into anything. Still, he could not miss this affair. That would be admitting to all of Dallas that he was suffering, which he was not. When his old friend the workaholic Sarah called, he had jumped at the chance to enjoy the evening's festivities with her. He was relieved to find that Bryan Carson had not added her to his list of successes with women. As a matter of fact, Sarah seemed decidedly uninterested in her business partner. Frank wondered if there were more going on here than met the eye. Perhaps she had fallen for him but was afraid to show it. But fear was definitely not in Sarah's vocabulary.

Frank chuckled at the memory of fifteen-year-old Sarah. She had given Bobby Thomas a black eye because he had grabbed her at the pool and kissed her in front of everyone. She liked Bobby just fine, she just did not want everyone knowing that she did. She felt he had shown poor judgment in making a public spectacle of both of them in front of the entire country club. Bobby's interest in her had cooled after that. Much to Sarah's despair, he transferred his affections to her friend Heather.

After that, Sarah had not had any serious teenage relationships that Frank could remember. She had stayed pretty much to herself, almost as if afraid to love. Then her mother had died and her father had married Mildred. Sarah had been pretty much alone, even during college, so her friend and assistant Holly said. Running the business had kept her pretty busy after her father's death, except for the ill-fated engagement to him. Glancing at her standing at his side, Frank hoped she would find some happiness now that Bryan was here to share the burden of Tillings Industries with her.

Sarah did not know that she was the focus of Frank's thoughts. She was too busy scouring the sea of faces for the only one that mattered—Bryan's. She wanted him to see her entrance on Frank's arm. She wanted to let him know that he was not the only drop-dead handsome man in Dallas. Frank, with his curly light brown hair, could stop hearts too, especially when his deep brown eyes looked from under the thick black lashes that fringed them. Many women had fallen for him. There had been times over the years when she had come close to falling herself.

With her hand resting lightly on Frank's arm, Sarah descended the steps and made her way to a table near the edge of the room. She had requested this seating so that she could see the goings-on, as well as be seen by all who entered. She wanted Bryan to notice every move she made, and to know that her happiness did not depend on him.

Passing one table after the other, she spoke to everyone along the way. The soft light from the chandeliers cast a glow on every bare shoulder. Carefully coifed hair shone in the candlelight. Perfume from only the best houses filled the air, like so many flowers from the garden. Jewels bedecked every throat, and every finger glittered with its own special ornaments, among which were the greenest emeralds, the reddest rubies, and the most luscious blue sapphires. The stars shone in the heavens, and in the grand ballroom tonight, in Dallas.

Her eyes eagerly searched the room for Bryan as she eased into her chair and allowed her wrap to slide off her shoulders, revealing her warm brown skin. Laughing, happy faces spread before her, but not one of them was his. Already he had managed to ruin her evening, without even knowing it. He had spoiled the excitement of her deliberately planned fashionably late entrance by not being there to see it.

With a sigh, Sarah turned back to Frank's conversation. They had known each other forever. She felt as if she were listening to her older brother. Yet he had grown into a strikingly handsome man. His shoulders and chest had broadened with age since he had been the skinny teenage boy she had chased around the pool.

Suddenly there was a great swish of clothes and a craning of heads toward the grand stairway. All eyes turned at once. Bryan Carson stood at the top of the stairs. The town's most eligible bachelor, with the most notorious reputation for being seen with fabulously beautiful women, had finally arrived. He did not disappoint either his admirers or his detractors tonight. On his arm was a disarmingly beautiful woman. Her chestnut-colored hair cascaded in soft ringlets down her back and around her sweet, heart-shaped face. A smile of nonchalant disregard for anyone in the room other than Bryan crinkled the corners of her perfectly painted lips. Almost translucent silvery blue silk wrapped itself around her divine figure, revealing all the decency would allow.

No one in the grand ballroom breathed as Bryan and this heavenly creature descended the stairs. As they made their way past the first table at the rear of the room, the silence was suddenly broken by whispered speculation. Could this stranger be the woman of his dreams? Where had Bryan found her? She certainly was not a resident of Dallas. She was not a local beauty.

Anger tinged some of the curiosity. "Why did Bryan find it necessary to invite a stranger to the most important event of the summer social season?" whispered women at all the neighboring tables. Their husbands had nothing to say; they were too busy ogling the vision in blue as she floated by.

Sarah watched as they slowly made their way to the empty seats at the head table. From her vantage point, she could see that the mystery woman did indeed possess striking beauty. Her skin was café-au-lait in color, with just a tinge of summer tan. Her makeup had been skillfully applied to cover any imperfections in tone. Her figure was hourglass perfect, each curve having its own special purpose.

Bryan looked neither pleased nor embarrassed by the stir

they caused. His face wore an expression of studied indifference, almost as if he were tired of being noticed—even if he did arrive late for that very purpose. He nodded his head, waved, and spoke to everyone along his path, gently holding the woman's hand in his.

As Sarah watched his procession, a fire from deep within her spread through her entire body. Her cheeks grew red and hot. The evening was not playing out the way she had planned it. She was supposed to be the one who turned heads as she floated in on Frank's arm. In her version, Bryan had sat at the head table, watching her. Instead, she had to endure the sight of him strutting to his place with this exquisite beauty on his arm. Worse still, she hated the thought that she looked at him with the same hunger in her eyes as did the other women in the room. She should have more control over herself—but when she was around him all reason, sense, and logic flowed from her body, to be replaced by a burning fire that started at her heart and continued to her groin.

Frank's reaction did not help matters one bit as he leaned over and said, "Wow, where do you suppose he met her? She's fabulous. Definitely not a Dallas woman."

Shooting him a killer look, Sarah answered, "She's a bit showy,don't you think? She must be one of his old girlfriends from his New York days. You're right about one thing; she's definitely not from Dallas. No one from here would dare to wear a dress like that in this heat. One drop of perspiration and the effect would be ruined. It certainly is bad form to arrive so late. I wonder if pretentious entrances are a habit of his." Once again, she had forgotten that she had planned to do the same thing.

In truth, Sarah had arrived almost as late as Bryan, hoping to cause the same stir. She had only just stopped sulking about her own ruined grand entrance when he arrived and upstaged her, throwing her into a totally foul mood.

Ignoring the darts that fired from her smoky gold eyes, Frank said approvingly, "Well, if you ask me, any woman who looks the way that one does can arrive as late as she likes."

Sarah kicked him—none too playfully—under the table.

"Hey, why did you do that?" Frank asked, rubbing his shin and chuckling. He had known Sarah long enough to recognize the sign of the green-eyed monster when he saw it. He was aware that they were on this non-date for only one reason—to make Bryan jealous. Now it looked as if the plan had backfired. Sarah was the one with the decidedly green tinge.

To save his leg any more abuse, Frank asked, "Would you like to dance?"

Quickly calculating the effect of negotiating the crowd to the dance floor, directly in front of the head table, Sarah accepted with a smile so bright that Frank almost forgot his painful shin. She certainly could be charming when she wanted to be, he thought. Whatever she had up her sleeve, he was glad it was not directed at him.

Frank was the envy of every man in the room as he escorted Sarah through the maze of tables. All eyes were on them as they twirled around the dance floor. The jewels at her ears sparkled brightly with every turn. Her feet barely touched down as they danced the waltz and the fox trot.

As Bryan watched Sarah smile into Frank's face, he felt anger swell within him. She had never gazed at him that way. She had never laughed at his jokes with that much enthusiasm. He could tell that she was relaxed with Frank in a way that she had never been with him. He tapped his fingers angrily on the white damask tablecloth. Even the beautiful woman at his side could not stop the feelings that surged within him. His companion, his place at the center table, and his chairmanship of the charity ball committee had been carefully calculated to draw attention to him and to make Sarah jealous. Seeing her this happy, he wondered if his plan was working. She did not seem to know that he existed.

Bryan did not suspect that Sarah's beguiling smile and her escort were parts of her own carefully orchestrated plan. She was aware of the reaction Frank would cause among the envious women. He was tall, handsome, broad shouldered, witty, and flashing-eyed . . . and unattached at the moment. Sarah could tell that all the women in the room, even those who knew of their former engagement and his relationship with Holly, wondered if she would be wife number five. She knew that the men would try to guess if she had ever plotted to snare Frank to save her company.

He had heard all of this and more. Bryan knew all the gossip that floated through black Dallas society. He had checked out the entire scene while he was deciding to buy controlling interest in Tillings. He knew who was sleeping with whom, which marriages were based on money, not love, whose finances were in shambles, who was seeing a psychiatrist, and who was in the process of getting a divorce. No one in the room had escaped his scrutiny. After all, taking control of a family-owned company in a tightly knit black community meant knowing everything about everyone. He had known who his allies would be before he had begun the take-over process. He also knew his enemies.

Bryan was not the only one watching Sarah tonight. Sitting at the table immediately to his right was Mildred, Sarah's stepmother. She stared at Sarah and Frank twirled around the floor. Never had she seen her stepdaughter looking so fabulous, so joyous, and so relaxed. Was it Frank's scintillating conversation? Somehow, she doubted it. Sarah and Frank had been friends too long for love to have sprung up between them now. They knew each other's flaws and foibles all too well. Someone else must be the source of her happiness or her charade.

Glancing to her left, Mildred saw her answer. At the neighboring table, with smoke all but coming from his ears, sat

Bryan Carson. She looked into Bryan's tormented face and knew immediately. He had fallen in love with Sarah. Did Sarah know, she wondered? Is that why she danced so freely with Frank? Sarah hated social functions. Why was she here tonight? Was Sarah playing a cat-and-mouse game with the man's emotions while dancing so provocatively close to Frank? Had she seen the look of mingled pain, unbridled affection, and rage that filled Bryan's face?

Mildred would make it her business to find out. This evening would not be the terrible bore she had expected it to be. Thinking back on the past five years with Sarah, she reflected that she had never liked the energy of her stepdaughter or her devotion to Tillings Industries. Although everyone considered her a calculating, conniving woman who would stop at nothing to get what she wanted, Mildred had felt wounded because Martin did not appreciate all she had done for him because of Sarah, Grace's memory, and Tillings. It had hurt her deeply when he had called out Grace's name at his death, when her face should have been the last thing on his mind.

Watching Martin's daughter whirl around the floor in the arms of a dashing old friend, while being glared at by a man who was even more appealing, made Mildred feel better somehow. She vowed to find a way to use Bryan's obvious love for Sarah to her advantage. If her suspicions were confirmed, and if Sarah truly did share his affection, she would have more ammunition than she needed. Until she was sure, she would sit patiently and watch. When the time was right, she would use that she knew to her advantage.

The band played the final cords of a waltz and then fell silent. The dancers returned to their seats, as Bryan stepped to the microphone. All eyes focused on him. Scanning the room, Sarah could see the admiration and longing on the faces of almost every woman in the room, while the men wore expressions of deliberate concentration. Sarah felt a tug of envy as she watched Bryan's date gaze at him with a rapturous expression of belonging.

"Ladies and gentlemen," he began, "on behalf of the Harmony House Hospital Capital Campaign committee, I would like to take this opportunity to thank you for giving of your time, money, and talents to make tonight's gala a success. With your help we have raised well over six million dollars this year to defray the cost of the new wing for the hospital. That brings our two year total to fifteen million dollars. With your continued support, we will reach our goal of twenty-five million by Christmastime. Construction will begin as planned in September; therefore, your continued devotion to Harmony House is vital.

"For tonight, however, let us put aside all thoughts except those of having fun. Eat, drink, dance, and mingle. We seldom have the time to come together as a community. Let's take advantage of these few hours together. Enjoy!"

With that, applause filled the grand ballroom. Waiters appeared, bearing trays loaded with caviar, pheasant, quail, oysters Rockefeller, salads, shrimp, and other assorted delicacies. Conversation quieted as the gathered members of black Dallas society consumed the tempting delicacies with relish.

Sarah stole a quick look in Bryan's direction. He did not look as if he were enjoying his dinner, or the company of the beauty sitting next to him. His brow was furrowed, and he hardly touched his food. His dazzling beautiful guest did not seem to share his distress, however. She consumed each mouthful with obvious glee, dabbing at the corners of her mouth and savoring every bite. Sarah wondered what could possibly be troubling the most admired and sought-after man in the room. She knew that, before the evening was over, many of the women would have discreetly slipped business cards bearing their private telephone numbers into his pockets. His telephone messages were the talk of the secretaries at Tillings Industries. According to them, more than half of his callers were women.

Again, Sarah felt the now-familiar tug at her emotions, and warmth spread across her cheeks. Silently, she scolded herself for reacting to the thought of other women finding Bryan desirable. Surely she was not the only one who knew he was the most handsome man in the room. Even Frank could not hold a candle to his good looks. Bryan was one of those men who was heart-wrenchingly handsome, but carried himself as if he never noticed the women who all but threw themselves at his feet.

Still, she could not stop the feeling that swept over her. Could she be jealous of the admiring glances from other women? The answer was a loud, screaming yes. She hated the way their eyes consumed every inch of Bryan's body, starting with that irritatingly appealing lock of hair. She despised the weakness and hunger that showed on their faces as they watched him through carefully veiled eyes. She resented the way they licked their red lips in preparation for the kisses of which they dreamed, but which would never become reality. Most of all, she grew angry with herself for having the same expression in her half-closed eyes, for the soft yielding set of her shoulders, and for the tongue that played at the corner of her all-too-willing, pouting lips.

Shaking herself slightly, Sarah turned her attention to a somewhat startled Frank. As her conversation became more animated and she repeatedly touched his hand and laughed a bit too loudly at his jokes, Frank chuckled to himself. It was true that he loved the attention. However, he knew what Sarah was doing. He had not missed either the looks she darted at Bryan or the soft sighs she breathed when their eyes met before she quickly turned away.

Frank had known her long enough to understand that she was a woman in love and denying it to herself. Yet he did not know why Sarah worked so hard at trying to ignore Bryan.

Was it his controlling interest in Tillings Industries, or the constant reminders that were plastered across every newspaper of his popularity with women that caused her to turn her attention from Bryan and toward him? Frank did not know, but he would try to find out.

Frank had secretly hoped to have Sarah for his own one day. He had thought that she would have turned to him for help when Tillings had fallen on hard times. He would have proposed more than just a financial arrangement. But, before he could act, the rumors of Bryan Carson's interest in Tillings had filled the financial pages and the gossip columns of Dallas. Still he waited, thinking that she would prefer combining her dwindling fortunes with his to being taken over by an outsider.

When Sarah did not turn to him, Frank realized that the opportunity had passed. He would have to wait until he found another chance to ask his old friend and childhood sweetheart to be his wife. She probably would not have had him, anyway, he consoled himself. His reputation with women and his many marriages made him almost as infamous as Bryan, especially in the small circle of the black elite of Dallas. Still, it was flattering to have this stunningly beautiful woman hanging on his every word—even if she were using him for her own purposes.

Frank looked into Sarah's sparkling gold eyes. His childhood friend had certainly blossomed. She had grown into her long calf-like legs and bony knees. The slender arms that used to climb trees faster than most boys were scrubbed clean of scars. Her flat, childish chest had filled out nicely, he noticed, as she leaned close and brushed her supple breasts against his arm. He felt his breath catch as her fingers traced the veins in the back of his hand.

Yes, Sarah was definitely not a child any longer. Whatever game she was playing with Bryan, he was more than happy to be her partner in it. Suddenly, a thought shot through him. How far would she go to make Bryan jealous? Maybe there was still hope that they could become something more than just friends. If she would not marry him to save Tillings, maybe she would take him as a lover to make her business partner jealous. Frank would wait and see.

Chapter Seven

When the last of the china and silver had been cleared away, the band sprang into high gear. Putting away the mellow sounds of Bach and Beethoven, it moved into music guaranteed to work out the stiffness of sitting and burn off calories. Dallas was a town that loved a good time, and a good time required good food followed by good music. Before the first notes could float to the high ceiling, the social elite of black Dallas, bedecked in jewels, satin, silk, and chiffon, was on the dance floor. Every foot tapped out the beat of music that rocked the soul and turned even the most reserved dowager into a Josephine Baker.

Diamond-encrusted hair caught the light of the chandeliers as the richest and finest twirled, bobbed, strutted, and bumped. Full uplifted breasts, tiny waists, and slim hips pressed temptingly against black tuxedoed partners who laughed at the tease, hoping for more than a fleeting promise of passion. Lips pouted, eyes fluttered closed, and manicured fingers snapped to the rhythm of soulful music and the throbbing of the drum beat.

The movers and shakers of black Dallas moved and swayed to the sounds of Smokey Robinson, Anita Baker, Nat King Cole, Luther Vandross, and Patti LaBelle, played by a band that knew its business, and wanted all of Dallas to know it, too.

With good spirits came open wallets. Looking around the room, Bryan knew that the money would flow tonight. Already the gold baskets on each table overflowed with discreet white envelopes containing generous donations. Harmony House Hospital would have no trouble making its financial goals this evening.

Bryan watched as Sarah skillfully played the game of flirtation. He did not miss seeing a laugh, a seductively leaned shoulder, or a caressingly placed finger. He felt his chest tighten every time he looked in her direction. Try as he might, he could not keep his eyes from returning to her table. He watched her fingers play along the back of Frank's hand, her shoulder press against his, and her eyes flash into his smiling, adoring face. With every move, Bryan found less to interest him on his dessert plate or in the face and figure of his date. He had planned to make Sarah jealous tonight. He had not counted on her obvious infatuation with Frank or the effect the sight of them would have on him.

Damn his assistant, Bryan fumed. He had ordered full profiles of Tillings, the company, and Sarah Tillings, the woman, before finalizing the take-over arrangements. He had wanted no surprises. The research had been thorough, or so he had thought. Every aspect of the company's workings and finances had been laid open for his inspection. He knew its strengths, its weaknesses, and its competition. He thought he knew its president, too. Obviously, there was a side to her that his assistant had missed in her research. No one had told him that there was a man in Sarah's life. He had thought that Frank and Sarah were simply old friends: nothing more. But old friends did not share spoonfuls of peach melba. Old friends did not dab whipped cream from the corner of each other's lips. Old friends did not dance with their bodies fused together. Old friends did not whisper into each other's ears and giggle provocatively. Sarah's head should not be resting on Frank's shoulder. Frank's hand should not be caressing the gentle curve of her bare waist. They were definitely not just old friends.

Bryan was not a man who liked surprises. He also did not like to lose. Tillings, the company, was not his only goal in the take-over. He could have bought controlling interest in any number of cosmetics companies. He wanted Sarah. And he would have her. If it meant going to battle to win her, he would. At least now he knew the name of his competition: Frank Rogers.

Almost pulling his startled date to her feet, Bryan joined the happy throng on the dance floor. He knew that any man in the room would give his eyetooth for a moment with her, for a dance, for the feel of her fingertips easing their way down the collar of his shirt. But Bryan was immune to her efforts and her beauty. The aroma of her perfume did not make his blood run hot. The sway of her hips did not cause fire to burn in his groin. The smell of her hair did not make him long to take her to bed. She only made him long all the more for Sarah, and despise the man who held her yielding warm body against his. He hardly felt her breasts against his chest or her thigh lightly touching his. Her fingers on the back of his neck only tickled, much as a pesky fly would if it danced across his slightly moist skin. They did not make his breathing difficult, his heart quicken, and his manhood erect, as Sarah's did.

Forcing himself to pay attention to the beauty in his arms, Bryan smiled into her large, lash-fringed brown eyes. He had plotted to break down Sarah's defenses against him by sweeping Alyce into his arms, laughing into her eyes, and whispering sweet nothings into her ears. Well, the gala was not over yet. There was still time—although, at the moment, Sarah seemed not to know that he was even in the room.

Bryan glanced at Sarah and pulled Alyce closer. Alyce gig-

gled at his tightening embrace and eased her hips into a slow
rhythmic pattern matching his own. She pressed against him
invitingly. Bryan closed his eyes and swayed against her, listening to the soulful sounds of the male singer croon Johnny
Mathis's old standby "Chances Are."

Sarah felt her heart sink. Bryan was enjoying himself in
another woman's arms, entirely too much. Had this afternoon's
kiss in the elevator, steamy with their long repressed emotions,
meant nothing to him? How could he hold this woman like
this after crushing his lips against hers? Had he only been
planning to add her to his list of conquests? Had he truly
planned to make her his next acquisition? And to think that
she had dropped her defenses—allowed herself to feel something for him and to need the security of his arms. She was
angry with Bryan, but mostly she was furious with herself. She
had allowed her resistance to weaken, her defenses to slip, and
her resolutions to dissolve. She had allowed herself to consider
caring about the enemy, the man who would take Tillings
Industries from her. She had wanted him and almost given
herself to him—in an elevator.

Frank led Sarah back to their table. The dance floor was too
crowded, and they needed a cool drink. At the bar Frank found
himself standing next to Bryan. He had never actually met the
inspiration for Sarah's deception. Taking the opportunity, he
introduced himself, saying, "Welcome to Dallas, Bryan. I'm
Frank Rogers, long-time friend of Sarah Tillings and her family.
I've heard so much about you, and it's good to have you join
our little circle. Dallas needs more farsighted men like you.
Men who can lead our companies and guide their growth.
You've got yourself a good company in Tillings Industries.
Martin Tillings built quite an empire. Gave his life to it. The
only thing he loved more than Tillings Industries was that
beautiful daughter of his."

Watching the two men, Sarah wondered what was transpiring between them. They were certainly the most handsome men in the room but, undeniably, Bryan was the more impressive of the two. His six-foot-five frame towered over Frank's, at six feet even. His darker complexion made Frank look positively pale. His broad shoulders dwarfed Frank, making him appear thin and frail. Yet Frank was holding his own against Bryan. Sarah felt a glow of pride for her old friend. Frank was smaller, but he had a certain carriage that said he knew who he was and that he would not back down. Frank was old Dallas money at its best.

She could not help but wonder what it would have been like to have married Frank before the long parade of wives had begun. Would their marriage have lasted, or would she have been the first of many? Maybe he just was not the marrying kind. He was very attentive, but maybe his interests were short-lived. Maybe he was better at the chase than the long-term working out of problems in a relationship. Fortunately, she had realized early that a marriage between them probably would not have worked, not so much because of the distractions of other women, but because they knew each other too well. There would not have been any surprises. It was best that they had remained friends through all the years without letting love and marriage get in the way. She hoped Holly would not be hurt by him.

Seeing the two men together, Sarah could detect a certain hostility between them. Maybe it was the way in which they looked at each other. Their stares were too intense, and their handshake too long. She wished she could be a fly on the wall and listen to their conversation.

Returning the solid grasp, Bryan answered, ''Thanks. It's good to be here. Yes, Tillings is a solid company, all right. There are a few problems, but nothing that can't be overcome.

By the way, I couldn't help noticing your devotion to Sarah. Mind if I ask the nature of your relationship? I like to know everything about the people I work with, and she keeps pretty much to herself.''

Frank eyed Bryan cautiously. What was his real reason for wanting to know about his feelings toward Sarah? When he had separated from his last wife, she had told him that they would always be friends and nothing else. Now that he was in a new relationship with Holly, Frank decided to have a little fun at Bryan's expense. Maybe Frank could find out his interest in his buddy. He replied with a wily smile, ''Sarah and I have been close since we were children. Most people, including our parents, thought we'd eventually marry. Unfortunately, I did not have the good sense to listen to them. Whenever I was between wives, Sarah was either in school or too busy. Still, it's never too late, you know. With you here to help with the running of Tillings, I might be about to catch up with her. She has never had the time to attend this gala but, tonight, thanks to you, she's here.''

Bryan thought back on everything he knew about Frank Rogers, the wealthy playboy who had already divorced wife number four. So this man had Sarah in his sights, might want to make her number five. Well, he'd see about that.

Taking their drinks from the bartender, Frank added, ''Again, it's good to have you on board. Enjoy your evening, Bryan.''

''Thanks, Frank,'' he replied, feeling his temper rise. Thanks to him! Thanks to him Sarah was in the arms of an old sweetheart who had every intention of marrying her. What a fool he was! Playing right into the enemy's hands without even knowing it. He had practically given Sarah to Frank by pulling those stunts in the board room and elevator. He had misread her feelings toward him, and pushed her to Frank by being too forward and too self-assured. From now on, he would tread more carefully.

* * *

In this contemplative mood, Bryan did not see Mildred Tillings until she stood beside him. She was the last person Bryan wanted to talk with tonight, but it was too late for him to get away. "Bryan," she oozed, "you and your committee have made this an absolutely fabulous night. The gala has never been so well attended. We've never raised so much money for the hospital in a single evening. First, saving my dear husband's little company, and then working miracles for the hospital's capital campaign. You're just too wonderful."

Bryan could see why Martin Tillings had been drawn to this woman. She was beautiful. Not the same way Sarah was. But Mildred Tillings had a flare, a way of looking at a man that made him instantly feel important. She was giving Bryan that look of admiration now. If Bryan were not already so taken with Sarah, he would have instantly been intrigued by Mildred. Her eyes were perfectly lined, her lashes lightly dusted with gold flecks, her perfume far from subtle but not overpowering, and her gown a second skin that accentuated every well-tuned curve. She was a very handsome woman—very appealing in every way, with looks calculated to appear younger than her fifty years.

She was from one of the first black families of Dallas and had been rich before she married Martin Tillings. She had been one of the most beautiful women of her generation. She was one of the most beautiful of the women of her age, now. She was a walking advertisement for Tillings Rejuvenation Cream, which she applied lavishly every night and morning. As the widow of the founder of the company, she ordered the sweet-smelling, terribly expensive miracle worker by the case, and it worked. No one would have guessed that she was almost fifty.

Even Mildred's body was firm. It should be. She worked out with a private trainer every day for four hours. Then she swam laps in her indoor pool and walked four-mile stints on the treadmill. Every other day she played either tennis or golf at the club, depending on which of her lady friends was available. Mildred loved to show off her fabulous figure under extravagantly expensive clothes. She never tired of shopping at the Green Door or Bladens, two of the most trendy shops in town. Her slender frame and frisky walk were the talk of the town whenever she left the room.

Yes, everyone liked Mildred at first sight. It was only after they came to know her that they saw through the glamour that hid a woman who was as cold as ice. Mildred had made Martin miserable during the years of their marriage. Some of the less-than-kind residents of Dallas said that she had even hastened his death from heart attack. They said that trying to keep up with her after living most of his life with Grace had been too much for him. His best friends always questioned what it was that had attracted him to Mildred.

Yes, there was something in Mildred's eyes, in the depth of her stare, that said she was not what she appeared to be. Her smile was a little too practiced. Her head tilted to hear every word a bit too intently. Her smooth hands clung a little too closely. Her bosom heaved with the excitement of meeting a man a bit too much. Bryan decided that this was a woman to be watched. She could either be a very powerful friend or a very dangerous foe.

He had heard that there was bad blood between Sarah and her stepmother. Mildred blamed Sarah, her dead mother, and the company for taking Martin away from her, for depriving her of a husband's true love and devotion. Sarah felt that her father had been bewitched by this hazel-eyed beauty. She thought he spent too much time with her, traveled when he should have been running Tillings Industries, and lavished money foolishly on her whims.

Bryan knew that Mildred had not initially been in favor of the take-over. She wanted to sell Tillings Industries to save her investment. Even after Sarah bought out most of her stake in the 49% they owned together, she remained hesitant, and determined to find a buyer for the remainder of her shares. When she learned of his plans for expansion, she changed her mind and became his advocate.

Looking into Mildred's upturned face, Bryan wondered what this woman had in mind. Her smile was too come-hither to be simply business. She looked as if she wanted more from him than good investments, stock growth, and profits. It was flattering, but it was also unnerving. Bryan liked to be the aggressor, but with Mildred he felt that she wanted to be in control.

"Dance with me," she purred, taking his arm.

"Certainly," he replied, allowing her to lead him through the crowd to the dance floor.

Mildred slipped into his arms as if they were old friends, rather than perfect strangers. She pressed her body against his, matching her sways with his own. As he guided her around the floor, she hummed softly into his ear, her warm breath sending sparks down his spine.

Yet, Bryan could not allow himself to enjoy her attention. He knew that Mildred was up to something, but he could not tell exactly what it was. Usually, when so attractive a woman threw herself at him, Bryan did not hesitate to accept her advances. This time, with this woman, he found himself on guard. He could almost hear her mind hashing out a deception as they stopped in front of Sarah's table.

"Don't hesitate to call me any time you have even the slightest question about Tillings Industries, or if anything else of concern arises. I'd be more than happy to help in any way I can, any way at all," Mildred urged, giving his lips a soft yet lingering kiss. Leaving him standing with empty arms and Sarah's eyes burning into his face, Mildred eased her swinging hips into the crowd.

* * *

Sarah could stand no more of the spectacle Mildred was making with Bryan. Grabbing her shawl, she stood and said, "Excuse me, Frank, but I have to get some fresh air. You don't need to follow me; I'll be okay as soon as I get out of here for a few minutes."

Frank knew better than to insist on accompanying her. He had seen that mixture of fear, anger, frustration, and irritation in Sarah's eyes when someone got under her skin. From her reaction, he knew that there was more between Sarah and Bryan than a business partnership. He wondered if that was why she had been so attentive tonight. More than that, he wondered if she had faced her feelings for Bryan. She was determined to keep him at a distance; she might be denying the depth of her own emotions to herself. He sat and watched her thin proud shoulders ease through the crowded dance floor to the open French doors that led to the balcony and peace.

Roses, carnations, daisies, lilies, and marigolds bloomed in mad profusion on the balcony. Hibiscus added lively color around the grounds. As Sarah stepped out into the warm Dallas evening, the song of the last mockingbird of the evening filled the air. In the pond that gurgled in the distance, night-blooming water lilies lent their sweet perfume to the night. The sky was wonderfully clear for that time of year. Stars twinkled brightly overhead. The night sky reminded her of when she had been a little girl and had sat on the back porch making wishes on the first star of evening. Her desires were simple then, and usually satisfied by her father and mother without her ever having to ask. She would wish for a special doll or a new pony. As she grew older, her wishes became more complicated and harder to fulfill. When she was twelve, she remembered wishing for world peace. She still waited for that one to come true.

She never wished on stars any more. No magic could turn her dreams into reality now. Hard work and determination mixed with luck and God's help would bring her wishes to reality. Besides, she had learned that she had to be careful what she wished for. Often, vaguely worded desires brought partial satisfaction. After all, she had wanted Tillings to be safe and protected, but, in making her request, she was not specific in saying how she wanted it saved. Now, she had Bryan Carson as her savior. Somehow, she was not sure if she had been better off before or since his arrival.

Before Bryan came, Sarah only had to worry about the health of Tillings Industries. She was too tired and busy to have any time for herself. Her social life was almost non-existent after she broke off her engagement to Frank. She seldom dated, except for the required attendance at charity balls.

Now that Bryan had joined her in managing Tillings, she was terribly confused to find herself falling desperately in love with the man who had taken over her company and her heart. True, he had made the financial picture at Tillings considerably more rosy, and he had freed her from the drudgery of figures to do market research and planning. But, along with helping untangle the mess her father had left her at his death, Bryan had also made her emotions into a jumbled, topsy-turvy collection of thoughts and feelings.

She was so confused she felt like crying almost all the time. Sarah constantly questioned her own reactions to him. How could she love the man who now controlled her company, her heritage, her father's legacy? Yet she was pulled to him by a force too strong for her to deny. When she was in his arms, she felt warm and secure. She forgot his reputation with women when his hands and lips caressed her body. When he was away from her, disturbing memories of his photographs with other women flashed through her mind.

Mildred . . . the thought of her in his arms made Sarah's blood boil. It was not enough that she had stolen her father's affections from her and Tillings; now she wanted Bryan, too.

And what Mildred wanted, Mildred got. Sarah was sure she would stop at nothing to add him to her list.

Pulling her shawl more tightly around her cold shoulders despite the warmth of the evening, Sarah shuddered. She knew she had to return to the ballroom soon. People would wonder about her absence. Frank would be hard pressed for an excuse. She had to build up the courage to face Mildred and Bryan. It would not be easy.

"Sarah, are you all right? I was worried about you," Bryan's voice broke into the silence of her tortured thoughts.

"I'm fine, thanks. I just needed some air. I'm surprised you noticed that I had left the room. You and my stepmother certainly seem to have hit it off well," Sarah almost growled from between clenched teeth.

Bryan looked down at her drawn face. He could see more than irritation in the lines around her mouth. Betrayal and hurt shone from her simmering tawny eyes. Barely disguised was something else.

"Do I detect a note of jealousy? I distinctly remember you pushing me away. I didn't think you cared enough about me to be bothered by my conversations with other women," he answered with a slight smile playing at the corner of his lips. His hand rested on the balcony railing behind her.

"I could care less about your attractions to other women. You're unattached and over twenty-one. Other than on a professional level, there's nothing between us. Why should I care what you do and with whom?" she responded, feeling the color rise to her pecan cheeks. The last thing she wanted him to do was to see her discomfort at his accusations and the closeness of his body. His arm was barely inches from her waist. Sparks of electricity leaped between them.

"But you do care, Sarah. I'd say you care a great deal. Why don't you admit your feelings so we can get on with our life together?" He slowly traced the swell of her breasts over the plunging neckline of her dress. His fingers sent shivers of pleasure through her body.

Her breath came in gulps. She was afraid of the passion that charged through her. She feared what her reaction to this man might be.

"The only reason I even noticed you was that you were talking with my stepmother, Mildred. She's notorious for eating men and spitting out their remains. You're new to Dallas. She might be planning to add you to her full plate. If you had not been with her, I would not have paid any attention to you at all," she responded, trying to look terribly unimpressed with the company he chose to keep.

"I don't buy that for one moment, Sarah. I watched you when Alyce and I entered the ballroom. You were a little green around the eyes, if you ask me."

"Oh, really? Well, it seems to me that your skin took on a different hue at the sight of Frank, too," she retorted. Never one to lose an argument, Sarah was ready for anything he had to dish out.

"I must admit I was a little surprised to find you so contentedly in Frank Rogers's arms. My research on Tillings and on you had told me that you had broken off your engagement with him years ago. I had made the false assumption that your friendship had ended as well. But, have no fear, one of the ladies on the charity-ball planning committee has completed my education by telling me that he's an old friend and nothing else. I understand he has been dating Holly for a while." Bryan was ready with a quick comeback, too. He, also, did not like to lose. In this struggle he was fighting for Sarah's love, something too precious to let slip through his fingers.

Sarah turned her back so that he could not see the pink color that spread over her cheeks and bosom. She began again. "You're avoiding the issue. Why were you with Mildred?"

"She's very friendly and most welcoming. I'm sure her knowledge of Tillings Industries would be a good resource for us,'' he replied diplomatically. His heart ached with the awareness of Sarah's discomfort, but there was nothing he could do to erase Mildred's kiss.

Warm now with anger at the thought that he might find Mildred attractive, Sarah pushed her shawl from her shoulders. In the moonlight, Bryan could see the soft glow of her soft skin. He was tempted to reach out for her, but something in her eyes warned him to stand back. Her eyes flashed brightly with every word. ''There's nothing Mildred can ever do for me. Besides, she has done enough already. She's the reason you're here, the reason you own fifty-one percent of Tillings, the reason my father's dead. If it hadn't been for her, Daddy would still be the head of Tillings Industries and you would be in Houston. Take some advice from me: stay as far away from Mildred Tillings as you possibly can. She ruined my father and almost destroyed the company. I'll fight you with all I've got before I let that woman back in my company again.''

Bryan reached out to comfort her, but Sarah pushed away his hand. He had never seen her so angry or so hurt. He had to do something before an impassable rift developed between them. Jamming his hands inside the pockets of his tuxedo, he said in a soft, caressing voice, ''I have no interest of any kind in your stepmother. Of all the women in Dallas—no, in all the world—you are the only one who makes my blood churn. You are the only one with whom I can envision any future. You must believe me when I tell you that I love you, Sarah, and would do nothing to hurt you. I love your fire, your drive, and your stubborn determination. If you'd just let down that wall you keep up between us, I'd be able to show you.''

''Don't try to get around me by speaking of love at a time like this, Bryan Carson,'' she fumed, barely able to maintain her anger at his unexpected confession. ''How can I ever trust the man who took over my company and is now building a friendship with my stepmother? You ask too much of me, Bryan. Excuse me, but I must return to my escort. Frank will start worrying about me if I stay out here much longer. All the tongues in Dallas will have us either engaged to be married or involved in a mad, passionate affair, too, if I remain,'' she said, trying to gather her composure and push past him.

"Sarah, look at me," he said, taking her fragile shoulders in his strong hands. "Won't you ever let me come near you? How long do you plan to keep me away?'' His fingers turned her face up to his as he searched her eyes for an answer.

"Bryan, I . . .'' He did not wait for her to finish. His mouth closed over hers in a deep, penetrating kiss.

Wrapping their arms around each other, Sarah and Bryan clung together in the warm Dallas night. Mindful not to wrinkle her gown, he gently caressed her bare shoulders and back while his tongue teased hers and made her moan softly. Her trembling fingers laced in the hair at the back of his neck, wanting to keep him with her forever.

"My, my, isn't this too cute. I was wondering what had happened to you, Sarah. You left the dance floor and poor Frank so unexpectedly. When I saw Bryan leave, too, I decided to follow. I missed you, Bryan darling. I'm not interrupting anything, am I?'' Mildred's voice, dripping with sarcasm, shattered the beauty of the moment.

Collecting herself quickly, Sarah looked into the face of her stepmother. "No, Mildred. You're not interrupting anything that shouldn't have stopped before it began in the first place. For the first time since I've known you, you've actually done me a favor. I'll leave you two to each other. Good night.'' She accepted her dropped shawl from Mildred's outstretched hand. Turning on her heels, she left Bryan and Mildred standing alone on the balcony. She did not see the look of triumph that flickered at the corners of Mildred's eyes and lips. She missed Bryan's expression of agony, too. His eyes followed her but he did not try to stop her from leaving.

Rushing to Frank, she said, "Let's go, Frank. I've had enough of Dallas society for one evening.'' With that, Sarah spun on her heels and stomped out of the ball room. She practically flew past a stunned Frank.

Frank stood and looked into Bryan's unhappy face as he returned to the ballroom. A smiling Mildred stood behind him before drifting away into the crowd. Her work had been done for the evening. "Maybe you should call it a night, too, Bryan. You're new here. You think you've checked out everything and everybody, but there are some things that don't show in investment portfolios and society pages. Mildred is dangerous. Be careful. You don't want to get mixed up with her, not if you want to have a good relationship with Sarah, anyway," Frank added, grabbing up the gloves she had left behind in her rage. He hurried to catch up, leaving Bryan looking after them.

Bryan had no intention of becoming involved with Mildred. It was her stepdaughter he wanted and always had. He would tread more carefully. He had thought Sarah to be a tough business woman in all regards, but she was much more fragile on the subject of Mildred than he had realized. Bad blood definitely existed between them. He had seen it in her eyes and in Mildred's. For Sarah's sake, he would find a way to buy Mildred out of Tillings totally and send her packing.

Sarah sat in total silence on the drive home. Frank was convinced that her feelings for Bryan were much deeper than she wanted to admit. For the first time in all the years he had known her, Sarah was quiet after an evening out. Laying his hand over hers, he asked, "Is there anything I can do to help, Sarah?"

Placing her right hand over his, she squeezed it and answered, "No, Frank. I have to work through this problem alone. Thanks for asking. Knowing that you care makes me feel better. Fortunately, I have too much to do to let Bryan and Mildred cloud my thoughts for long."

Kissing him lightly on the lips, she stepped past the doorman and waved good night. Tears slid unbidden down her cheeks on the lonely ride in the elevator to her condo. Brushing them away hurriedly with her white kid gloves, Sarah closed the door behind her. She had finally reached the safety of her home. Here Bryan and Mildred could not get to her, confuse her, play with her emotions.

Easing between the cool sheets, her thoughts were once again drawn to Bryan. He had said there was nothing between him and Mildred. Could she believe him? Deep in her heart, she wanted desperately to trust everything he said. Yet Mildred was a very convincing woman. She had turned her father's head. Was it possible that Bryan was a stronger man?

Sarah knew that Mildred disliked her with the same intensity with which Sarah loathed her. Each blamed the other for Martin's lack of devotion. But tonight Sarah had seen a new level of venom in her eyes. Mildred had almost delighted in separating them, had rejoiced in throwing herself between them, had relished the pain she caused Sarah to feel. Had Mildred deliberately set out to cause trouble? What else did she have in mind? Sarah had never trusted her. She doubted she ever would.

Bryan paced the floor of his suite at the club. He had to do something about Mildred. He could feel that she was potentially bad news for Tillings Industries and for Sarah. Never had he felt anger and hostility as deep as that which sprang from Mildred and engulfed Sarah.

Making a mental note to find out more about her, he slipped into his lonely bed. After tonight, he knew that Sarah's happiness had not been threatened by investors and creditors alone. Frank was right; there was much he did not know about the infrastructure of Dallas society. Now that this was his home, he would make it his business to find out all he could. He had to protect Sarah at all cost.

Chapter Eight

Sarah was too busy preparing for the introduction of her namesake perfume to think very much about Bryan and Mildred. When she did, it was to wonder if an attachment really did exist between them. Since she had never liked Mildred, she found it difficult to imagine anyone else caring for her. Yet, Bryan was new to Dallas and did not know her treachery first hand. He had heard the rumors and knew her as a stockholder, but the real woman remained a mystery to him. Perhaps she intrigued him. Perhaps he found her sexually appealing. In the recesses of her heart, she hoped he was simply being polite at the hospital gala, and did not find Mildred in the least interesting. If she believed his words and kiss, he had eyes only for her.

Still, she was painfully aware of his presence. Each Monday morning he sat opposite her at the board meeting. His confident smile, proud carriage, and runaway lock of hair served as constant reminders of her attraction for him and her weakness in the elevator and in the board room. Now, added to that, was the balcony scene that played like something from an old movie. She could feel her cheeks grow red as his gaze and slow easy smile showed that he harbored the same thoughts, too. All Sarah knew for certain was that she should never be alone with him. She did not know if she could resist his pull or her desire to give herself to him.

Never in her life had she felt this way about any man. She could feel his hands on her body even when she was not consciously thinking about him. She could hear his voice even when she sat in her silent condo. She could taste his kisses, although days had passed since she had savored them first hand.

Sarah constantly had to remind herself that Bryan Carson was the enemy. He owned controlling interest in her company, and appeared to want to control her, as well. Try as hard as she could, she could not completely separate her feelings and reactions to him from her position as the president of Tillings Industries. She knew that, out of loyalty to her father's memory and to his company, she should find Bryan totally repulsive. She should loathe him and find his presence repulsive.

Yet, she did not. In fact, she longed to be with him. If she had not been so busy with preparing her speech for the ceremony to introduce "Sarah," she would have found it difficult to stay away from him. As it was, she struggled to keep her distance every time he came to her office to brief her on financial matters or touch base on the preparations. She almost jumped out of her skin whenever their hands touched. She grew warm at the sound of his voice. By the end of their meetings, she had to struggle to regain her composure before continuing her work. No other man had ever had this effect on her, and she had to remind herself that he was not to be trusted and certainly not loved. He was the enemy, not her lover.

This morning as she slaved over the tenth revision of her speech, she did not hear the door open and Bryan enter with his usual cat-like gait. He stood in front of her desk looking down on her before she knew he was in the room. He carried a long white box with a wide gold ribbon under his arm.

Waving her hand impatiently at his presence she said, "Just a minute. I'm on a roll and can't stop right now."

"No trouble. I have plenty of time," he answered casually.

Her father's Montblanc pencil, the one she always used to compose speeches and her thoughts, fell from her fingers at the sound of his voice. Her heart pounded in her chest so loudly that she was instantly afraid he heard, and knew the effect he had on her. Her mouth went dry and her lips felt chapped under her red lipstick.

Looking up, she greeted him, saying, "Bryan, I didn't hear you come in. It's not time for our appointment, is it? I've been awfully busy, but I don't think I missed it. What brings you here?"

He took a seat in the chair across the desk from her. His eyes never left her face. The smile that crinkled the corners of his mouth flickered at her obvious surprise at finding him in her office. He crossed his legs and smoothed the crease of his black-on-black Armani suit before answering her query. He was obviously enjoying the flustered expression on her face. He had not missed the pen that dropped from her fingers like a hot potato when he spoke her name. He knew that the sound of his heart galloped in his ears every time he looked at her. He wondered if he affected her the same way. Her reaction said he did.

Offering her the box he said, "These are for you as a peace offering, if you will. Sorry to bother you. I just wanted to explain about the other evening at the hospital gala. You've been so busy preparing for the introduction of 'Sarah' that I haven't wanted to interrupt. I decided that bad vibes between us might be noticed by the press and the investors. I don't want anything to interfere with the success of your announcement," Bryan only took his eyes from hers long enough to look at her tempting lips. He wanted very much to save on words by taking her into his arms, but was afraid that Sarah might misunderstand his intentions. She was still fragile and untrusting. She had to give him a sign of willingness before he touched her again. She had come to him in the elevator but pulled back after the gala. The next move had to be hers.

Sarah was quite surprised by his uncharacteristic thoughtfulness and did not immediately know what to say. Lifting the lid from the box and taking a deep breath of the apricot roses, she took a few moments to compose her thoughts. The heady brandy fragrance of the flowers immediately filled the room.

"The roses are exquisite. Holly must have told you that they're my favorites. Thank you for the concern. I'm really very busy, but I guess I can stop for a little bit. This revision isn't going very well anyway. A break might do me good," she said as a slight smile played at the corners of her mouth. "You really don't owe me any explanations. The incident in the elevator was isolated and not in any way taken as a sign of commitment by either of us. I'm partly at fault for the loss of composure in the board room. Your social interactions are entirely your affair, if you'll pardon the pun. At any rate, they don't concern me any more than my relationships should concern you," Sarah said, crossing her hands delicately on top of the much-edited paper on her desk and pushing the roses aside. Bryan could see that she had, indeed, been busy.

"I still want to clear up any areas of confusion. We can't have outsiders thinking that there's disharmony in the top levels of management at Tillings Industries, and there are things you need to know about me. First, I'm not in the least attracted to your stepmother. In fact, I've heard plenty about her and about her marriage to your father that would prevent any sane man from becoming involved with her. She came on to me; I resisted as much as was civil. I certainly did not encourage her in any way. Friendly sources have warned me about the web she weaves around men. She's not the Tillings I want to know more personally; you are."

Sarah's heart took flight at the straightforward way Bryan discussed the feelings that flashed in his eyes. She wanted to listen to more but was afraid her resolve would melt if she did. She could not afford to allow herself to wind up his his arms again—not if she were to complete her task. She had to make Tillings a financial success again without his help. Her self-respect counted on it.

"I saw the level of your resistance, and so did everyone else. Dallas is a big city with a small town's interest in other people's business. Take my advice and stay as far away from Mildred as possible. Finding yourself linked with her will do nothing to further your standing in the eyes of the black community. Everyone still resents the way she drove my father away from the company and me. She's not a very nice person, Bryan," Sarah said. Beneath the anger, Bryan could see something more . . . hurt pride.

Sarah resented the side of her father's personality that Mildred had brought to the front, the side that would run wild and shirk responsibility for the sake of having a good time. Sarah had been deeply hurt by her father's abandonment of Tillings and of her. Bryan could see that the same fear lurked behind those amber eyes now. Sarah was afraid that he would leave Tillings and her for Mildred, although her pride and determination to make Tillings great again without his assistance would never allow her to admit her feelings.

"Thanks for the advice. Just remember, I'm not your father. I'm not about to allow Mildred to ruin my dreams of a future with you and Tillings Industries. Remember that, the next time you think I might be interested in her," Bryan remarked, walking to the window behind her desk. He stood looking out on the city that was now his home. He knew all about Dallas, its warm welcoming nature, its hospitable reception of strangers. Sarah's father Martin had painted vivid pictures of this ideal place for doing business. Yet Bryan had found in his own dealings with the African-American society here that it could be very unforgiving of anything it perceived as a breach of trust. Although Mildred was invited to every social function, and no one could resist the pull of her great wealth, she was not well respected. Her business and personal affairs had been too well documented and too shady.

Sarah could feel Bryan's body against hers even though he stood a good four feet from her, looking down on the sun-bathed city below. She wanted him to turn and take her into his strong arms, to crush her against his body, to make her forget her resolve to keep him at arm's length. She fought against her own need to surround herself by him and to draw strength from him. He was so skilled at convincing investors to part with their money; she could have used some of his acumen today. She needed his ability to manage a situation to rub off on her. She was undeniably in love with this powerful man who owned controlling interest in her company, but she could not permit herself to take him until she had proved her authority over Tillings with the introduction of the new fragrance. She sat fighting the battle between her desire, her need, and her determination.

Bryan sensed her struggles and fought some of his own. He wanted Sarah in his life. He had saved Tillings for her and come to Dallas to be near her. He could have remained in Houston, safely managing the company from a distance. He controlled his other interests through trusted advisors stationed in the companies and hardly ever visited them. Yet Tillings was different. His devotion to Martin Tillings's memory and his determination to make Sarah his wife had forced him to take a more proactive role in this company and Dallas society. He had immersed himself financially and emotionally in the running of Tillings without regard for any future except one spent with her. He took pride in the company's achievements and the woman who made them possible. Unfortunately, his dealings had thrown him into contact with Mildred, too. Now, sensing Sarah's discomfort, he wondered if he should not have stayed away until she was ready to accept him.

He knew about the new perfume on which Sarah had placed so much hope of pulling Tillings out of the red. She had tried to stall the takeover by using revenue projections to win the confidence of her creditors. But when the vultures ignored her efforts and circled tighter, he had been forced to make a move or lose Tillings and Sarah forever. If only Sarah would stop fighting against him and realize that he did not plan to take control of her company from her, everything would work out as he had planned. Her resentment of his presence in her company kept her from being able to admit to herself that she needed him, financially and emotionally. Until she did, Bryan felt helpless to do more than just watch and wait.

Turning from the wall of windows, Bryan gazed at her thin frame sitting straight and tall in her father's massive leather chair. Her shoulders held the weight of a struggling company, yet he never saw them sag under the load. She loved Tillings. He wondered if Sarah would ever love him as much.

As he watched her, he could see her determination in her profile. The straight back, golden thick-lashed eyes, high cheek bones, dimpled chin, and luscious lips transmitted a regal air. He longed to take her into his arms and watch the mask dissolve as desire and love for him overpowered her control.

"Sarah," he whispered in a deep, guttural voice filled with emotions that bubbled from deep within him, "you have to understand that I love you. Everything I've done for Tillings has been for you. I'm not interested now, nor will I ever be interested in any other woman, as long as there's a chance that you might love me. I've lived a carefully programmed life of lies as the happy bachelor surrounded by desirable women. It was all a sham, a cover, to give you time to grow up. Since I first met you, when you were still a teenager, I've wanted no one but you. You must believe me."

"For the good of our working relationship and the success

of Tillings Industries, I'll try to be more thoughtful of your
feelings. However, at this time, I am not in a position to add
my name to your well-known list of women. I have Tillings
to think about, and my pride. I cannot become involved with
you now, and I doubt that I ever will. You tried to take my
father's company from me. I know you say you were trying
to save it, but I still doubt your intentions. Maybe in time I'll
see things differently, but for now this is all I can offer you. I
am grateful to you for keeping my company out of the hands
of others who would probably have thrown me out on my ear.
Still, I cannot not forgive you for not waiting until after the
introduction of the new fragrance. If you had only waited a
few more months, we would have met under different circum-
stances. As it is, we're on opposite sides until Tillings is completely mine once again," she retorted without once turning to
look at him. Her shoulders remained stiff and straight.

Bryan could hold back no longer. He could hear the agony
in her voice and knew only one way to remove it. Covering
the space that divided them in one step, he took Sarah by the
shoulders and lifted her from the chair. Turning her around,
he turned her face up to his and looked into her tear-filled eyes.
As her control broke, he covered her quivering lips with his
and kissed away the taste of salty tears that lingered at the
corners. Then he gently caressed her neck and ears while his
hands lingered over her back and shoulders before coming to
rest on her tight buttocks. She trembled slightly as he pulled
her against his protruding manhood and whispered into her
hair, "I love you, Sarah. I've waited this long; I can wait for
you as long as it takes for you to love and trust me."

She could fight against her stubborn pride no longer. Holly
had told her about the maneuvers, the plans, and the contacts
Bryan had made to help Tillings gain a larger market share
and to convince investors that they should place their trust in
her management. He had spent long hours on the telephone,
making his case, calling in favors, and staking his own reputa-

ion on her behalf. Sarah knew that he spoke the truth in saying
hat his concern was only for her. She had refused to drop her
defenses long after she knew in her heart that she could trust
him.

Sarah melted into his arms, her body answering him in ways
hat her words could not. She pressed the length of her body
along his until no space existed between them. She reveled in
he soft moan that escaped her lips as her fingers played in the
hair at the back of his neck and tantalized the lobes of his ears.

His lips once again covered hers and his hungry tongue
darted around her mouth. His hands caressed her undulating
buttocks as he crushed her against his painful groin. Every fiber
of his body screamed of his need for her. And hers answered.

As his mouth traveled from hers to her neck and, further, to
her cleavage, Sarah moaned at the thrill of his tongue on her
soft skin. She tangled her fingers in his hair to urge him forward.
He unbuttoned the criss-crossed jacket of her cream silk suit,
and then Bryan's fingers left hot trails on her breasts as he
struggled to unhook the front opening of her bra. Finally he
released her straining breasts and covered her tender nipples
with his mouth. The nipples quickly stood erect as his hot wet
tongue made circles around them and his teeth nipped the soft
skin.

"Bryan," Sarah whispered in a breathy whisper as her fingers
ran up and down his thighs until they found the protruding
hard lump that strained against the fabric of his suit. He groaned
as she stroked and squeezed the throbbing mass that longed to
bury itself in her soft womanliness.

His hands reached eagerly under her skirt and caressed her
thighs and buttocks through the thin film of her stockings. His
palm rubbed against and mound of pleasure until she shuddered
and moaned, pressing herself even harder against him. Her
fingers fumbled with his belt and zipper as he ground his
throbbing manhood into her thigh.

Just as his fingers reached the waist band of her panty hose, a voice from the speakerphone violated their world, shocking them back to reality. "Sarah, sorry to interrupt, but Dr. Morris is on line two for you. He says it's urgent. Something about the new fragrance. Jenny passed the call to me so as not to disturb you, but I couldn't help him. He said he needed to speak with you personally," Holly, her assistant, interrupted. Jenny, Sarah's secretary, routed all of her calls to Holly whenever she was in conference and did not want to be disturbed. Holly usually handled all of them skillfully. This one even Holly could not field.

"Thanks, Holly. I'll take it right away," she called in a voice that shook with the passion that still burned in her groin. Giving Bryan a quick look of apology, she rushed to the phone, refastening and adjusting her clothing as she walked.

"Dr. Morris, Sarah Tillings here. What seems to be the problem? Is anything going to delay the announcement?" she asked, taking her seat at the desk. Immediately, her shoulders straightened and she became Sarah Tillings, president of Tillings Industries. The woman who had so recently melted into Bryan's arms and craved the release that only he could give her had vanished.

Bryan turned away from the desk and refastened his pants. The fire in his groin would have to wait until the next time they could be alone. At least he hoped there would be a next time. Sarah had dropped her defenses very briefly, and he had taken advantage of the moment. He might not be so lucky next time.

Walking to the door, he turned and waved good bye before closing it behind him. Sarah looked up briefly and gave him a quick smile and a shrug of her shoulders. Then she returned to the conversation with Dr. Morris.

"Can't that be solved, Dr. Morris? Certainly it's not something that will jeopardize the success of the fragrance," Sarah said in a very worried tone. She counted on the new fragrance, bearing her name, to be the salvation for Tillings. If it failed, she would too.

"No, I don't think it will affect the longevity of the scent. I just wanted you to know that between now and the day of the announcement, I'll be busy every minute trying to find a way to stop the oils in the fragrance from staining silk. Most women know that perfume sprayed directly on fabric can leave a spot, but we had tried hard to keep "Sarah" from doing it. We'll keep working. I just didn't want you to be caught off guard or say something at the introduction that we can't deliver."

"Well, I appreciate your consideration and, as always, your dedication to Tillings. I'm confident that if there's a way to overcome this problem, you'll work it out. Keep me posted as you deem appropriate, Dr. Morris," Sarah commented and hung up the phone.

Returning to the speech that lay waiting on her desk, she could not stop thoughts of Bryan from rushing to her mind. The only thing that had stopped her from giving herself to this man, her enemy, was Holly's voice over the speakerphone and Dr. Morris's call. If they had not interrupted her, she would have made a terrible mistake.

Yet, as the comforting heat of the memory filled her with warmth and added a rosy color to her cheeks, she was not sure that it would have been a mistake. She questioned her reasons for wanting to keep Bryan at a distance. She knew she loved him and wanted him as she had never loved and wanted any other man. Still, she had a driving need to show him and herself that she could successfully run Tillings without his help or anyone else's. Yet, she needed to be a woman and fulfill her womanly desires, too. For so long she had denied herself the companionship of men while she gave herself totally to restoring Tillings to its rightful place as a leading cosmetics firm.

She had attended the weddings of her friends, but never dreamed of having one herself some day. Tillings Industries came first. When her company was safe and once again financially sound, she would be able to think of herself.

Now, with Bryan capably handling the financial end of the business so that she could spend her time in product management and marketing, she wondered if she had to postpone her personal happiness. Deep within her, she knew that, without him, Tillings would have been swallowed up by a hostile takeover. She blamed him for owning the controlling interest in her company because, out of loyalty for her father, she could not blame him for mismanagement of the company that had been left her as her legacy. Bryan had truly saved Tillings for her. His infusion of cash had rescued the company, and her, from oblivion.

She needed to prove to him that she could manage more successfully than her father. Until she launched the new fragrance and it proved itself as successful as she thought it would, she had to keep her distance from Bryan.

With a sigh, Sarah walked to the window that only a few minutes ago had been filled by his presence. "Oh, Bryan," she whispered to the empty room, "it's so hard to stay away from you. I want so much to give myself to you, to feel you holding me, to love you, to possess you. If only I could—and still feel true to my dreams. I hope I don't lose you while reaching for professional success. That's the chance I have to take, but I don't know if I could be happy without you, any more than I could be without this company. You're as much a part of me as Tillings is. I never thought I could love like this. It hurts so much."

She stood for a few minutes looking down at her city until the tears stopped flowing down her cheeks. Then she returned to her desk. She had a speech to edit before going home tonight. Forcing her mind to move from the smell of Bryan's cologne, the taste of his kisses, the touch of his hands on her body, and the feel of him in her arms, she returned to the task that lay unfinished on her desk. Sarah picked up her father's Montblanc and began again.

Chapter Nine

The morning of her thirtieth birthday dawned bright and hot. Summer was hitting Dallas with a vengeance. Sarah rose from her cool beige satin sheets, her legs shapely beneath the short batiste nightie. Walking to the window, she threw open the mauve silk curtains and stretched leisurely. Despite the bad taste last month's gala had left in her mouth, she knew today would turn out great. Nothing could spoil her plans for today, not Bryan, Mildred, or anything. She would introduce the perfume named for her at noon during a carefully arranged press conference. Chuckling softly, she threw off the nightie and stepped into the spray of the cool shower. It was a stroke of advertising genius on her part that "Sarah" the perfume would come into the world on her birthday. The connection between the woman and the fragrance would be inseparable.

Sarah lathered herself all over with a gel of "Sarah." The heavenly scent of apricots, roses, spices, and sensuality filled the bathroom. Even her shampoo was "Sarah," a fragrance that promised to appeal to women from every walk of life. The marketing tests had shown that all who tried it could hardly wait until they could purchase quantities of "Sarah." The perfume was neither too pricey nor too inexpensive. Its price stood well within the budget of every woman. The fragrance was light enough for the heat of summer, yet it lingered with the staying power of a heavier perfume. Even the cologne and eau de toilet had body, unlike so many other fragrances whose power disappeared almost as soon as the wearer applied them.

Toweling her hair and body vigorously, Sarah looked at her smiling reflection in the mirror. She did not look thirty. Looking at her figure in the full-length mirror on the opposite wall, she was pleased with what she saw. The hours at the gym had paid off. Her arms were firm, her breasts were still perky, her stomach was flat, and her thighs and buttocks were rock hard. Gravity had not begun to do its worst with her.

Foregoing the usual towel to cover her nakedness, Sarah pranced into the walk-in closet. She knew exactly what she would wear today. Everything down to the color of her underwear had been carefully coordinated for the presentation.

Wrapping herself in the apricot-colored silk, thoughts of last month's hospital gala rushed through her mind. Shaking her head, Sarah tried to dismiss the thought of Bryan Carson. Today was her day, and "Sarah's." She would not allow him to take over her thoughts.

All the reports on Bryan led her to believe that he was ruthless in business. Yet not once had he shown anything but kindness toward her, and honest concern for the future of Tillings Industries. Who was he really? He had taken over the company but had made no attempt to reorganize, as usually happens. No one had been fired or demoted. She had kept the president's office while he had been content with the smaller one at the opposite end of the hall. Everything was exactly as it had always been under her father's leadership and hers. If she did not sit opposite him in the board room every Monday, she would not even know he existed. She ran the company and made all the decisions; he only advised, when consulted, and managed the finances. Except for that one time that they had been carried away by their passions, there had been little interaction between them.

What did he really want with Tillings Industries? Could she believe his explanations, spoken so passionately? Bryan owned more than enough companies all over the country to keep him busy. Yet, he spent all his time in Dallas. Since coming to town, he had conducted all his business from his office in the Tillings Tower penthouse. He never traveled out of town to check on the other businesses. All his affairs were conducted by telephone and fax. His secretary and special assistant were kept busy until late hours, keeping him posted on all the activity in the other companies.

Looking at herself one last time in her bedroom mirror, Sarah was pleased with what she saw. The apricot of the silk suit brought out the peachy tones in her warm brown skin. Her heels, dyed to match her suit, flexed the muscles in her calves and made them even more shapely. Her legs glistened in the apricot stockings.

"Just who is Bryan Carson, anyway?" Sarah asked her reflection.

She had to admit one thing. The man was loyal. When he first arrived, she had doubted his sincerity and his intentions toward Tillings. She thought this takeover would be just like all the others she had read about. She had expected to have her interest in Tillings Industries bought out by him as soon as he unpacked his briefcase. She had been warned that he would probably make her the titular president and call her out annually for press conferences and flower shows. Instead, he treated her with professional courtesy and respect. Naming the new fragrance after her had, after all, been his idea.

A sudden chill caused by her runaway thoughts gave her goose bumps. Maybe he had waited until today to make his move. Maybe this was the beginning of a long list of appear-

ances for her. Sarah knew she could not afford to drop her
defenses where Bryan Carson was concerned. Maybe he was
the man he appeared to be, but just maybe there was more to
him than had yet met the eye.

Well, whatever the truth was, that was enough of Bryan for
now. This was her day. Whatever thoughts still swirled around
in the recesses of her mind about him would have to wait until
later. Sliding into the coolness of the apricot limousine with the
glove-soft apricot leather interior, Sarah put this mysteriously
intoxicating man out of her mind.

Workmen had draped the main entrance of Tillings Tower
with a massive banner. Letters six feet high spelled out the
words HAPPY BIRTHDAY, SARAH. Bryan thought the connection between Sarah Tillings and the perfume named for her
and introduced on her birthday should be established immediately. Everyone would celebrate the birthday of the two Sarahs,
from the time the first rays of sun hit the apricot marble of
Tillings Tower, until counter-sales women wearing the taste-
fully elegant apricot shifts, the trademark of Tillings cosmetics,
distributed the last sample in its apricot-colored bottle at every
store around the country. The full press would begin as soon
as the stores opened and would end when they closed.

Every major newspaper carried an ad celebrating the birthday
of the two Sarahs. Photographs of Sarah Tillings holding an
oversized bottle of ''Sarah'' adorned the sides of buses, bill-
boards, and magazines. Expensive sixty-second television com-
mercials ran continuously during the soap operas and again
during prime time viewing hours. No expense had been spared.
''Sarah's'' big day was destined to make a loud splash in the
cosmetics world.

Inside the conference room, the lights from the video cameras
blinded Sarah, causing her to blink repeatedly. Flash bulbs
popped in her face, creating multi-colored spots before her

WE HAVE 4 FREE BOOKS FOR YOU!

ARABESQUE

(If the certificate is missing below, write to:
Zebra Home Subscription Service, Inc.,
120 Brighton Road, P.O. Box 5214, Clifton, New Jersey 07015-5214)

FREE BOOK CERTIFICATE

Yes! Please send me 4 *Arabesque* Contemporary Romances without cost or obligation, billing me just $1 to help cover postage and handling. I understand that each month, I will be able to preview 4 brand-new *Arabesque* Contemporary Romances FREE for 10 days. Then, if I decide to keep them, I will pay the money-saving preferred subscriber's price of just $16.00 for all 4...that's a savings of almost $4 off the publisher's price with no additional charge for shipping and handling. I may return any shipment within 10 days and owe nothing, and I may cancel this subscription at any time. My 4 FREE books will be mine to keep in any case.

Name _____

Address _____ Apt. _____

City _____ State _____ Zip _____

Telephone ( ) _____

Signature _____ AR0997
(If under 18, parent or guardian must sign.)

Terms and prices subject to change. Orders subject to acceptance by Zebra Home Subscription Service, Inc.
Zebra Home Subscription Service, Inc. reserves the right to reject or cancel any subscription.

ZEBRA HOME SUBSCRIPTION SERVICE, INC.

120 BRIGHTON ROAD

P.O. BOX 5214

CLIFTON, NEW JERSEY 07015-5214

AFFIX
STAMP
HERE

eyes. Her cheeks ached from constant smiling. Her lips felt stretched and dry. Yet her reflection told her that every hair was in place. The apricot suit had not wrinkled in the car ride to the office. The "Passion Fruit" lipstick had not caked or cracked. She continued tirelessly to smile, wave, and answer questions about the new fragrance named for her. If the customers reacted as favorably to the new fragrance, "Sarah," as the news media was, Tillings Industries would have a best seller.

Looking from the podium into the crowded auditorium, Sarah saw many faces she knew from other press conferences. Among the rows of people sat many strangers, too. Journalists from every major magazine and newspaper, buyers from every department store chain, and fashion correspondents from all the corners of the earth filled the room. Everyone sniffed appreciatively at the sample vials distributed to them as they entered. From the expressions on their faces and the aroma of "Sarah" that wafted through the air, she could tell that they found the fragrance pleasing. Every female reporter and store buyer covering the announcement dabbed a few drops of "Sarah" behind each ear and on wrist pulse spots. Men covering the event gently placed the fragile glass sample vials into their briefcases to give as tokens to a favorite woman later tonight. "Sarah" was a success.

"Ladies and gentlemen, I want to thank you for taking time from your busy schedules to join me on this day of beginnings," Sarah began, lightly tapping the microphone to silence the gentle murmurs that filled the auditorium. "This is a truly auspicious occasion, as Tillings Industries unveils a new fragrance—a fragrance designed to knock your socks off and revolutionize the perfume industry.

" 'Sarah' is a gentle blend of only the best essences, acquired with the modern woman in mind—a woman who works from nine to five, cares for her children, makes fabulous love to her significant other, heads PTA committees, chairs the boards of numerous corporations, hosts talk-of-the-town dinner parties, raises prize-winning roses in formal gardens, writes award winning novels, grows agriculturally phenomenal crops, and pumps her own gas. In short, 'Sarah' is not a fragile perfume 'Sarah' is bold, adventurous, courageous, yet she does not overpower or intimidate. She represents the many faces of every woman and accepts the challenge of today's fast-paced life and brings out the best in all who experience her power.

"We gather here today to greet a new beginning for the fragrance industry—a new awakening of smells, a celebration of the new woman, a recognition of the power within us to do great things, to be whoever we want to be and to reach new heights. Tillings Industries has instilled 'Sarah' with all these traits and more. A woman can make this her signature fragrance and feel equally comfortable dabbing it on when wearing jeans or when wearing an evening gown, in her nightgown as well as in a business suit, in mink or in cotton.

"For the first time in its distinguished history, Tillings Industries has named a fragrance after a member of the family. I'm thrilled to lend my name to this exciting and innovative fragrance. In a way, 'Sarah,' Tillings Industries, and I are celebrating together. Today is not only the introduction of a remarkable new fragrance, but the beginning of the end of worries about the future of this company. Today Tillings is saying with 'Sarah' that we have seen the enemy of financial restrictions, labored under near-bankruptcy conditions, and risen above all of the obstacles to stand before you, stronger than before. On my birthday, I stand before you to announce that Tillings Industries is stronger financially than in the last ten years. We will not be counted down and are definitely not out.

"So let the champagne flow. 'Sarah' and I welcome you to a new page in perfume and Tillings Industries history."

The curtains behind her opened and the slide of Sarah Tillings holding a huge bottle of "Sarah" flashed on the screen for all to see. Deafening applause filled the room as apricot balloons floated down from the netting overhead. As the enthusiastic crowd rose to its feet to give her a standing ovation, waiters wearing apricot-colored jackets and carrying silver trays eased in among them, bearing glasses of apricot champagne.

Sarah blinked into the lights as she accepted the praise. The members of the management team whistled their tribute to their leader. Bryan stood a bit away from them, wearing an expression of pride. The press conference was a huge success, and "Sarah" looked as if it would take the perfume industry by storm, just as they had hoped it would. Yet his eyes were focused, not on the fragrance or the admiring crowd, but on the vision in apricot silk standing at the podium. Sarah's face was flushed with excitement, her bright gold eyes sparkled with fire, and her body radiated an undeniable energy. She stood every inch the brave young warrior leading her company into battle against financial setbacks and industrial rumors. She was poised to take aim at those who thought they had seen the last of Tillings.

Now that "Sarah" had restored Tillings to its former glory, the stock was bound to surge ahead. He wondered if she would ever come to him, ever realize that everything he did, from the takeover to allowing her to remain the president of Tillings Industries, was motivated by the love he felt for her. Would she ever trust him? Would she ever turn to him with outstretched arms? The expression in her eyes over the crystal champagne glass filled with apricot ambrosia flashed the answer. He would rot in hell before Sarah Tillings ever needed him or trusted him. His arms would stay empty, never feel the heat of her yielding body. He would never drink of the sweetness of her kisses. He would never bury his head in her breasts and feel her heart pounding in unison with his. He would never see her run barefoot in the park, splash in the ocean, or sun on the beach. Worse, he would never see their children sleep in her arms.

Sarah did not realize how deeply the look cut into Bryan's very core as she turned her back on him and concentrated her attention on the reporter from a leading fashion magazine. She could feel Bryan's eyes burning into the back of her jacket, but she refused to turn around. She was afraid her resolve would weaken. She was afraid of the power this man had over more than just the company. She would not, today or any other day, admit her attraction to him. She had worked hard to make "Sarah" a success, to increase the stockholders' revenues, and to buy Tillings Industries away from him.

Now was her chance, and she would not allow a moment of passion in an elevator with a man whose list of female conquests was longer than the listing of the New York Stock Exchange to sway her from her deliberate purpose. This was her day. She had engineered it, planned it, given birth to it. Today "Sarah" and Tillings Industries were hers alone. All she had to do was meet with Mildred and get her to sign the papers. The value of their combined stock at the new price would be more than enough to buy out Bryan Carson.

Mildred. Sarah's eyes searched the crowd for signs of her stepmother. She knew that Mildred would not miss this day for anything, and she was right. Surrounded by a small gathering of reporters near a huge bouquet of apricot roses, Mildred's laugh rose above the din of conversation. She looked radiant in a deeper shade of the Tillings's trademark apricot. Her skin was as flawless as her outfit.

Sensing Sarah's eyes on her, Mildred smiled and waved. No one would have guessed that there was no love lost between these two. They played their parts well. No one in the room would have thought that "Sarah" was not the only plan that had been born today. Mildred had a few tricks up her sleeve, too. She would watch carefully for the right moment. Then she would strike. Maybe today. Maybe tomorrow or next week.

She would wait. She was not in a hurry. She would make Martin Tillings's daughter sorry she had ever heard the name of Mildred Banning. Sarah was not the only one with plans for Tillings Industries and Bryan Carson. Mildred had a few of her own. She had waited until the company was back on its feet before setting her plans in action. Judging from the reception the new fragrance had received today, the time was right.

As the flash bulbs burst in Sarah's face, she did not suspect the thoughts that lurked behind Mildred's dark apricot-colored lips and sparkling white teeth. If she had, she would not have enjoyed her day. As it was, Sarah allowed the flowers to be piled in her outstretched arms by Holly, her assistant. All she saw were the tears of joy on Holly's lashes. They had worked so hard, and for such long hours, that the relief flowed freely through both of them. They hugged, and left the room with their arms around each other. The morning had been exciting, but they still had much work to do.

Bryan watched as Sarah and Holly walked from the hall. He had seen something in the corners of Mildred's too-friendly smile that disturbed him. He had encountered that expression before on the faces of opponents across the table in card games and corporate board rooms. As he eased from the room, leaving the assembled press in the hands of the public relations and marketing people, Bryan wondered when she would show her hand. He would make it his business to find out what Mildred was up to, and when she planned to pounce. He wanted to make sure he would be at Sarah's side when she played her cards.

The elevator ride to the penthouse floor was long and lonely. Bryan could not help but think of how short it had been only a month ago when he had held Sarah's warm, pliable body in his arms.

Bryan adjusted his tie and walked down the polished floors.

As he passed Sarah's office, he remembered the blanket he had snatched up that morning, that lay in the trunk of his car. He had already phoned Duke's and made all the arrangements. Everything would be ready by the time they arrived. All he had to do was convince Sarah, but that would not be easy.

Taking a deep breath, he turned the knob and entered the reception area leading to Sarah's office. Her secretary was at lunch, so he entered without being announced. Bracing himself for rejection, he said cheerfully, "Let's go for a drive. It's your birthday. No one should celebrate alone, especially not the thirtieth."

Looking up with disbelief flickering in her eyes Sarah replied, "I can't leave the office now. The phones are going crazy. Marketing is swamped with orders. This is not the time for a drive."

"Oh, yes, it is. There's no better time. Frank and Holly are probably already there waiting for us. Grab your sunglasses. Let's go," Bryan responded confidently, taking the pen from her hand and laying it on the stack of papers in front of her.

"They're waiting where? Where are you taking me?" she protested as he guided her out of the office and into the hall.

"It's a surprise. You'll see soon enough. This is one time that you're not in control of the situation and you'll have to live with it. Be spontaneous, just once in your life," he teased as the elevator door closed.

"Bryan, this is the most irresponsible thing I've ever done. You didn't even give me time to leave a note. You just whisked me away from everything. No one will know what has happened to me. They'll think I've been kidnapped or something. I have work to do," she complained again as they reached the lobby and headed toward the waiting limousine.

"Not today, you don't. Today isn't special just because of the perfume. It's your day, too, and you're going to relax a little and have some fun before you're back on display tonight at your party. My secretary knows where to find us. I'm wearing my beeper just in case she needs me. We're as close to the office as the phone in the car. This afternoon, you're going to be a little girl again. We're going on a picnic,'' Bryan beamed. He was really quite proud of himself for having pulled off the surprise without Sarah's knowledge. In a company like Tillings, it was so difficult to keep anything a secret. He had feared someone would spoil the day.

"A picnic?! I'm not dressed for a picnic. Bryan, I appreciate the thought, but I really don't think this will work," Sarah replied, looking down at her suit, stockings, and heels. Her matching purse sat demurely in her lap.

"Don't worry, Sarah, you're dressed perfectly," he responded as the car stopped. As the driver opened the door and beamed at them, Bryan lead her into the clearing of a little wooded area not far from the office. He had seen a family having a picnic Sunday dinner here one day, and had thought Sarah might enjoy the serenity of the spot. The scowl on her face as she stepped over fallen branches in her three inch heels and straight skirt said that she was not having fun yet. Bryan spread the blanket on the ground with a Sir Walter Raleigh flourish to keep her from ruining her shoes.

As she stepped into the bright sunshine, Sarah heard music from the quartet seated at the far side of the clearing. The sunlight glinted off their highly polished instruments. Then she saw the table spread with an apricot damask cloth, champagne glasses, bone china place settings for four, and sparkling silver. Five waiters hovered, ready to serve the meal. Sarah wondered what kind of picnic this would turn out to be. It certainly did not remind her of any she had ever experienced during her childhood. There were no paper plates and cups and plastic utensils anywhere in sight. The only similarity was the bugs that tickled her legs.

"Surprise!" shouted Frank and Holly, stepping from the bushes carrying gifts wrapped in bright paper and adorned with ribbons and flowers. They joined Bryan in leading Sarah to the table while the quartet played the birthday song.

"How did you keep me from finding out about this? Holly, you're such a sneak! I thought we were friends. And Frank, you never used to be able to keep anything from me," Sarah bubbled as the waiters filled the glasses with apricot champagne.

"Don't blame this on me. I didn't have anything to do with the plans. Bryan did all the work. He planned the menu with the chef at Duke's and arranged for the music, too. All I had to do was show up," Frank laughed.

Holly added, "Isn't this a great idea? We should go on picnics more often. Bryan was so sweet to plan this for you."

Sarah felt her eyes mist as she looked at Bryan. It was so thoughtful of him to go to all this trouble for her birthday. She knew she was often difficult and preoccupied with the company. She appreciated all the time he had taken from his busy schedule to arrange everything.

Lifting his glass in a toast, Bryan said, "To Sarah, who is more precious than the oils of any fragrance and more bewitching than any moonlight. Happy birthday."

"To Sarah!" Holly and Frank echoed.

"Open your gifts," Holly coaxed.

To Sarah's delight, she found a lovely silk scarf in one box and a pair of apricot kidskin gloves in another. She thanked her dear friends, who beamed lovingly at her. With the introduction of her new fragrance and the lovely picnic, this was certainly turning out to be the best of days. Bryan had done a wonderful job. For the first time in their association, Sarah did not want to distance herself from him.

Quietly, Bryan placed a long, thin, burgundy velvet box on her plate. He watched the expression on her face as she opened it. Inside, nestled among the black satin, lay the most exquisite diamond tennis bracelet she had ever seen. Leaning closer, he fastened it onto her wrist. The sun sparkled brightly among the brilliant stones.

"Bryan, it's beautiful. You shouldn't have—after all you've done for Tillings and for me," she whispered, planting a kiss softly on his cheek.

"This is just the beginning, if you'll let me. We'll have more picnics, go to baseball games, and take exciting vacations. I'll even learn to ski," he said, laughing. His eyes lovingly devoured her face while his hand lightly rested on hers.

As they gazed into each other's eyes, Holly cleared her throat and said with a laugh, "Excuse me, but lunch is getting cold."

The waiters served the crab imperial as the music broke into the strains of show tunes. The fragrance of flowers filled the air and birds chirped in the trees. Sarah was happier than she had been since she was a little girl and her parents had taken her on picnics. She wondered if life with Bryan could really be this wonderful.

Chapter Ten

When Sarah returned to the office, she found that the phones had not stopped ringing all day. Sarah, and the perfume named for her, were a huge success. The sales department reported more advance orders of "Sarah" than for any fragrance ever introduced by Tillings Industries in its history. The New York Stock Exchange heralded it as a red-letter day for the company. Happiness rang through the halls of Tillings Tower. Everyone knew that good times lay ahead.

Mildred, sitting in the parlor of her massive estate, knew that today was special for her, too. At exactly 3:45 P.M., she would place a call to her new stockbroker, ordering the sale of her shares of Tillings Industries. She chuckled with sadistic glee as she thought of the panic she would cause. All the papers and news bureaus would report that a major stockholder had abandoned the company at its hour of triumph. Maybe an enterprising reporter would discover that she was behind the sale. The scandal would be devastating. Everyone would suspect that things were not as healthy as they appeared before the cameras and microphones.

Stock prices would fall, people would sell, and she would sit back and wait. When the price fell far enough, she would use her vast fortune to buy all the shares she could get her hands on. When she owned controlling interest, she would confront Sarah. Revenge would be sweet as she dethroned Martin Tillings's precious daughter. With the ruin of Tillings Industries, Mildred would make Sarah pay for all the times she and the company had stolen Martin's love from her.

Smoothing the wrinkles from her skirt, Mildred smiled and took a sip of her champagne. Chuckling softly, she twirled the pale yellow liquid around and around in the glass. It was not the loathed apricot champagne favored by the Tillings. To Mildred, the ambrosia in her glass symbolized her break with the family and the company that had robbed her of her husband's love and devotion.

Mildred did not feel any regret for what she was about to do to Sarah and the company. They deserved it. Sarah had never welcomed her into the family; she had always resented her for marrying Martin. She had never forgiven her for not being Grace, his first and beloved wife. Well, two could play that game. Today, and in the days to follow, Sarah would find out just how awful it felt to be on the outside looking in.

Another equally vicious possibility began to take form in her mind. She might just wash her hands of Tillings Industries for good. She might sell her shares and watch the prices fall from a cruise ship in the Mediterranean. She was tired and bored with all of this business foolishness anyway. She really did not want to expend too much energy on vengeance. Too much ugliness made one's skin age, her mother always said. She would be perfectly satisfied if a panic leveled the company and Sarah. Her satisfaction would come from the results; she did not have to be the one stirring the stinky mess. If she never owned another share of that stock, she would be all too happy.

Suddenly Mildred's smile faded. Bryan . . . now he was a different story altogether. He had been warm and friendly to her from the first day he arrived in Dallas. He had even consulted her on the best neighborhood in which to live, and the most impressive restaurants in which to dine, when he first came to town. He was a kind person, even if he had the bad taste to be infatuated with Sarah. She was sorry that he would have to suffer also. Maybe she could soothe his pain by taking him with her to Europe. She was skilled in making men forget their troubles. She had eased Martin's distress until Sarah intruded in their tranquillity.

Stretching, Mildred flexed her long, slender hands. She looked like a cat as her long, red, manicured nails raked through the air. Curling her legs under her in the large floral tapestry-upholstered chair, her mind returned to Bryan Carson. Too bad he was so smitten with her stepdaughter. He was a fabulously handsome man. His combination of sophistication and boy-ishness was as difficult to resist as his dark skin and flashing gray eyes . . . his broad shoulders, thin waist, and narrow hips. She sensed that he was not a man who could endure weakness, in himself or others. He would learn to hate Sarah when he saw Tillings Industries fall into chaos with her at the helm. Then Mildred would watch his infatuation with the little twit turn into disgust. With Sarah out of the picture, she would show him what a real woman could do for him.

Searching her face in the gold compact she pulled from her pocket, Mildred considered the fine lines at the corners of her mouth and eyes. Not bad for a widow who was the stepmother of a thirty-year-old. Her cheeks were still firm, without a single trace of jowls. Looking down at her firm breasts and flat stom-ach, Mildred knew that her figure was still young and trim, the result of daily workouts with a personal trainer.

"Not bad, not bad at all," she muttered to herself, raising her glass in a salute. "He'll forget all about Sarah by the time I finish with him."

Moving slowly and deliberately, Mildred reached for the telephone. It was 3:45. Her hands shook with anticipation as she dialed the number of her broker, Sherwood Michael. "Sherwood," she began as soon as the secretary connected her call, "I'd like to sell all my shares of Tillings Industries. Yes, you heard me correctly. All of them. That's right. I know the Exchange closes in only a few minutes. You'll have to hurry, darling. Sell them now. Call me if you have any problems, but don't have any. I want to unload Tillings today."

Mildred's cheeks were flushed with excitement as she hung up the phone. Now all she had to do was wait. She could envision Sherwood Michael cursing her under his breath as he scurried to make the bell. At four o'clock, she would turn on the radio, but for the next few minutes, she would sit and sip her champagne.

Unaware of Mildred's actions, Sarah sat in her office, her father's office, with Holly at her side. The room was filled with telegrams, flowers, and candies from well-wishers celebrating the success of "Sarah," the latest fragrance addition to the Tillings family. Kicking off her shoes, Sarah leaned back in her chair and unbuttoned her apricot jacket. She closed her eyes and sighed deeply. The strain of the past months and of today's press conference had been harder on her than she had anticipated. She rubbed her eyes, feeling tired and drained. The first time she had felt this exhausted was the day she first found out that her father had left Tillings Industries in financial ruin at his death and that takeover rumors ran rampant.

With a soft chuckle, Sarah said, "I guess we showed Bryan Carson, didn't we? He may have taken over the company, but we saved it without him. We started work on 'Sarah' before he came here. He had nothing to do with it. 'Sarah' saved Tillings Industries, not Bryan's money. Maybe now he'll see who runs this company. The nerve of the man to kiss me in the elevator as if he owned me, too. Well, I've shown him. No one controls a Tillings except a Tillings. The next time I see his arrogant face, I'll remind him of that. This has certainly been a birthday to remember.''

"Here, Sarah, have another. These chocolates are fabulous.'' Holly's voice interrupted Sarah's thoughts of Bryan. "Trust Frank to send something so deliciously sinful. He knows you so well, doesn't he? Who else would have sent milk chocolates filled with these delectable apricot preserves?'' Holly said, licking the stickiness from her fingers. She was tired, too, but excited at the same time for her friend. In her heart, she had never doubted that Sarah would be able to pull it off, to put Tillings Industries back in the black financially without the help of Bryan Carson. Still, she knew that Bryan had flexed his corporate muscle and infused considerable amounts of cash to keep the company afloat. So much rested on the success of one fragrance. Now that preliminary figures showed that "Sarah" would be a success, they could all rest a bit.

"No, thanks. I can't eat another bite if I want to fit into the evening gown for tonight's dinner party. Besides, I'm too tired to eat anything else. All I want is a nap. What time will the press conference be aired? I'll stay here long enough to watch the television coverage, then I'll go home,'' Sarah said, barely able to open her eyes, she was so tired.

"Four o'clock news, I think. It's almost that now. I'll turn on the television,'' Holly responded, dragging herself from the soft leather armchair into which she had sunk.

Immediately, the visage of a somber-faced newscaster filled the screen. At first Sarah could not understand his words through the fog of fatigue that filled her mind. Then, slowly, they began to penetrate.

"The stock market was sent reeling at the close of business today by an unexpected transaction. A major, as yet undisclosed, Tillings Industries' stockholder sold all shares on the day that this historic African-American-owned company introduced a new fragrance that itself rocked the cosmetics industry. The fragrance, named after the president, and daughter of the founder of the Tillings dynasty, Sarah Tillings, was touted as the most promising addition to the cosmetics world in many years. It was expected to put Tillings back on the map following the death of the founder, Martin Tillings, a near financial ruin, and a recent takeover. In the wake of this new and much-needed success, the sale of so large a block of stock comes as a major upset and a tremendous set-back for the company,'' he closed.

Sarah sat open-mouthed, slumped in her chair. What had happened? Who was this stockholder? Why had the sale been ordered today, of all days? Who hated her enough to try to ruin Tillings when everything was going so well?

Suddenly, her telephone began to ring. Holly answered in a shaky voice. The caller was the editor-in-chief of the *Dallas Century,* asking for an interview. Holly begged off, claiming that an official statement would be forthcoming as soon as Sarah had time to assess the situation. No sooner had she hung up then the phone rang again. This time it was the television station manager demanding an interview. She gave him the same answer.

Sarah stood with slumped shoulders at the window, looking out onto her town. Today had started out with such promise. Everything had gone so well at the press conference. ''Sarah'' was a huge success. She buried her face in her hands and sobbed. Why this? Why now?

The takeover had been something she could fight against. But, now, there was nothing she could do to stem the tide of further sales. The defection by a major stockholder was a sign of lost confidence in Tillings Industries and in her management. The stock market would shudder from the impact. Tillings was lost, ruined. Who could have done this to her? Who owned enough stock to cause this run of panic? Bryan? Mildred? An unknown enemy?

No, not Bryan. He had too much of his own money tied up in Tillings to do something like this. Besides, she had not missed the look of pride on his face as he watched her standing before all those cameras and reporters during the press conference. She had seen his eyes follow her everywhere she went, even as she refused to acknowledge his presence. No, Bryan was not the one.

Mildred? She hated Sarah. She thought that Sarah and Tillings Industries had kept Martin from truly loving her. She had never realized that it was her own hunger for money that had prevented Martin from finding happiness with her. Could Mildred have done this? Why would she? Her fortunes were tied up in Tillings, too. She and Sarah owned considerable holdings together, but Sarah always suspected that her father had given her several hundred lots as a wedding present. Sarah never knew the exact extent of Mildred's financial involvement in the company. Did she hate Sarah enough to ruin her reputation in Dallas to get back at her?

Was there someone else? Sarah racked her brain for the answer. In the business world, there was always someone who wanted to see a competitor fail. Yet, when Tillings was at its lowest point before the takeover, no one had tried to bury it. Who was trying so hard now to ruin her?

Through her gulping sobs, Sarah did not hear Holly leave, or Bryan enter her office. She only felt herself being enfolded in a warm blanket of security as he turned her around and took her into his arms. She rested against his chest and allowed him to stroke her back. The closeness of his body, the smell of his cologne, the strength of his arms, and the soft deep murmuring of his voice quieted her sobs. She rested her weary body against him and drew strength from his solid warmth.

"What can I do to help?" Bryan asked as he held her tightly, trying to blot out the pain of the announcement.

"Nothing. There's nothing anyone can do. It's over. We both tried to save the company, but this last is too much for even our combined effort. Someone has completely shaken stockholder confidence,'' Sarah replied. Her hopes had been totally shattered.

''Don't give up yet,'' Bryan urged confidently. ''I still have some untapped resources. Give me a few hours. We might pull this off, yet.''

Looking into his strong face, Sarah whispered, ''Do you really think we might make a success of this shambles? You know there's nothing in the world I want more than to restore the company to its former glory. I know 'Sarah' would have done that for us. The initial success was too positive. Someone else must have thought the same thing and decided to pull the rug from under us while we weren't looking.''

''Don't worry, darling. I'm going to do what I can. Leave everything to me,'' he said as he softly stroked her hair and shoulders. He could feel the tension fading from her body as she began to rely on his strength.

Gently, Bryan tucked his fingers under Sarah's chin and lifted her tear-streaked face. Looking deeply into her brimming eyes, he saw all of her pain and despair. She had worked so hard to save Tillings Industries. He knew that she had wanted to prove, not only to herself and the financial world, but to him, as well, that she could manage her father's company. He was not blind to the fact that she saw him as the enemy. Even after their conversation, she still considered him the one who had stolen Tillings from her. She knew that her father had all but turned his back on the management of the company when he married Mildred. Yet Bryan knew that she could not allow herself to tarnish the memory of her beloved father by blaming him for the financial failure of Tillings. It had been easier to blame him for the takeover.

Bryan understood everything. He had waited patiently these past months for Sarah to let down her guard and for her to reach out for him. In the elevator he had thought that the heat of the day and the tension of being together had finally worn her down. He had taken advantage of her weakened state. She had yielded to him so completely that he had hoped that they had begun a new phase in their relationship. But, that night at the ball, she had seemed more determined than ever to push him aside, to show that he meant nothing to her. Days later in her office, she had again yielded to his embrace, matching her passion to his. That time an emergency phone call from Dr. Morris had saved her from him, and from herself.

Slowly, he kissed her eyelids and tasted her sweet, salty tears. Then, he kissed her cheeks and the trembling corners of her mouth. Finally, he slid his lips over hers and pressed her to him. Sliding his arms around her trim, womanly frame, he pulled her against his chest and held her there. For the moment, he would not try to analyze her feelings. He would not wonder if Sarah would pull away from him again or reject him as she had after the elevator ride. For this moment in time, she was his.

Sarah had no desire to resist Bryan's arms and probing tongue. She needed his strength, his clear-headedness, and to have his arms around her. She needed to know that he was with her, that he was not the one who wanted to take Tillings from her. Something in the way he held her, in the way his hands caressed the curve of her back and shoulders, told her that she was right. Finally, she could believe him. Bryan had not betrayed her and taken from her the dream of restoring Tillings Industries to its old glory.

As Sarah returned his kisses, her tongue darted playfully against his. Her lips teased and begged for more. She clung to him, dug her nails into his back through his jacket. She pressed herself against his hard thighs and felt his manhood respond to her closeness. In the midst of her pain, a need to belong and to be loved filled her very being. She needed Bryan; not for his money; but for the love he could give her. She felt a warmth grow deep in her groin, something she had only fleetingly allowed herself to admit she felt for him during the brief elevator ride. She wanted him! She wanted to hold him in her arms, to feel his naked body against hers, to give herself to him, and to rest spent in his arms.

"Sarah!" he whispered into her neck.

"No, Bryan, not like this," Sarah eased herself away from his warmth. Her world was cold once more. "I can't come to you knowing that I've failed Tillings Industries and myself. I know now that I was wrong about you all along.

"I think part of me knew from the first time I saw you. You were so careful never to make me feel as if I had failed the company. I can admit that to myself now. But I had to keep you at a distance, to treat you as an outsider and the enemy. I couldn't admit that, had it not been for you, Tillings would have folded, slipped through my fingers, not because of something I did, but because my father mismanaged the company.

"But now I can't think about myself, about us, when someone is threatening the security and the future of Tillings. I just can't. No matter how much I long to hold you, to love you, I can't until this is straightened out. I just can't."

Fresh tears glistened on her eyelashes as she stepped back, wrapping her arms around herself for warmth. Bryan saw the determination in the set of her thin shoulders and almost pulled her to him. She needed his strength, but Sarah had to finish what she had started. He understood and loved her for her determination. He knew that she could never be his until Tillings was safe. Just as he had helped her before without her understanding why, he would help her again now. They would unite with one purpose to save her beloved company and her father's memory.

Bryan took her elbow and led her across the office to the couch. He carefully seated himself at the opposite end of its great length.

"Sarah, we have to plan our strategy against this attack on

the company but, before we do, there's something you must know about my takeover of Tillings Industries," Bryan began. "This may be difficult for you to believe, but you must hear me out. My interest in the company began years ago when I first met your father. I was incredibly impressed by his business savvy and his ability to build a successful company when all the odds were stacked against him. In a world where black men are feared and doubted, he managed to succeed. More than his business sense drew me to him. I admired the love he showed his family. He never put the business ahead of you and your mother; he loved you both more than he loved Tillings."

Bryan continued, "As I studied Martin, I found myself in the company of a charming teenager: you. You were tall, poised, beguiling, vivacious, and far too young for me. To you, I was a friend of your father's and nothing else. I promised myself that, one day, when you were older, I would tell you how I felt about you. I watched as your father and the company fell on hard times. When it looked as if you'd have to file bankruptcy or be bought out by a competitor, I stepped in. I never intended to take Tillings from you. In fact, I had planned to give it to you as a wedding present, if you'd have me. I've loved you for years, Sarah. All I want in life is to make you feel safe and to restore the comfort you knew when your father was alive."

"What about all the stories about you and the long string of women? The society pages have been filled with photos of you escorting one beautiful woman after another to various functions." Sarah inquired. She looked away so that Bryan could not see the blush that colored her tired cheeks.

Bryan smiled. He was quite thrilled that his careful planning had not gone unnoticed. "All part of the plan. I had to appear the carefree bachelor while I waited for you to grow up. The society editors would have had a field day if they had thought I wasn't interested in women. They accepted a worldly man much more easily. I played the part well, don't you think?'' he replied.

"And the takeover? How did you engineer that?''

"That was easier than arranging the photo sessions with the glamorous women. Jason Parson, your father's old friend, banker, and benefactor, knew of my devotion to your father, Tillings Industries, and you. He kept me informed of the financial situation as word spread throughout the industry that your father was in trouble. After he died, Jason contacted me regularly with status reports on your efforts to straighten out the mess he left behind. You almost succeeded, you know. When the wolves started to circle, he called me with word that it was time to act. With his help, I made my move. Your father was special to me, Sarah, but you were even more important. Tillings Industries had to be saved for you.''

Sarah gazed into his soft, gray eyes and believed him instantly. She had, deep inside, known that Bryan Carson had not meant her any harm in taking over her company. Still, her pride and anger had not allowed her to show how much she appreciated his help. She was ashamed of the way she had acted and, yet, she knew in her heart that she could not have done anything else. Even now she could not follow the dictates of her heart. She could not throw herself into his arms and wrap herself in the security she found there. She could not allow herself to fall completely for him until Tillings Industries was safe. She knew she loved him, but love would have had to wait. She had to save Tillings first.

"Thank you, Bryan, for all you've done for my father's memory, for Tillings Industries, and for me. I would have lost everything sooner if you hadn't stepped in. I can understand why you never mentioned knowing my father. I'm not always . . . approachable . . . when I've made up my mind to do something, and I was determined to save the company single-handedly,'' Sarah whispered, her throat tight with the tears of gratitude she would not allow to fall. Her gold eyes sparkled more brightly than ever.

"Nothing is lost yet, Sarah my love. My sources at the Exchange are hunting down the origin of the sales transaction. From there, we'll uncover the identity of the seller in no time at all. Once we know that, we'll know the reason. Then we'll do whatever it takes to turn this around. Don't give up yet. There's still too much work to do," Bryan answered. He spoke with a confidence that belied his misgivings.

"I wish I were that confident. Even if we find the person, there's a lot of money at stake here. The stock has all but bottomed out. I don't know if we can raise enough cash to buy up the outstanding stock," Sarah said with a shake of her head. With a shy smile she added, "I doubt that even you have enough ready cash for that."

Bryan was happy to see her old biting wit begin to return. "I might not be able to pull this off alone but, with a few well-placed phone calls, anything is possible. I'll go to my office now and get started. I'll keep you informed of my progress. In the meantime, you and Holly should get that press release ready. It's important not to look defeated. You have to remain confident in the face of this new assault. Another conference might not be a bad idea if you think you can carry it off. Stockholder confidence is one thing we can't afford to lose now. We have to stop the possibility of a stampede on Monday morning."

As he rose to leave, he placed a gentle kiss on her forehead. In his heart, he wanted so much more than this chaste peck, yet he knew that nothing more was possible now with Tillings Industries under siege.

Sarah wanted more, too. She longed to pull him down to her and feel his weight crushing against her. She wanted to feel his hands exploring her body, pulling her under him, making her cry out his name. Now that she knew the truth of Bryan Carson's involvement in her life all these years, she could admit her feelings. She loved him.

Now, when he was in reach and wanted her as much as she wanted him, something stood in the way of their happiness—her love of Tillings Industries. He had saved her father's company for her. Now that very company kept them from sharing their love.

Watching him leave, Sarah knew that they were up against serious odds. It did not take much to shake stockholder confidence. She had seen it happen when news of her father's death had hit the market. When she had been named president, the stockholders had again wavered in confidence. Would a woman be able to stem the tide of the weak financial picture left by Martin Tillings's neglect of the company? When she proved herself, they returned.

Yet she knew they watched and waited. They had breathed a sigh of relief when a man had taken over the company. A man had run it into the ground and a man would save it. Yet, she needed everyone to understand that she, Martin Tillings's daughter, had taken the helm. That was why the success of "Sarah" was so important. She had let everyone know that the fragrance was her design. Bryan had not helped her. She knew they might not remember the success of "Sarah" in the wake of this fiasco. Holding another press conference was a good idea. Taking out ads in the newspapers and trade magazines was a good strategy, too.

Sarah squared her shoulders with the old determination as she rose from the sofa. Bryan was right. She was not licked yet. Pressing the intercom button, she said, "Holly, come in, please. Call Toni Wilson in marketing and tell her to alert her contacts that I'm calling a press conference for six o'clock. I want print coverage, too. Tell her that I'm preparing an open letter to the stockholders that I want published in all the newspapers. It'll be on her desk in half an hour. Make sure every department head knows that we have only just begun to fight.

We will not fail to turn over every single rock in this hunt for the viper that has reared its ugly head against Tillings. This is war!''

''Gotcha!'' Holly replied, happy to hear the old passion in Sarah's voice.

She would fight this unknown enemy's attack on Tillings Industries with the same energy with which she had fought against Bryan. Whoever it was that had planned to ruin her business would be sorry he had ever crossed Sarah Tillings.

Chapter Eleven

"Ladies and gentlemen, if you will take your seats, Miss Tillings will be with you in a moment," Holly shouted. The atmosphere in the conference room was somber. All the apricot bunting, carnations, and roses from earlier had been removed. This would be a working press conference—serious in nature, and vitally important to the future of Tillings Industries.

Polite applause greeted Sarah as she entered the room. Flash bulbs popped, but not with the wild abandon of earlier. Sarah, too, looked different. She had removed the apricot silk suit of earlier and replaced it with a navy blue twill with brass buttons that closely resembled the uniform of the captain of a ship. She hoped no one would miss its statement. She was still at the helm of Tillings Industries. She was still in control of the situation, regardless of how catastrophic it appeared. She was its captain and was not about to go down with the ship.

"Thank you for coming on such short notice," she began. "I'm sure by now you are all aware of the happenings on the stock exchange this afternoon, but I will clarify for those who need it. At approximately three fifty-five today, a large sell order was placed by an as-yet-unidentified Tillings Industries stockholder. It amounted to the sale of several thousand lots of Tillings stocks. The reason for this sale is unknown, and I can only speculate.

"Tillings Industries, as you all know, suffered some ups and downs, financially, in the last years of my father's tenure as president. When he died and I took over the management of Tillings, there was much to be done to right the effects of his absentee management style. The physical plant and the laboratories needed to be upgraded and brought into the future. The employees needed improved benefits. Dividends needed readjusting to make the stock more attractive. We made all of these improvements and more. I hired new scientists, researchers, chemists, and marketers, the best money could buy, to bring us out of the doldrums quickly and efficiently. The plant underwent extensive modernization. The laboratory now sports the best equipment in the industry.

"However, my efforts could not stem the tide of a friendly take-over. This infusion of new talent at the upper management level allowed me to concentrate on the product end of Tillings while Bryan Carson managed its financial affairs. Our teamwork has paid great dividends. Today, we introduced 'Sarah,' the newest, most exciting fragrance to hit the cosmetics industry in years. The stock market rallied around Tillings, following the announcement. The price of stocks soared all day. All of you sampled the fruits of our labors. Tillings is on sound footing once more. We are out of the red for the first time in five years. All capital expenditures have been amortized, all investors paid, and all employees covered by an improved health program.

"Yet that was not enough for whoever is trying to undermine the security of all of us. Bryan Carson has called in a top team of analysts to get to the bottom of this treason and find the person who would so deliberately scuttle our efforts. He is meeting with them as we speak.

"As president of Tillings Industries, I tell you with all confidence that we are in sound condition. There is no need for a wholesale panic. Tillings is not in jeopardy from any source other than a mean-tempered, vindictive person who for some reason has decided to try to bring us down.

"Believe me when I tell you that Tillings Industries has weathered many storms. We will pull through this one. I apologize for not being able to answer any questions at this time. However, as soon as we know the identity of the person behind this insult to our integrity and future, I will inform you.

"Again, thank you for coming, and good evening."

A stunned silence filled the room as Sarah left the podium. Then the assembled press corps started firing questions from the floor. With a wave of her hand, she dismissed them and closed the door.

Hurrying down the hall to Bryan's office, Sarah realized just how much she needed him. They had decided that she would face the press alone. She had spoken with them many times and knew most of them personally. Bryan was still a newcomer to Dallas. His appearance tonight might have undermined her strength. He had deliberately kept a low-key profile, professionally, since arriving in town. This did not seem to either of them to be the time for him to flex his muscles.

But now, alone with only her worries, she needed him. She needed the sound of his voice, the strength of the set of his jaw, and the touch of his hand. Bursting into his office, she found Bryan huddled around the conference table with the financial wizards he had brought in to help them decipher this mess. He looked up immediately. When he saw Sarah, the scowl between his brows faded. His face lit up with a gentle smile. He could tell that the press conference had gone well. There was never any worry about that. Sarah was a master at working people. Yet he had worried about her. She was so fragile. He was not sure how much more she could take. He remembered the feel of her trembling and sobbing in his arms.

Looking into her eyes, Bryan found a renewed strength. This was the Sarah Tillings whose flashing eyes had greeted him in the board room on the day of his arrival. This was no delicate flower. The navy captain's suit was the perfect touch. She was at the helm of Tillings Industries and always would be. This was her company; he was now and always would be her first mate and, one day, he hoped, her husband.

"Good news, Sarah. We've identified the stock broker who made the transaction and are about to track down his client. Seems as if he's here in Dallas. Holly tells me he has become quite well known in the short time he has lived here. Moves in only the best social circles. He lives in your neighborhood, I think. With any luck, the stockholder will reside locally, too," Bryan said, not allowing himself to look into her flashing amber eyes.

Sarah leaned closer for a better look at the printout spread open on the table. Her shoulder brushed against his, sending sparks of desire through his body. She saw the name of the local stockbroker, Michael Sherwood, highlighted in bright yellow. His name was familiar yet somehow strange at the same time—almost like a fading memory. Maybe she recognized it because of his reputation in town. She must have met him at the country club or at social gatherings. She might have seen him when she jogged through the neighborhood. Despite it's size, everyone knew everyone in Dallas.

She stared at the name . . . Michael Sherwood . . . Michael Sherwood. The letters pulsed beneath the yellow highlighter. In the tired recesses of her mind, she knew him but could not make the connections, regardless of her effort. She could see him coming toward her through the fog but could not make out his features or his connection with her. She must have worked on some committee or other with him. Maybe she had danced with him once at a gala. She would continue to search her memory for the connection when she was not so tired.

Bryan watched the struggle play out on Sarah's tired face.

"Do you know him?" he asked when he could stand the silence no longer.

"I'm not sure. I have some vague memory of meeting him. But I'm too tired to pull it all together. This has been a long day, and it's not over yet. I still have that dinner party at nine," she replied, sinking into the chair he offered her.

Bone tired though she was, Sarah Tillings was still a beautiful, exciting woman. Bryan watched as she slipped off her heels and gently massaged her tired toes. He reached over and took her foot in his hands and did the job for her. He could feel the warmth of her foot through the sheer navy nylon of her stockings. She started to relax as he wiggled each toe in turn and carefully ran his knuckle down the center from toe to heel. She sighed as he applied gentle pressure to her Achilles tendon. She smiled contentedly as he repeated the process on the other foot, all the while imagining his fingers traveling up the length of her legs until he reached the hidden treasure between them.

Straightening her jacket, Sarah rose from the chair and walked slowly toward the door. She carried a shoe in each hand. Calling back over her shoulder, she said, "I'm going home now, Bryan. I'll see you later tonight. I have to get changed and try to put on a face for later. Call me if you find out the name of the stockholder."

"Right, Sarah," he called after her. He forced himself to concentrate on the work at hand rather than the sway of her hips as she walked from the room. There would be time for passion later, he hoped.

Sarah soaked in a hot tub overflowing with "Sarah" bubble bath. Her head rested on a pillow balanced on the rim of the tub. Her eyes were closed. Soft jazz from the stereo in her dressing room floated in to soothe her nerves. What a day, she thought. What a way to spend her thirtieth birthday. The day certainly had not gone as she had thought it would. She had planned it as her chance to show Bryan Carson that she and Tillings Industries did not need him. Her new fragrance had taken off like gangbusters. Stock prices soared. Sales orders came in by the tens of thousands. The press conference had been a huge success. She had the reporters eating out of her hand.

And then the bubble had burst. Someone had sold thousands of lots of Tillings stock. Once again she found herself needing Bryan to bail her out, just as he had saved her from financial ruin with his takeover of the company. The one person on the face of the earth she had wanted to tell to go to the devil, she now had to rely on to save Tillings Industries one more time.

Wiggling her toes in the warm, soapy water, she thought about the unanswered questions that plagued the day. Who had sold those lots of stock and why? Who wanted to hurt her so badly that he waited until her birthday and the biggest day in Tillings Industries' history to do something this destructive? Who was determined to drive her into bankruptcy?

Her tired mind slowly sifted through the possibilities one more time. Mildred. Bryan. The two most obvious possibilities and the two most unlikely. Mildred had as much at stake as Sarah if Tillings folded. Why would she want to do something like this? Sarah knew that her stepmother still did not hold any love for her, but to hurt herself at the same time was ridiculous. More than that, the act was sick and self-destructive. Still, Mildred was capable of engineering a diabolical plan like this one. She was very dangerous and extremely crafty. To take her for granted would be a huge mistake. She could easily have started this panic with the right inside help.

In her heart, Sarah knew that Bryan could not be involved in this blatant attempt to ruin her. Not only did he have a fortune tied up in Tillings, he was working his tail off to find the person behind the stock sale. He would not be doing all this if he were the one. Or would he? Her mind would not stop churning out questions. Could he be searching for the culprit to throw her off his track? Could he be covering up his own involvement in this mess? Was he hiding evidence that would point to him? Was this part of his master plan to take over Tillings Industries totally?

Who was Michael Sherwood and how did he fit into this puzzle? Did he act alone or was he someone's foil?

Her body shuddered as if a cold draft had blown through the bathroom. In spite of the nagging uncertainty, she could feel Bryan's arms around her. She remembered surrendering herself to him and seeking comfort against his broad chest. She had found herself unable to resist his strength, and the solace from the world, that were in his arms. He was always there when she needed him.

Yet, she continued to hold back, to keep herself away from him, to give only so much but not all. She wondered if she would have broken down her self-imposed defenses if the telephone call from Dr. Morris had not interrupted them.

Through the tangle of thoughts, she could hear a voice reminding her that she loved Bryan and that he loved her. She remembered him saying that he had waited for her to grow up, to need him, and to love. Well, she needed him, now, all right, but love would have to wait until Tillings was safe. Only then could she think of herself. Only then would she be able to silence that nagging little voice that questioned Bryan's sincerity.

Slowly Sarah enfolded herself in the thick apricot towel and stared at the face in the mirror. The bath had relaxed her tired muscles but had done little for the shadows under her eyes. Well, skillfully applied make-up would solve that problem. She had to appear confident tonight. None of her guests must ever guess just how damaging today's sale had been to either the financial future of Tillings Industries or to her self-esteem. They had to think everything was under control, as she had said it was in her last press conference. After all, many of them owned stock in Tillings, too. She could not afford to panic them even further. Besides, one of them might have betrayed her.

Slipping into her apricot silk gown and adjusting the strap that covered one shoulder, Sarah thought about the list of Dallas notables who would be arriving in about fifteen minutes. Everyone from judges and corporate executives to the most in-demand plastic surgeons had been invited to tonight's celebration of the birth of the two Sarahs. She had arranged everything perfectly for the maximum effect. The selection of every flower, tablecloth, napkin, piece of silver, crystal stem, and bottle of wine had been supervised by her. She wanted to let the world—and Dallas society, white and black—know that Sarah Tillings was alive and well and in control of Tillings Industries.

Sarah's hands shook slightly as she fastened her mother's diamond necklace around her long, thin neck. Scolding herself, she said, "You'll have to do better than that, old girl. People will know you're worried if your hands shake. Buck up. You can pull this off. You've gone through worse and come out smelling like a rose. Don't give up now."

She knew she had faced worse than this. Her mother's death when Sarah had been a teenager and had needed her most had been a terrible blow. Her father's death and the discovery of the mismanagement of Tillings Industries' finances had left her reeling for months. The takeover by Bryan Carson had sounded like a death knell, ringing for Tillings and for her. Somehow, this was worse. She had been able to put faces on her fear when her mother and father died and when Bryan took over the company. Now out there somewhere lurked an unknown traitor who had the power to crush her with a simple phone call. For the first time in her life, Sarah was terrified and unsure of her next move.

Squaring her shoulders and putting on a happy smile, Sarah slowly descended the stairs to the first of her waiting guests. She knew that if she could get through tonight, she could handle anything.

Sarah was not surprised to find her stepmother carefully surveying the buffet table, daintily sampling each delicacy. Mildred's performance would have been comical if Sarah had felt more secure about this evening.

Mildred was always among the first to arrive at every party in town. She liked to check out the surroundings before the presence of others cluttered up her view. If she found something not to her liking, she shared her opinions with everyone as she greeted them. She was the unofficial queen of gossip. Everyone feared her critiques; one negative word from Mildred could cause a party to die before it got started.

Tonight, Mildred surveyed the condo with an expression of something close to admiration on her face. Although she did not care for Sarah, she was the first to admit that she knew how to throw parties that were second only to her own. Sarah had filled the massive three-bedroom penthouse duplex with flowers of every type and description. They sat in pots on tables, on pedestals, and on the stairs leading up to the bedrooms, even providing extra color to the powder rooms. Waiters flowed among the guests as smoothly as the apricot champagne they poured. Caviar graced several tables around the room. Foe gras overflowed on one end of the buffet table, while fruit and rich chocolate cakes filled the other. Dim sum, chilled spiced shrimp, thinly sliced roast beef, and ham urged the guests not to hesitate to satisfy their hunger. The quartet discreetly stationed in the corner of the living room by the window played soft jazz music as the guests arrived. The carpet had been rolled up to expose the shining bare floors and create a dance floor in front of them. A gold cage of white doves cooed on one side of the front door and a small table laden with a departing gift for each guest stood on the other. Although not needed, the gas fire flickered behind the fireplace doors, radiating cheer to all. Sarah had rearranged the furniture into conversation-inspiring clusters. Mildred could find nothing to criticize in the party preparations.

Holly and Frank had arrived together. They had started dating a few months before the hospital gala. Now, from the way they interacted with each other, they appeared to be having a serious romance. In the midst of the day's turmoil, it made her happy to see her two special friends together. Frank was a wonderful man whose life had been filled with one broken romance after another. He deserved the happiness and camaraderie someone as kind and thoughtful as Holly could give him. Holly was just the right woman for him. She had a well-developed sense of loyalty and a level head. She had experienced her share of pain and suffering since her parents' death.

The guests drifted in . . . respectably late, of course. No one wanted to be first, except Mildred, and no one dared to arrive last. The crystal tinkled and the diamonds sparkled. Satins and silks adorned every sleek body. Black Dallas was out in force tonight to watch Sarah Tillings put on the show of her life. Sarah was ready for them. She laughed just loudly enough to appear confident but not too loudly, for fear of being fake. She flirted just enough with every man in the room, married and single. She was charming and carefree, rather than desperate and worried. She danced with all who asked her, and chatted gaily. She joined the other women in shared confidences and shamelessly gossiped with everyone about everyone else in the room.

Between dances, Sarah scanned the room for Bryan. She was disappointed when she did not find him. His absence had been noticed by the others, too. She saw several women with their heads together. She wondered if he had uncovered the name of the person who sold the stock through Michael Sherwood.

The old nagging thoughts about Bryan refused to leave her as she moved about the room crowded with laughing guests. Did Bryan's absence mean that he was the one who had betrayed Tillings and her? Had he left town before she could find him out for herself? She could not allow herself the luxury of truly trusting him . . . not yet, until she overcame this last hurdle standing between Tillings and success.

Watching her chatting gaily with John Fraser, no one would have suspected her fears. Looking over his shoulder, she stared right into Bryan's face as he stood in the doorway dressed in a perfectly tailored tuxedo. But he was not alone. Beside him stood a tall, willowy brunette.

Sarah could not believe her eyes. Bryan had brought a date to her birthday celebration. After the elevator kiss and their long conversation that afternoon, he had arrived with another woman. He had promised her his loyalty and his love, only to arrive on her special night with another woman on his arm. She felt as if someone had thrown cold water on her at the end of a hot Dallas day.

John interrupted her thoughts. "Are you all right, Sarah?"

"I'm just fine, John. Forgive me for stepping on your toes. I'm just a little tired. Too much excitement in one day, I guess," she managed to say through clenched teeth and smiling lips. She would not let anyone know the pain that filled her heart and threatened to tear her apart, not even John.

As the quartet finished playing the waltz piece, Sarah excused herself and calmly walked to the part of the room where Bryan and his lady friend stood. She tried to remember what Bryan had said about the perfect orchestration of his appearances with women. Somehow, the words seemed hollow as she watched this beautiful woman smile lovingly at him.

"Bryan," Sarah cooed, aware that all eyes in the room were on them, "so glad you could make it. Better late than never, I suppose. Won't you introduce me to your friend?"

"Sorry we're late, Sarah. I had a little trouble getting away from the office. A last-minute fax kept me from leaving. This is Courtney Paige, an old friend from Washington, D.C. She's here on a modeling shoot. I thought I'd bring her along and introduce her to Dallas society. Hope you don't mind," Bryan answered with an ingratiating smile that grated on her nerves.

Turning to Courtney, Sarah said, "Welcome to Dallas and my home. I hope your stay will be long and happy. You'll find that we're a congenial group. We're always eager to make new friends."

"Thank you, Sarah, and happy birthday. I've wanted to meet you for some time. I love your new fragrance. Bryan gave me a sample. I hope you don't mind. As a matter of fact, I plan to wear it during the shoot tomorrow. I'm modeling lingerie tomorrow. A splash of 'Sarah' will make me feel sexy," Courtney replied in a soft accent tinged with a hint of Virginia.

Sarah could not help but like someone who had the good taste to appreciate "Sarah," but she was still annoyed at Bryan for bringing this vision of loveliness in red satin. She was aware that he was watching her every move. She wondered if he were waiting for some sign of jealousy, perhaps. Well, he would never see that from her. Not in a million years.

"Well, have a good time, you two. Happy to meet you, Courtney. Bryan, maybe we can talk later about any new discoveries. Enjoy yourselves," Sarah chirped in mock happiness, and eased away to check on her other guests. She thought her face would crack from the weight of the smile plastered on her lips.

Black Dallas society had stopped waiting for Sarah to dissolve in tears of devastation and was having a good time at her party. Even Mildred seemed to be enjoying herself. She had stopped looking for any flaws in the preparations and was engaged in animated conversation with a man Sarah had a nagging feeling she should recognize. He was about forty, dressed in a perfectly tailored dinner jacket, and obviously interested in every word Mildred uttered. In his hand was a pipe from which smoke trails, smelling of cherry tobacco, escaped. His mustache was carefully trimmed and his nails newly manicured.

As Sarah made her way toward them, she heard Mildred

say, "It's all going very well, don't you think? I've never enjoyed anything more."

"Enjoyed what, Mildred?" Sarah asked, taking her place between Mildred and the unknown man. She was curious about the identity of her stepmother's companion.

"Why, the party, of course, dear," Mildred replied with her usual heavy dose of syrupy sweetness.

Turning to her companion, she continued, "Sarah, I'm sure you remember Sherwood Michael. He was on the hospital's presidential search committee with me."

Sherwood Michael. That name was awfully familiar, but somehow different, too.

"Yes, I think I do remember. How are you, Sherwood? Welcome to my birthday party."

"Doing quite well, thanks. Happy birthday, Sarah. You'll have plenty to tell your grandchildren about today," he added with a chuckle.

As he spoke, Sarah studied this stranger. She had a vague memory of seeing him at the hospital gala, but another more pressing thought nagged at her tired mind. Sherwood Michael . . . Sherwood Michael. She could not figure out why alarms sounded in her head at the mention of his name.

"What do you do in Dallas, Sherwood, besides work on committees, I mean?"

"Oh, Sherwood's a very busy man, Sarah. He does a little of this and a little of that," Mildred interrupted. She looked a little anxious at Sarah's question.

"Mildred's right, in a way. I do have a number of interests, and I own a few companies, too," Sherwood answered confidently.

Sarah was poised to ask for specifics when Mildred broke in again, "Sherwood, that's my favorite song. You haven't danced with me at all tonight. You won't get away with that, you dear man. You'll excuse us, won't you, dear?" she purred at Sarah, slipping her arm through Sherwood's. She propelled·

him through the crowd to the little dance floor on the other side of the huge living room.

Sarah watched as they vanished into the crush of people. She tried hard to recall what Bryan had said to her earlier. She had to tell Bryan as soon as she could. He would remember even if she could not.

She searched the room for him and finally found Bryan and Courtney standing at the bar. He stood gazing deeply into his date's warm brown eyes. Occasionally he allowed his eyes to fall to her ample bosom. A pang of jealousy coursed through her body at the sight of Courtney touching his arm in a very familiar manner.

Sarah started walking toward them, but stopped when she saw Bryan lean forward and gently place kisses, first on the tip of Courtney's nose, then on the corners of her mouth. A stab of pain shot through her heart. She could not walk any closer. She could only watch as he took Courtney's arm and led her to the seclusion of the verandah.

Standing there in her living room, Sarah felt hot and cold at the same time. Her face burned as if on fire. Her cold hands shook with rage. How could he do this to her? Bryan had held her and claimed to love her earlier today—and now this. Just when she thought that maybe she could trust him, he showed that she really meant nothing to him at all. He had only been playing with her emotions, trying for yet another conquest, another notch on his belt.

Well, Sarah Tillings would not be a notch on any man's belt. She would show Bryan Carson that she did not need him. She had come this far without his help. She would work through this problem without him, too. She had plenty of friends who could advise her . . . Holly, Jason, and Frank, just to name a few. She would show Bryan Carson that she could save Tillings Industries without him. Besides, she admitted: from the looks of things, she would have to do just that. In her anger, Sarah forgot all about the name Sherwood Michael.

Chapter Twelve

Bryan and Courtney were the first to leave. As if on cue, the other guests quickly followed. Sarah could not bring herself to feel sorry that he had left, although she had looked forward to some time alone with him. He had paid no attention to her. He had not even noticed her new dress. He had been too busy looking deeply into his date's eyes to give her more than a few passing glances. She was glad they had left. She needed time and space before seeing him again.

Tossing her apricot silk dress across the back of her bedroom chair, Sarah pulled her nightgown over her head and climbed into bed. She was too tired even to pull the drapes. Her mind was a blur of thoughts, all of which were about Bryan. The condo was strangely silent after so much music and laughter. Everything had been cleaned up and put away. The doors had been secured, and all the lights turned off. Even Hilda, her housekeeper, had turned in for the night.

Sarah was just settling down to sleep when she heard the ringing of the front door bell. At first she thought she had fallen asleep and had only dreamed the sound. Then she heard it again; more insistent this time, and a little louder.

Pulling on her dressing gown, she quickly walked down the hall and into the condo's foyer. Who could it be at this hour? She had not noticed that a forgetful guest had left anything behind. Surely whatever it was could wait until the morning.

"Yes, what is it? Who's there?" she called through the closed door.

"Sarah, it's me—Bryan. Open the door. We have to talk," the voice answered.

Standing on her tiptoes, Sarah looked through the peephole. It was Bryan, all right. And he was alone.

Opening the door, she said, "What do you want, Bryan? I'm awfully tired and sleepy. Besides, I thought you'd be in bed by now."

Her sarcasm was not lost on Bryan. He could see the pain and distrust in her tired eyes. "I took Courtney home and came back. The doorman let me in. We need to talk," he answered, closing and locking the door behind him. The lock made a heavy, final sound as it slid into place.

Stepping to the center of the foyer, Sarah leaned against the table in feigned exhaustion. "There's nothing for us to talk about that can't wait until Monday. We've done all we can for Tillings Industries tonight. Anyway, I'm too tired to talk to you about any more of your stories," she replied with determination.

"Fine, then I'll do all the talking. There's so much you need to understand about me . . . about us. I know it's late, but now's as good a time as any for you to hear everything," he insisted.

"Can't it wait? I'm too . . ."

Bryan's hungry lips cut short her words. The sight of Sarah in her dressing gown, with her eyes a mellow amber, was more than he could stand. She looked so vulnerable, and sexier than any woman had a right to look.

"Better still, we won't talk at all," Bryan added, sweeping

Sarah into his arms and carrying her down the hall toward her bedroom.

Once there, he gently placed her on the bed. Sarah lay perfectly still as he removed his tie and jacket. She watched as he quickly unfastened the onyx studs on the front and cuffs of his tuxedo shirt. He threw them impatiently on the floor. He kicked off his black patent leather tassel loafers and flung off his socks. Sarah's breath caught in her throat at the sight of his broad mahogany shoulders, rippling with muscles.

Sitting on the side of the bed, Bryan leaned over and gently kissed her eyes. He softly touched each of her cheeks with his hot lips. Holding her captive in his strong arms, he lifted her until she sat on his lap, cradled against his bare chest. His breathing quickened as he eased his mouth over hers. One hand burned into the small of her back while the other tightened in her hair. She could feel the hardness of his manhood pressing through the silk of her nightgown.

Against her will, Sarah felt her arms ease around his shoulders. Her fingers pressed into his shoulders and back, clinging to his strength. She closed her eyes and allowed her body to melt into his. Her will power dissolved with the heat of his caresses.

Slowly, Bryan slipped the tiny straps of her gown from her shoulders. He kissed her breasts and teased the nipples until they stood erect. Skillfully lifting her hips from the folds of fabric, he placed her naked on the bed. Quickly he removed his trousers and briefs. The sight of his newly freed manhood caused her to utter a soft gasp.

Bryan settled himself onto the satin sheets beside Sarah and took her into his arms. He held her and caressed her body until she trembled with desire. His lips left trails of fire along her shoulders, breasts, and stomach. His hands alternately heated and cooled her skin as thrills of the most painfully delightful warmth ran through her. Probing fingers sought her center of passion and caressed it in slow gentle circles that quickened with her breathing and the movement of her hips. As she called his name, they entered her moist depths, causing her to arch her back and scream with pleasure as the tide of desire began to wash over her. She was on fire and only he could put it out.

Her hands darted over his body, exploring every curve and muscle. He groaned when she touched his sweaty thighs and eased upward to his throbbing manhood. Whispering her name, Bryan gazed down into Sarah's smoldering gold eyes. With a barely audible sigh, she pulled him toward her and directed him into her source of passion. As they joined, she matched the movement of her hips to the hungry thrusting of his body. Her nails raked his body from shoulders to buttocks as the flames roared high and higher. She screamed his name as her body arched and fused with his. His face contorted with painful ecstasy as they clung together . . . their bodies, voices, and souls united in the pleasure they gave each other. She felt his strength flow out of him and into her. For the first time in years, Sarah did not think about Tillings Industries. She was not its president, its captain. She was a woman in love.

As the moonlight streamed through the window, Sarah and Bryan lay together on the rumpled satin sheets. Neither wanted to move or speak. They were afraid of breaking the spell or disturbing the fragile bond that held them together. Yet, even in the silence, each knew that there were many unasked questions that needed answering before their relationship could go any further. Still, they snuggled closer under the sheets and kept quiet. They were both too tired from the events of the day and the emotion of the evening. Questions would wait until the morning. Pushing the stray curl from his forehead, Sarah snuggled into the fold of his arm and fell into a gentle, sound sleep.

The next morning while Bryan slept, Sarah busied herself setting the little table in her bedroom with sweet, tempting treats for breakfast. She threw open the windows to admit the intoxicating smells of the Dallas morning. When the coffee was ready, she woke him with quick little kisses to the corners of his mouth.

"Wake up, sleepy head," she said, pulling the covers from his sleep-warm body. "Breakfast is ready. How do you like your coffee?"

Bryan stretched every muscle like a great, sleek, seal-colored cat. He smiled into Sarah's sparkling gold eyes and pulled her into his arms. Breakfast would have to wait. "Cold," he answered, untying the sash of her dressing gown and burying his face in her breasts. Sarah sighed contentedly and gave herself up to his warmth. She had neither the strength nor the desire to deny her need for him, her thirst for the pleasure he gave her, and the love she felt for this man who, only a few hours ago had been the enemy.

All thoughts of food and coffee were long forgotten. Lazy afternoon sun streamed across the bed, and a soft breeze filled the curtains. Sarah did not want to get up and risk breaking the spell. She lay contentedly in Bryan's arms as he stroked her shoulders and back. She stretched out one lazy arm toward the folded newspaper that lay on the bedside table.

"Don't move. What's the hurry? This is Saturday. There's nothing to keep us from spending the whole day together," Bryan urged her to return to his arms. His words reached her too late.

"It's him!" Sarah gasped. On the cover of the Saturday edition of the *Dallas Century* was a photograph of the man she had met last night with Mildred. Under the picture was the caption which read, "Sherwood Michael makes his mark on Dallas society." She turned to page two and read the story with great interest. Sherwood Michael had just settled in Dallas from Austin. He was single, rich, and available. Quickly scanning past the other trivia about his sporting interests, Sarah arrived at the information about his line of work. She had been introduced to that same man last night.

"Read this while I take a shower," she demanded, thrusting

the paper into Bryan's hands. "Looks like the rest of our leisurely day will have to wait." Sarah dashed naked into the bathroom.

Bryan chuckled, watching her shapely buttocks vanish behind the closed bathroom door. His manhood rose, unbidden, at the sight. He wondered if he would ever have enough of Sarah Tillings. Somehow, he knew that he never would grow tired of holding her, looking into those changeable gold eyes, and feeling her supple body merge with his. He listened as the water in the shower drummed full force. With difficulty, as the shower door slammed shut, he allowed his concentration to turn to the open newspaper. Without much interest, he read the caption under the photograph. Suddenly the name seemed very familiar. Sherwood Michael . . . Sherwood Michael . . . Michael Sherwood!

The name on the printout had been backward, last name first. The name of the stockbroker who had engineered the sale of thousands of lots of Tillings Industries stock was not Michael Sherwood, but that of the same Sherwood Michael who had attended Sarah's birthday party. The same man had been Mildred's guest. If only he had made the connection last night, he could have questioned the man then and there.

Quickly, Bryan jumped out of bed and joined Sarah in the bathroom. Through the steam, he could see her soft skin glistening with water droplets. Bryan felt his manhood respond as he reached for her. All thoughts of Sherwood Michael flew from his mind. He pulled Sarah into his arms and kissed her cheeks, lips, and dripping breasts. Taking the soap from her hands, he lathered it over her shoulders, around her breasts, and down the gentle slope of her stomach. She gasped as he reached the site of her pleasure just beyond.

"Bryan, stop. We have work to do. We have to find Sherwood Michael before he gets away from us," Sarah protested half-heartedly, pushing away his exploring fingers. She could feel the heat building between her thighs as his hand made lazy tracks over her body and his fingers darted into her moist recesses.

"That can wait. He won't get far. Besides, we can always trace him through the newspaper or the SEC," he answered, his voice a husky whisper on her neck. He continued the slow journey down her thighs. With soapy hands, he grasped her buttocks and crushed her slippery body to him. A groan escaped his lips as her petal softness closed around his throbbing manhood.

Gently Sarah pried the soap from Bryan's fingers and began to soap his hot, slippery body. Her small hands made ever-widening circles along his shoulders, back, and stomach. He whispered her name in a voice that came from the depths of his being, as she soaped his thighs and flickered around his groin.

Swooping her up into his trembling arms, he carried her back to the bed, dripping water and soap along the way. Lying on the wet sheets, her body arched to meet his. Her hands reached up to pull him closer, to guide him into her softness. She gasped for breath again and again as his hands made the heat swell between her legs and her mouth grow dry from calling his name. With one great surge of energy, their thrusts reached a crescendo, causing a fire to blaze out of control within them, consuming them in its heat as it gave them release. They clawed at each other and held on for the ride. As they joined, the page with Sherwood Michael's photograph fluttered to the floor unseen.

Hours later, Bryan stopped the car in front of Tillings Tower. Planting a kiss on Sarah's nose, he said, "I'll see you back here by five o'clock. Call Jason and Holly. They need to be here too. I don't trust anyone else. I'll see what I can get from Mildred."

"Okay, we'll be waiting. Be careful."

"Scrounge up everything you can about Sherwood Michael while I'm gone. The reporter who wrote that story would be a good place to start. Don't worry about me. Besides, something tells me that you're more hazardous to my health than she is. I haven't eaten all day. Remember? I've been up against tougher cookies than Mildred Tillings," he said with a deep chuckle.

"Just the same, watch your back," Sarah called over her shoulder as she walked through the revolving doors and into the apricot marble foyer of Tillings Tower. She wondered how Bryan could think about their lovemaking session at a time like this.

Mildred Tillings sat perched majestically on the edge of the sofa in her little informal parlor. She had not expected company today but, as usual, she was dressed to the nines and dripping with jewels. She smiled and put away her novel as Bryan entered the room. The sight of his broad shoulders enclosed in the black suit filled the flowered room to overflowing.

"Thanks for seeing me on such short notice, Mildred," Bryan said, enclosing her extended hand in his. He accepted the offered seat in the overstuffed armchair, across the flower-heaped coffee table from her.

She watched as he filled her parlor and settled his long muscular legs. It was clear from the smile that played at the corners of her mouth that she found him a fine specimen of a man. Mildred had not seen him since the night of the gala, and so much had happened since then. She hoped he would not suffer too much in this latest scandal. After all, it was not Bryan she wanted to hurt and to destroy.

She had never been driven to a state of desperation by people who did not understand her need to love and be loved. Mildred was not a vengeful woman. They had brought out the worst in her by keeping her at arm's length, never opening up to her, and never making her one of their own. Sarah, especially, had been unkind to her, and had never accepted her as either a mother or a companion, and certainly not as a friend.

Sarah would pay.

Settling against the cushions, Mildred studied Bryan and tried to guess the purpose of their meeting today. Her face was perfectly composed, belying any uneasiness she felt. Could he have discovered her connection with the stock sale? She would wait calmly and see.

"Mildred," he began, "I'll come right to the point. I have reason to believe that you and Sherwood Michael are involved in the sale of Tillings Industries stocks." He paused to watch for a reaction. When Mildred's expression did not change, he continued. "What do you know about him? He's a stockbroker, isn't he? Did he encourage you to sell, or was it your idea?"

So he knew about Sherwood and about her involvement with the stock sale. Well, he would have found out sooner or later anyway. Mildred quickly assessed her losses and decided on a strategy. Crossing her long brown legs so that the slit in her skirt revealed just enough muscular thigh, she spoke calmly as she said, "Bryan, I never meant to hurt you in this mess. You're an innocent bystander. I wanted to get back at Sarah. I'm terribly sorry that you got caught in the crossfire."

At first, Bryan could not believe that her admission of guilt had come so fast. There had to be more than what Mildred spread before him. "Start from the beginning, Mildred. I'm not sure I understand," he said. "Why do you want to hurt Sarah? Why did you take out your anger on Tillings Industries? What could a corporation have done to you?"

Mildred felt herself under a magnifying glass and knew that she was ready for any scrutiny. She took a deep breath, thrust forward her ample bosom, and began her tale. Her voice quivered ever so slightly as she told of the insults and injuries at the hands of Sarah and the Tillings empire. "Well, you see," she began, dabbing at the corners of her well-made-up eyes, "when I first married Martin, I had all of the new wife's hopes of happiness and family. Sarah was a such a welcoming young woman at first. She was so warm toward me. She and Martin included me in everything. He discussed all of his decisions with me, all of his plans, everything.

"Yet, that wasn't enough. We never had any time for ourselves. We were always Tillings Industries, never just Martin and Mildred. We entertained constantly, and traveled on business, from one conference to the other, incessantly. We seldom spent time at home alone. Sarah and crowds of others were always with us. For a new wife, that was very difficult.

"I tried to tell him, but he only replied that his first wife, Grace, had loved being involved with the business. She had shared the running of Tillings with him. I couldn't convince him that I was different; I needed more. I needed him, not the company."

Mildred paused long enough in her story to allow a stray tear to run down her cheek. It left a track in her make-up before splashing softly on her hand. Through fluttering eyelashes, she gazed at Bryan. She tried to assess the effect of her words, but he sat expressionless in his chair.

Fingering her lace-edged handkerchief, she began again, "I had needs that were not being met. There were long, lonely nights when I went to bed alone. Martin had work to do. He stayed up late on business calls with clients from around the world. Sarah was always at the house, too. She would never leave us alone. She was always demanding more of his time. They were precious moments, that should have been mine. The company had fallen into difficulty, nothing too serious, but Martin needed to straighten it out himself, or so she said. Sarah nagged him until he gave up all his free time to work on making the company healthy again.

"I know this sounds selfish, but I had desires too. I needed the feel of his arms around me, the comfort of his body next to mine at night. He wasn't there for me.

"Finally, I told him that he had to make a choice. It was either me or Tillings Industries. Martin was a very private man. The thought of divorce and scandal horrified him. Besides, he loved me. He knew I was only demanding what was rightfully mine. I only asked that he give me his love."

Again, Mildred stopped to wipe a tear and adjust the deep V of her blouse. She watched Bryan from under her eyelashes as she shifted ever so slightly in her chair. She wanted her figure to show to perfection.

"Martin placed more responsibility on Sarah's shoulders, where it belonged. After all, she wasn't a child anymore, and she was single. He had worked hard all his life and deserved a rest. We traveled to New York, Los Angeles, Boston, Chicago, Philadelphia, Washington, Hawaii, and San Francisco. We were together all the time without a phone. Not even Sarah could reach us. No one could contact us. We were lovers every day and every night. It was heavenly! I couldn't have dreamed of more.

"I guess he felt guilty about not helping out more, because he started drinking heavily. Yet, I knew he loved the life we lived. He especially loved London and Paris. His face lit up as we walked down the Champs Elysées. We went shopping in all the stores: Gucci, Baccarat, Armani. He was like a kid at the Tower of London, running from one building to another. His first wife had been all business, and I was all fun. We were so carefree, so much in love. Finally, he belonged to me. I no longer had to share Martin with Sarah and Tillings Industries.

"But Sarah did not like that. She hounded him by telegram to come home. She faxed newspaper articles to him. When that did not work, she came to us. She followed us everywhere until Martin finally agreed to return home. Our tranquillity was broken."

Mildred paused in her story to dab the tears that welled in her big, brown eyes. She peeked over her handkerchief to assess Bryan's reaction. When she saw that he sat stone-faced, she allowed the tears to flow down her cheeks. Her shoulders shook as she sobbed into the arm of the sofa.

Bryan did not know what to do. Should he let her cry or

comfort her? He hated to see a woman in pain, yet he needed the information that was flowing so freely from her. If he held her, would she stop spilling the information he needed so desperately?

He could stand the sound of her sobs no longer. Moving to the sofa, Bryan took Mildred into his arms. She melted against his broad chest as she sobbed forth even more pain and anguish. Stroking her back, he muttered soothing words that slowly began to quiet her.

Mildred looked up into Bryan's face. Her heart leapt when she saw the look of concern written there. He was falling into line nicely, she thought. She wanted him to feel for her . . . to want to comfort her . . . to believe in her innocence. Maybe then he would join forces with her against that conniving witch of a stepdaughter. With an ally of his wealth and position, she could squash Sarah.

"Oh, Bryan," she muttered, "I've been so lonely since Martin's death. All of Dallas hates me and blames me for the downfall of Tillings Industries. Some mean-spirited people even think I drove Martin to an early grave. I've been so miserable. There were days when I didn't think I would make it."

With that, Mildred threw herself into Bryan's arms and wrapped herself around his neck. Then she did something totally unexpected. Mildred pulled his head down to her and kissed him. She pressed her lips against his until Bryan thought they would fuse together. She ran her left hand over his back and shoulders. She trailed her fingers delicately down his arm and stopped at his thigh. Then she allowed them to dart upward toward his groin. Reaching their destination, her red-tipped fingers made tantalizing circles on the black silk.

This was not the first time a woman had thrown herself at Bryan, but it never failed to catch him off guard. He was used to being the aggressor. With Mildred, he wondered about her motive. Sarah had warned him that she was dangerous, but she had not said how completely the venom poured from Mildred. Mildred was poison from the tip of her coifed head to her pedicured toes.

Sensing someone standing in the door, Bryan glanced over Mildred's head and into Sarah's stony face. Her yellow eyes glared with the anger of a caged lion. Her hands clenched into furious fists. She held her thin shoulders straight and set and her usually luscious lips in a line of determined rage.

Sarah never came to Mildred's house, but today she had arrived to lend him support and to explain that she had found Sherwood Michael's address. Instead of delivering good news, she found Bryan locked in a passionate embrace.

Liberating himself from Mildred's probing tongue and grasping fingers, Bryan called out, "Sarah, let me explain." His words were answered by the clicking of her high-heeled shoes as she hastily retreated along the oak floors to the front door. Before he could reach the door, Sarah had jumped into her car and sped away.

"Don't fret over her, Bryan," Mildred cooed, massaging the back of his neck with her hot fingers. "She's of no importance to people like us. I remember hearing Martin tell stories of your exploits, both with women and finances. Sarah's not enough woman for you, and she certainly can't be of any financial help. She's weak. She couldn't even hold on to Tillings Industries without your help. I can introduce you to all the right people. I know how to make a man happy."

"The way you made Martin happy, I guess," Bryan replied, his voice tinged with sarcasm.

"Yes, Martin was very happy with me," Mildred continued as if in a daze. She did not notice the sarcasm in his voice. The angry words poured from her like champagne from a freshly uncorked bottle. "We did everything together at first. We would have stayed together forever if it hadn't been for that daughter, that Sarah. I told you she spoiled everything for us with her whining and nagging. She took him away from me. But I've gotten even, now. I've taken Tillings Industries from her. It took me five years of patient waiting for the right moment, for the right situation to present itself. Finally my chance came."

The expression on Mildred's face frightened Bryan. He had seen it during his tour of duty in Vietnam on the faces of soldiers in combat. He had see it in board rooms, a combat of a different kind. He had never seen a woman's eyes gleam with such joy at the thought of hurting someone who had never wronged her. He watched silently as Mildred paced the room. Her body was charged with raw, unbridled energy. At that moment, he realized that he had underestimated her, seeing only that she was beautiful. Sarah had been right. Mildred Tillings was dangerous.

"You almost spoiled it for me, you know," she continued. "Yes: I was all set to strike when you took over the company. I was ready to pay her back when you came on the scene. I had hoped you'd push her out, take over totally. Instead, you gave her time to regroup. The press conference introducing that new perfume made me see that drastic measures were my only hope. Sarah had pulled off a major feat. She had saved Tillings Industries. She had made herself a star. She didn't need you or your money any longer. Her plans, made long before you arrived, had come to fruition.

"So I did it. I called Sherwood Michael and arranged the sale of the shares of Tillings that I owned independently of her. I timed my move for the close of business on her birthday. My plan was perfectly legal. Any stockholder can sell her interests at any time. There's nothing anyone could have done to stop the panic I've caused. She took Martin from me, but I've had the last laugh. Happy birthday, dear Sarah, happy birthday to you," she sang. The frost in her voice made Bryan's blood run cold.

Mildred returned to her spot on the sofa and sipped daintily at her champagne. She twisted her diamond-encrusted wedding band around and around her finger. On her face, a smile of total contentment played at the corners of her crimson lips.

Bryan felt a chill run up his spine as he watched Mildred's display of cold hatred for Sarah. She had risked her own financial security to ruin Martin Tillings's daughter. Sadly, he realized that there was nothing he could do. Mildred had been very cunning. She had not broken any laws. She had not even indulged in insider trading. The sale of the stock was perfectly legal. He felt helpless.

Mildred watched Bryan's discomfort over the rim of her glass. He was a handsome man even when his brows were knit in concentration. She could almost hear the wheels turning under his smooth brown skin. Breaking the stillness, she said, "We would make a good couple, Bryan. Your brains, money, and drive, teamed with my flair. I'd introduce you to everyone in the know in Dallas and the world. We'd travel and live. You could leave every concern behind, now that Tillings is finished. Come Monday morning, there won't be anything left to keep you here. Martin always said you were a smart man. Cut your losses while you can. Sell your shares of Tillings Industries early, before the stock crashes. We can book a flight out first thing. The Côte d'Azur is fabulous this time of year."

Bryan watched as she licked her lips. Mildred savored the sweet taste of her anticipated victory. He wondered how she would like the bitter gall of defeat he and Sarah would soon generously ladle out.

Sarah! In his fascination with this conniving woman, Bryan had all but forgotten the expression on Sarah's face when she found Mildred in his arms. Now he again saw the pain in her eyes and the quiver of her chin. He could see the strength in her brave shoulders as she walked with dignity from the room. That Sarah was so different from the woman whose every curve and pleasure spot he had memorized last night and again this morning. He remembered the feel of her body against his during their long night of lovemaking and again this morning as the coffee cooled and the eggs hardened. He had all he needed from Mildred. It was time to run to Sarah's side.

Nothing to keep him here? Mildred did not realize that it was never the company, never Tillings Industries, that had brought him to Dallas. It had always been Sarah and his love for her. He had nurtured that love from a distance until the time was right. He had waited until she needed him financially. He had watched and waited until she wanted him emotionally, even though he had a reputation for being a confirmed bachelor and a ladies' man. He had maintained his resolve to take it slowly with Sarah when what he really wanted to do was force her to love him. All this Mildred had underestimated. She could never replace Sarah in his heart or his arms. No matter how well toned she was and how flattering to his ego it was for her to throw herself into his arms, she was not his Sarah.

There was much to keep him in Dallas, but he would never tell Mildred. She would find out soon enough. For now, he would play along, let her think he was interested in her. She must never tip off Sherwood Michael that Byran was on to him.

"I need some time, Mildred. I can't just run off into the sunset. Tillings Industries isn't my only holding, you know. There are arrangements to be made and people to appoint as executors while I'm away. Give me a few days to get my affairs in order," Bryan answered, watching her expression. To his surprise, Mildred, crafty as she was, did not realize that he was playing a game.

"I'll be waiting, Bryan," she purred, looking at him with warm anticipation. "There are a few things I need to do, too. I'll make all the reservations. Maybe we'll go to Paris. I'll show you all the sights and then some. We'll have a wonderful time, you'll see. Soon we'll both forget all about Tillings Industries and Sarah."

"I'll leave all the plans in your capable hands. I'm sure you know how to make a man forget," he said planting a chaste kiss on Mildred's forehead as he left the cloying sweetness of her parlor. Outside, he took deep breaths of the warm Dallas air. He tried to rid himself of her smell. He had much to do in the next few days. His head had to be completely clear. He had to reverse the effects of Mildred's stock sale.

Chapter Thirteen

The elevator ride to the penthouse offices of Tillings Industries seemed longer and lonelier than usual. The silence of a Saturday evening was deafening. Bryan forced himself to walk to his office instead of to Sarah's. He longed to go to her and take her in his arms. He needed to assure her that Mildred had thrown herself on him without any encouragement. He ached to hold her and make everything right between them. He hated the thought of causing Sarah any further pain. Yet he could not take the chance that someone within Tillings Industries was a spy and would report back to Mildred. Even in the best of firms, there were leaks. She had to think that Sarah was miserable. She had to believe that any relationship between them was through—at least until he could finalize his plans.

Taking his seat behind the imposing mahogany desk, Bryan reached for the phone. Dialing a number known only to himself, he knew the risk he was taking. He had planned drastic measures for a catastrophic problem. It was a chance he would have to take to save Tillings Industries and Sarah from Mildred once and for all. He had to do this even if it meant losing her and his fortune.

Down the hall, Sarah sat in her darkened office. The drapes were drawn to block out the late afternoon Dallas sunshine. She slumped in her chair, listening to the silence that filled the office. She knew that she should meet with her banker, Jason Parson, and John Fraser, the Senior Vice President for Finance, who waited for her in the board room. They needed to rally all possible sources of revenue to fight against any further sale of stock on Monday.

Yet, she could not bring herself to move from where she sat, idly twirling a pencil between her fingers. The irony of the moment was not wasted on Sarah as she watched the black Montblanc slide around her hand. It had been her father's. She had seen him think with this pencil in his hand many times. She had watched him plan new products, sales strategies, corporate moves while juggling this instrument. Now, she sat twirling it and thinking nothing. Her mind was too cluttered with random unrelated thoughts to focus on any one thing for long. Saving Tillings stock from any further sales should have been foremost in her thoughts, but she could not think of the company without thinking of Bryan. She could not think of him without thinking of Mildred.

Mildred . . . she had poisoned her father and destroyed him. She had stolen him away from his company and his daughter. She had made him forget his responsibility to the company and to her. Now, she had set her sights on Bryan. She had warned him that Mildred was dangerous, yet he had not listened. He had been lured into her trap.

Bryan . . . he had saved Tillings for her, or so he said. She had believed him, loved him, made love to him, and given herself to him. Her every instinct said she should distrust him. Yet she had gone into his arms willingly, freely, and found comfort there. She had loved only two men in her lifetime . . .

her father and Bryan Carson. Both had betrayed her with the same woman. Both had left her alone to fend for herself.

Sarah buried her face in her hands and wept. She thought her heart would burst. She felt lonely and foolish at the same time. How could she have trusted him, believed in him? How could she have let her guard down?

She did not hear the door open or see Frank enter. Holly had sent him with a message. He stood watching her from the center of the darkened room. Poor Sarah, he thought. She has been through so much. She had endured first her mother's death, then her father's; and then the near financial ruin of Tillings Industries. This betrayal by a stockholder and the latest setback for the company and finding Bryan in Mildred's arms threatened to crush her.

Frank had never thought highly of Martin's second wife. She was too self-centered and too self-absorbed to notice the needs of others. She had driven Martin to an early grave and robbed him of the greatest love of his life, Tillings Industries. Martin had shown his weakness, and she had taken advantage of it. She had used his loneliness when his wife Grace died as a way to wheedle her way into his heart. Then, when she had him, she had used him, instead of helping him. She had all but taken him away from Tillings Industries and Sarah. She had caused him to neglect the company until there was almost nothing left. Now, she wanted Bryan, too. From the look of dejection sitting on Sarah's shoulders, she had succeeded.

Gently, Frank took Sarah into his arms. Holly had told him all about Bryan's betrayal. He hated himself for not being able to save Tillings Industries for her. He had money, quite a nice fortune actually, but not enough to bail out the suffering cosmetics giant.

Sarah's streaming gold eyes looked into his and almost melted Frank's heart. He had loved Sarah when they were younger. He had been heartbroken when she never seemed to notice him as anyone other than a friend. He had long ago learned to accept their relationship for what it was and not to ask for more. He had dated and married other women, not to make Sarah jealous, but to make a life for himself. Still, the sparkle of her eyes and the twinkle of her laughter never left his heart. No woman could match Sarah Tillings. It was not fair to expect anyone to replace her. His marriages had failed because he could not accept his wives for themselves and for the love they could give him; he had wanted Sarah. Only when she told him that they would forever be best friends and nothing more did he finally give up hope of having her.

When she set him free, he finally saw Holly, standing quietly in her friend's shadow. Holly was so much like Sarah. Both were determined women, both had suffered the loss of their parents, and both had known financial setbacks. Holly was tall, thin, and beautiful, just like Sarah. Maybe her hazel eyes did not sparkle as brightly, and perhaps her laughter lacked the bell-like quality of Sarah's, but she needed him. Frank, for the first time in his life, was happy. They planned to announce their engagement as soon as things settled down at Tillings.

Stroking Sarah's hair and cradling her in his arms, Frank thought of all the times he had wanted to hold her, not as friends, but as lovers. Now, his love for her was different; he wanted to protect Sarah, not possess her. He still found her to be one of the most attractive women he had ever known, and certainly one of the most desirable. But true friendship had replaced longing.

Gazing over the top of Sarah's head, Frank looked at the portrait of Martin Tillings hanging on the far wall. It had been painted before Mildred entered his life, while happiness and determination still shone in his eyes. A similar portrait of Sarah hung to the right. Her eyes showed the same fire and sparkle. She was definitely Martin Tillings's daughter. The same determination curved her lips and the same easy manner illuminated her face.

"Frank, what am I to do?" Sarah asked, easing out of his

arms. She blew her nose noisily before continuing. "Tillings is in trouble, under attack just when everything was going so well. I think Mildred is involved somehow. And to top it all off, I found Bryan in her arms. Just when I thought I could trust him. Oh, Frank, the sad thing is that I've fallen in love with him. I tried not to . . . I was determined not even to like him. But I couldn't help myself. Now what can I do?"

Even with her eyes red from crying, Sarah Tillings was strikingly beautiful. Frank could not help smiling as he wiped her tear-stained face. "Don't worry, little one. Everything will work out. I have good feelings about Bryan. You know I did not want to like him when he first came here. I resented his ability to help Tillings when I couldn't do it myself. But I've learned to trust him. I know you found him with Mildred, but I don't believe he'd betray you with her. Everything he has done so far says he loves you. Still, you have more than enough to do right now without worrying about him. Tillings is in trouble. You know that the company means more to you than anyone . . . even more than Bryan. You're Martin Tillings's daughter, remember. Go wash your face. You have work to do. Holly says you're late for a meeting with John and Jason."

Sarah looked into Frank's calm, understanding face. He had always been there for her, even when she rejected him as a lover. She had always known she could count on him. She consoled herself with the thought that good friends were harder to find than lovers, anyway. She was lucky, despite Mildred's efforts, that she had good friends like Holly and Frank. She was happy that they had found each other.

Just then Bryan broke into the room, shattering the moment. "Sarah, I have to . . ." he began. Seeing her in Frank's arms, he stopped in his tracks.

"Hello, Bryan," Frank said. "Sarah was just . . ."

"Don't try to explain, Frank, I'm not blind. I should have suspected that your relationship with Sarah was more than just friendship months ago when you escorted her to the gala. Like a fool, I believed that everything was over between you two. I thought that Tillings was my only competition. Now I see I was wrong,'' he said as the pain of betrayal tore at his heart.

''Bryan,'' Sarah whispered, ''It's not the way it looks at all. Frank was just trying to comfort me. I was upset about you and Mildred and Tillings. He's one of my best friends and Holly's boyfriend. You know I'd never do anything to hurt her. Please listen.''

''Maybe not, but you wouldn't hesitate to accuse me,'' Bryan retorted bitterly, giving Sarah a look that froze her heart. ''I'll give you the same chance you gave me this morning when you stormed out of Mildred's house. My situation was quite innocent compared to this.''

''You've got it all wrong, man,'' Frank called to him as Bryan turned quickly and left the office.

Sarah stood frozen with Frank's arm around her shoulders. She could not believe what had just happened. Bryan had twisted everything to make her seem guilty instead of him . . . or had he? Maybe he was innocent; but, then again, he could be trying to cover up his relationship with Mildred by pretending to be angry. Sarah was even more confused now.

''Now what should I do?'' she asked, hoping that Frank would have the solution.

''Leave Bryan to me. You have a meeting. Remember?'' he said, giving her a shove toward the bathroom.

''You're right, Frank. Tell Holly that I'll meet the gentlemen in thirty minutes, please. Let's the three of us grab a quick dinner right after the meeting. Suddenly, I'm starved. I haven't eaten since . . . a long time,'' she smiled at him. She would not allow herself to think about the cold coffee and eggs that went untouched that morning.

''It's a date,'' he answered. By the time he reached the door, Sarah had opened the drapes. Dallas sunshine flooded the office and held her in its rays. He smiled as he watched her straighten her shoulders beneath the gold silk suit that matched her eyes to perfection. Sarah Tillings was back!

"Gentlemen," Sarah said, striding confidently into the board room exactly thirty minutes later. She took her place at the head of the long mahogany table and spread out the printouts of investors Holly had prepared for her. "I hope I did not keep you too long. Please be seated. I appreciate your devotion to Tillings Industries on a beautiful Saturday. There is much to be done. In the last few hours, I have personally contacted the major stockholders. I have assured them of Tillings's financial security. Each has faxed to me a written vote of confidence. They have promised to give us until the end of next week to sort out this latest attack on Tillings. They have promised not to sell any of their holdings on Monday. However, we are not out of the woods yet. Considerable numbers of shares are owned by smaller investors. Their flight could still drive the price per share to an all-time low. We must work quickly to forestall any unfortunate reactions.

"Also, we have learned the identity of the person who made the sales transaction on Friday at the close of business, and identified the disgruntled stockholder. If we can publicly respond to this person's concerns and eliminate any further rumors of instability, we should be out of the woods. Unfortunately, I am not at liberty to divulge the shareholder's identity to you at the present. As soon as I can, I'll let you know."

Sarah's eyes sparkled golden with the confidence she felt. Only an hour ago she had thought that everything was hopeless, that all was lost. Now she was in control of herself and her company. Frank was right. She was Martin Tillings's daughter. Her father had been felled by a beautiful, conniving woman, much like Samson had fallen to Delilah. She was not going to fall or to surrender. Not even to Bryan Carson.

Yes, she loved him passionately, with her whole heart and

every fiber of her being, but Sarah loved herself even more. She loved the feel of his hands on her body and his lips on hers. She relished their coming together as he lowered himself over her and took her in his arms. But she knew that she could not love him so much if she did not love herself more. She had to be whole to give herself to someone else. She had watched her father crumble and fail his company and her because of his love for a woman. He forgot to love himself and to take care of himself first. She would never forget again.

Sarah continued, "In the meantime, let us assume a worst case scenario. How are we fixed for capital? Is there a reserve on hand? Is it sufficient to carry us through if sales bottom out in reaction to the stock transaction? What is our borrowing power? Which of our friends would be willing to advance us a loan to cover expenses, if necessary?"

John Fraser spoke first. "There are a few resources that I have not touched as yet. You might have to give up some control of your personal stocks to get their help. Maybe even sell some of your holdings to them. Still, I am sure—considering the immediate success of the new fragrance—that we can float some short-term personal loans from our friends."

She nodded in agreement and looked at Jason Parson. He had been involved with Tillings Industries since her father had first come to him for a loan to build Tillings Tower. Jason had introduced Martin to the country-club set and helped him move into the Dallas professional elite. More than that, Jason was a good friend, almost a father to her now that her father had died. Still, he was the president of the largest commercial bank in Dallas and had to protect his investors' interests.

"Sarah," Jason Parson began clearing his throat. She could see the pain his words caused him as he said, "I will be painfully honest with you. The board of the bank would probably be more inclined toward advancing funds to Tillings Industries if you could show a good-faith effort to secure a buyer for the majority of the stocks sold on Friday. Not all of them, mind you, but a sizable portion of them. That was a major sale, Sarah, and it set Wall Street on its ear. Who knows what Monday will bring, even with the promises you have from investors and customers. As you've stated, a retreat of smaller stockholders would be just as damaging to Tillings's financial future as the loss of confidence by major holders. The bank would be willing to advance you operating capital as needed, once the majority of those stocks were covered. I am sorry, Sarah, that I cannot be more promising than that."

Sarah saw the pain on Jason Parson's face, and knew that he was right. "Well, gentlemen, it looks as if I have my work cut out for me. The first thing to do is find a buyer or several buyers for most of the lots sold on Friday," she responded.

"How does Bryan stand on all of this, Sarah?" John queried. "I hate to ask, but you know news travels fast in the financial market and even faster in Dallas. There's some talk that he and Mildred are an item. Everyone knows how she feels about Tillings Industries. That could mean that he sides with her. She never hesitated to say that she wanted to divest herself of any interest in Tillings stock."

"Bryan stands firmly behind Tillings Industries and supports my decisions totally. He has as much to lose as we do in this mess. He wants to find the person who made that sale and expose the motives behind the act as much as I do. He has hired investigators to search through information on all major stockholders. He has some leads and is pursuing them at this moment," she tried to sound convincing and was surprised when even she believed it.

"And Mildred?" Jason asked. He knew the long history of ill will between them. He also knew that she was a major stockholder in her own right.

Sarah considered her response carefully then said, "She knows only as much as is necessary for any stockholder to know at this time. She has received a personal letter from me, as have all the major stockholders, detailing the steps being taken in the effort to halt any further sales of Tillings Industries stock. The same letter, as you know, appeared in the business section of all major newspapers today. It will run again tomorrow and on Monday as well. Aside from that, knowing that Mildred has never been concerned with the day-to-day management of the company, I did not feel it necessary to share anything more with her.''

The men looked satisfied that all bases had been covered. Rising, they bid Sarah good afternoon and returned to their plans for what was left of this beautiful sunny day. Each knew that the success or failure of Tillings Industries rested squarely on the shoulders of this brave young woman. Only Sarah could convince stockholders that Tillings was safe.

Sarah gathered up her papers. She was exhausted but there was no time to rest. She had put at least five stockholders on her list who might be interested in purchasing more shares. She had to contact them before trading began on Monday. She had to forestall any further large sales.

As she left the board room for her office at the other end of the hall, Sarah noticed that the door to Bryan's assistant's office was open. Beyond it lay his office. She knew that he was probably alone. She needed to talk with him about Tillings Industries and about Mildred, yet she was not sure that she could handle either discussion without dissolving into tears. She was not ready yet to work with him as only a business partner and not see him as the man she loved. The sight of Bryan in Mildred's arms was still too fresh. It hurt too much. His arms were for her only. She should be the only woman to feel the bulge of his muscles as he pulled her closer, and smell the spice of his cologne as his lips crushed hers. Mildred had no right invading her territory.

Advancing toward his office suite, she heard Bryan's voice booming in the stillness as he shouted into the telephone. ''I don't care how much it costs me. Sell. I have some business here that needs my immediate attention. Sell all my shares first thing Monday morning. You heard right, all of them. I don't want any more mistakes. Call me as soon as you complete the transaction. I know I can count on you, Michael.''

Her heart stopped . . . Michael. Sherwood Michael was the name of the stockbroker who put through the sale transaction for the Tillings Industries stock yesterday. He was the same man who had escorted Mildred to her party. She could not believe it. Bryan was on the phone with the very man who had helped orchestrate this disaster. Bryan was involved in the sale of Tillings stock!

Sarah stumbled down the long hall to her office suite. She closed her door and fell onto the glove-leather sofa. Bryan Carson had saved Tillings for what? To do this, to ruin it totally. Why? What would he gain by destroying Tillings? His money was tied up in the company's welfare, too. Had Bryan and Mildred planned this together? That would certainly explain what she had seen earlier today in Mildred's parlor. They had probably staged that show, too. They had planned for her to see them, a final coup de grâce.

She had felt that her heart would break and that her world would end when she had seen Bryan holding Mildred in his arms. But now, hearing him planning to sell his shares of Tillings Industries stock, she was livid with rage. What kind of demon was he?

Thinking back over all his actions, Sarah's confusion increased. What kind of man would profess love to a woman and for her company and then team up with someone else to destroy it? What kind of person destroyed what he had helped to save only a few months earlier? Bryan was not exactly a shrinking violet. He had escorted another woman to her birthday party, returned and made love to her when it was over, and then played loose and free with her stepmother. Now he was planning to sell his holdings in her company. To top it off, he had been arrogant and uncaring enough to leave his door open while plotting against her.

The man's conceit and arrogance were maddening. Everything he had ever told her must have been either a lie or, at least, part of a larger plan to win her confidence and then betray it. He said he had surrounded himself with beautiful women to detract people from finding out his devotion to her. Bull! He was never emotionally interested in her. He only wanted her confidence and her company. But what did he have to gain?

Sarah thought back on what she knew about him. From her agitated mind, she extracted the fact that Bryan Carson was a buyer and seller of struggling companies. He bought them at a low price when they needed his money for financial security. Sometimes he broke them into pieces and sold off each division individually. Other times he raised them from the ashes with an infusion of cash. After their stock prices soared, he sold them in one piece to other less adventurous investors. All the facts about him were there in the background material Holly had dug up on him. She never realized until this minute that Bryan must have had the same plan in mind for Tillings. Buy low, restore, sell high. Or maybe even break up and sell in little bits and chunks.

Questions flew around in Sarah's mind. Why had he teamed up with Mildred? Were they partners long before he came to Dallas? Was he part of Mildred's plan to get revenge on Sarah? How did Sherwood Michael fit into the plan? Did Bryan only pretend to be angry when he found her with Frank?

Suddenly, Sarah had answers to most of her questions. She remembered hearing Bryan shout over the phone. "No more mistakes!" They had planned to sell all of their combined shares of stock at one time. Sherwood Michael must have become confused and sold some of Mildred's, but none of Bryan's.

Sarah wondered how long Mildred and Bryan had been working together. Were they already a team when Mildred married her father? Had they planned to ruin him, take over the company, push Sarah out of the picture, and sell off Tillings?

She leaned back against the sofa and stared at her father's portrait. Had he found out about Mildred before he died? Is that really what had killed him? Did Martin know that he was being used by that conniving gold digger? Well, at least Sarah had found out before it was too late. What was next in Bryan's plan if selling the stocks and causing a panic failed to crush her? Did he mean to marry her and control and sell her shares in Tillings Industries, too?

"Not in a million years!" Sarah heard herself say aloud. "Bryan Carson will never take Tillings away from me. I'll find a way to stop him."

Hearing voices in the outer office, Sarah pushed the button that connected her to Holly. Hearing Holly's tired voice, she said, "Holly, you and Frank should go to dinner without me. I have some calls to make. I'd appreciate it if you'd bring me back a chicken salad. Okay?"

"Sure, Sarah, but I hate to leave you. Anything I can do to help? Frank can pick up salads for both of us."

"No, thanks. I have to do this myself, but thanks for asking. I don't know what I'd do without good friends like you and Frank."

"You were there for me. Remember?" Silence fell over the room as Holly clicked off the intercom. Sarah needed time to think, to compose her thoughts, to plan her retaliation against Mildred and Bryan, and to develop a sales pitch designed to win investor confidence. With Holly and Frank out of the office, she could work without interruption.

She studied the list of potential investors. Everyone in town had seen the television coverage, read the business section of the paper, or heard about it by now. A direct approach was the only option. She would tell them what they needed to know and ask for their help. She would leave out her suspicions about Mildred and Bryan until she had proof. Then she would expose them as traitors to Tillings Industries.

Sarah hated Mildred and Bryan for putting her in this position. The idea of begging investors to have confidence in her ability to manage Tillings Industries was offensive to her. Tillings was a good company with a bright future because of her hard work. "Sarah," her flagship fragrance, was a success. If it had not been for their treachery, she would not have to convince people that Tillings was sound.

Martin Tillings's portrait looked down on her as Sarah reached for the telephone. From where she sat, the usual smiling eyes looked sad as she dialed the first digit. Her hands began to shake as a feeling of desperation for what she was about to do washed over her. She was throwing out a life line and hoping that someone out there would pick it up. She shuddered at the thought that if one of these five investors did not help her, Tillings Industries was lost. The grandfather clock, which stood in the corner, sounded eight o'clock in its deep sonorous tones. To Sarah, it was almost like hearing a death knell for Tillings.

Chapter Fourteen

Just as Sarah was about to dial the last digit, her office door swung open. Not waiting for her to speak, Bryan strode confidently into the room. He wore a freshly pressed suit and looked as if he had just had a shave. He exuded confidence as he perched on the edge of her desk. The gold cufflinks sparkled in the light from the desk lamp. He certainly did not look worried about the future of Tillings Industries. No wonder, Sarah thought; he was planning to sell out. He had nothing to lose, and he looked the part.

Against her will, Sarah had to admit that he was certainly a handsome man, with that curl lightly brushing his forehead. She remembered pushing it away this morning after they made love. Involuntarily, she took a deep breath and inhaled. The smell of his cologne made her head feel light. He was the one she turned to for advice. Now that she needed him the most to help save Tillings Industries, he was not there for her. He was part of the problem.

Damn the man! He was too real, too alive. She wanted him

too much. She hated him for betraying her with Mildred, o
all women. Yet, she needed to feel his arms around her s
desperately that she was almost willing to forget everythin
and give herself to him. If only Tillings Industries were not a
stake, she would allow him to take her into his arms. Bu
Tillings came first, and he had threatened the thing she hel
most dear. The memory of her father and mother was in ever
stone of the building. She could not forgive Bryan for betrayin
Tillings and their memory.

"Put down the phone, Sarah. I want to talk with you," h
ordered calmly, without any sign of remorse for his actions.

"I don't have time right now, Bryan. I have calls to mak
and investors to woo. I have to find someone to buy the share
sold yesterday. I think you and Mildred have taken enough o
my time already," she responded without looking up. Her lip
were a hard, tight line of determination. She knew she woul
be tempted to forgive and forget if she looked into his dee
gray eyes. She did not want to remember the way they undresse
her and made her feel warm and special.

"I said for you to put down the phone, Sarah. We hav
things to talk about that can't wait. You have to hear me ou
now, before the confusion and deception go on any longer,'
he replied, gently taking the phone from her fingers. His voic
was even more deliberate and controlled than hers. She ha
never heard that tone directed at her. This was a new Bryar
Carson. Maybe she would finally meet the real man. Mayb
now he would stop hiding behind the glamorous facade, the
women, the photographs on the society pages, and the Arman
suits.

Sarah was an expert at hiding, and recognized the sam
ability in other people. She had skillfully kept her true feeling
about Bryan secret from everyone, even herself. She had beer
afraid to let them show. She had to remain in control at al
cost. Too much was at stake. She could not take the chance o
following in her father's footsteps into a tragic relationship.

She knew that Bryan was hiding something, too. His poise was too complete, too unshakable. Only once had she seen him rattled or worried. He played a high-stakes poker game every time he acquired or sold a company. In his personal life, he was equally well guarded in his actions. The only time she had seen him totally relaxed was this morning when they made love. But that was only one side of this complicated, secretive man. She needed to know more if she were to forget seeing him with Mildred in his arms and ignore the conversation she had overheard with the stockbroker.

"I can't imagine what you have to say to me, Bryan. I saw plenty this afternoon at Mildred's. You certainly don't owe me any explanations for your actions. We're adults. From your reputation, I shouldn't have expected anything more from you than this. Devotion and loyalty to one woman don't seem to be your strengths. Your usual operating procedure is to date an assortment of women at one time. One night stands are probably part of your charm to many. They probably call you love 'em and leave 'em Bryan. I don't hold it against you. I just should have seen it coming, that's all."

Moving from the edge of the desk, he pulled a white envelope from his breast pocket and placed it in the center of her desk. Standing beside her, Bryan said, "You've got it all wrong, Sarah. For all these years I've been nothing but faithful to you. I dated many women but never loved any of them. I never married; I couldn't even pretend to be faithful to anyone else. They were beautiful and tempting, but not one of them was you. I told you, Sarah: from the time you were a teenager, I knew that you were the only woman in the world for me."

"And Mildred? How does she fit in?" Sarah asked scornfully. She reminded herself that she had to be very careful around this man. Her head said to stand her ground and to refuse to accept his story, but her heart called out to him to take her in his arms. She needed him to make her forget everything except their coming together and their love. She needed to be able to trust him again.

"She means nothing to me and never will. She told me her version of life with your father then she threw herself at me. I never would have taken her into my arms at any time and certainly not after last night and this morning. No other woman would fit the way you do, or feel the way you do when you press against me, or smell the way you do when you've just awakened from sleep. I don't want anyone else, Sarah. There can't be anyone else."

Damn the man! he looked so believable and Sarah wanted so much to trust him. She sat looking into his deep brown eyes. For the first time, she noticed the lines that fluttered at the corners. He looked tired and a little worn down, as if the weight of Tillings Industries and of her resistance to his affection had finally used up his strength. Deep crags outlined his mouth, too. Bryan's shoulders in the beautifully tailored suit were not as straight as usual either. She saw that trouble weighed heavily on them and they slumped under the weight. She wanted to put her arms around him and kiss away the crags and the lines and lift the baggage from his shoulders that made him look older than his forty-five years. Yet she could not. Too many unanswered questions lay between them.

She could not afford to take the chance that Bryan was really not involved with Mildred. She dared not believe that he did not plan to destroy Tillings. He might be weaving an elaborate tale to throw her off guard just as their lovemaking had this morning. Sarah was torn between her love for him and her devotion to Tillings Industries. She floated helplessly in a sea of uncertainty.

Breaking the silence that filled the space between them, Bryan spoke in a voice edged with fatigue and strain. The look of confidence had left him. "Look, Sarah, we got off on the wrong foot from the very beginning. You saw me as the enemy when I took over Tillings Industries to save it from bankruptcy.

It's quite natural that you wouldn't trust me with your company. It's even logical that you wouldn't trust me personally. After all, I've dated other women since moving here to Dallas. I haven't exactly lived the life of a monk. I've told you that my interest in those other women was only to keep alive the careful facade I created over all these years. I can understand that you would have a hard time believing me, but it's all true.

"I wouldn't do anything to hurt either Tillings or you. I organized the take over to save the company for you, not to take it from you. It's your company. You proved that with the success of the new fragrance. Your touch is everywhere, just as much as your father's was when he ran Tillings Industries. I want to help you in any way I can, but never would I do anything behind your back. I may own controlling interest, but I would never sell a single share of Tillings with the intent of causing the company harm. You must believe me."

Bryan paused briefly to allow his words to sink in. To Sarah, the moments of silence stretched into painful stillness. Her heart pleaded with her to reach out to him and to tell him that she believed him. She wanted to kiss away the pain that filled his eyes and her heart. Yet, her mind argued that Bryan was a consummate ladies' man. This well-crafted speech could be one of his games, played out to perfection to confuse her and throw her off guard again. She had seen him with Mildred only hours after he had held her against his sweaty body, still smelling of their lovemaking. He had held Mildred in his arms only hours after swearing his love for her. She would force herself to listen and wait. She had to be right this time. Her heart could not take any more disappointment.

Bryan waited for some sign of forgiveness to sparkle in those cold, golden eyes of hers. Seeing nothing there for him, he walked to the fireplace and rested wearily against it. "As for Mildred," he continued softly, "I watched her turn your father into a man I didn't even know. When I first met Martin Tillings, he was a strong man who thrived on control and power. He was driven by dedication to his family and to Tillings. He loved both deeply. He was never the same after your mother's death, Sarah. He lost heart and focus. When he married Mildred, all of his old friends hoped that she would be able to give him back some of his old energy and his old vitality.

"At first, it looked as if she had. They went everywhere together, as you remember. They seemed very happy. Then things started to go sour. He spent money he did not have and moved funds from one account into the other to deceive the auditors. He dug himself deeper and deeper into debt and despair.

"When he died, he left the company's finances in even worse shape than you ever knew. Jason Parson and John Fraser took it into their own hands to clean things up as much as they could. They pumped their own money into Tillings without telling you. They didn't want you to know what a mess your father had made of things.

"They called me when even they couldn't keep Tillings afloat. They knew that I bought and sold companies. They thought that I might be interested in Tillings since it was a basically sound company. They were right.

"That was the opportunity I had been waiting for. I paid them back and moved all of my business dealings here to Dallas. I could be near you and pay respect to an old friend by saving his company all at the same time. Your father was a trailblazer in industry. I could not allow his name to be tarnished."

Again, Bryan paused. This time he did not wait for her to respond but walked toward the door. The cold, yellow emptiness of her eyes showed no warmth for him. Any more explanation was a waste of effort. Sarah had made it clear by the way she hugged her arms around her thin body that she wanted nothing more to do with him.

Placing his hand on the knob, he turned and added, "I talked with Sherwood Michael. He told me about Mildred's order to sell all of her stock. Being new in town, he did not know that she was connected with Tillings when he first took the sell order for her stock. Although the transaction was large, he had no idea she was planning to cause a panic. At the time, he was more curious than suspicious, so he placed her order as requested. After he found out that 'Sarah' was being announced on the same day and made the connection between Mildred, Tillings Industries, and you, he started worrying about possible insider trading conflicts. The last thing he wanted was the Securities and Exchange Commission on his back. By then he knew for sure what she was up to, but it was too late. He had already done her dirty work. He was one scared man when I talked with him late this afternoon.

"You don't have to worry about Tillings any longer. I've taken care of everything. Monday, she'll be all yours . . . lock, stock, and barrel . . . and I'll be out of your hair. You once said you tried to wash me out, remember? Well, this time you won't need the shampoo. The details are in that envelope. I don't blame you for not trusting me, but you must believe me when I say that I've never loved anyone except you. Good bye, Sarah."

Sarah watched as Bryan closed the door with a gentle whoosh. The sun had set and the lights of Dallas twinkled in the streets below Tillings Tower. She sat in the silence of her office without moving or even thinking . . . only feeling. So much had happened in twenty-four hours. She did not know how to sort it all out. Her birthday had come and gone. "Sarah" had been introduced to the world. Its success had promised to save Tillings, until someone betrayed them. She had given herself to Bryan, only to find him, the next day, in the arms of her stepmother. Mildred had betrayed her and Tillings Industries. Sarah did not know where to begin to unravel the confusion that tormented her mind and heart.

Rising slowly, she turned to the window and looked out. Down below people went to dinner, to parties, and to the movies. They played with their children, watched movies together, and ate late suppers in their cozy kitchens. Up here in Tillings Tower, Sarah was alone. Bryan's last words echoed in the stillness. The sight of his tired, hurt face played through her memory. There had been something painfully ominous in his last words, "I'll be out of your hair," and something final in his good bye that made her shudder in the warm evening. Now that he had left, she wanted him back.

The grandfather clock reminded her that it was nine o'clock. Holly and Frank would be returning from dinner soon. She still had not called the investors. She had so much work to do and so little heart or energy for it.

With a tired sigh, she turned from the window. The envelope on her desk glowed in the light from her desk lamp. Gingerly, Sarah picked it up and turned it over in the palm of her hand. She opened it and pulled out two sheets of paper. They felt light between her fingers. Her eyes scanned the few simple hand-written paragraphs on Bryan's letterhead stationery. Her lips moved silently as she read, "Dearest Sarah, I have tried my best to convince you that my intentions toward you and Tillings Industries have been honorable. Unfortunately, nothing I have done has worked out as I envisioned.

"Through all the years of planning our future, I dreamed of our running the company together, just as your father and mother did when Tillings Industries was young and healthy. It would seem that all of my efforts have been for nothing, since my past haunts me. I created an elaborate charade to hide my comings and goings from prying eyes that might wonder why I never settled down. I let the world think I was a confirmed bachelor and a ladies' man when all the time what I really wanted was to be as happy with you as your parents were together. This charade keeps you from me. There is nothing I can do to erase the picture I've painted from your memory. I now painfully realize that all is lost.

"Yet, you have not been totally blameless, my love. While

my goal was to spend the rest of my life with you, yours was to save Tillings at all cost. You put the company ahead of everyone who tried to come near you. It looks as if we will both have to live with our choices.

"Therefore, I am returning to Houston where I can live in peace and, perhaps, find some of that happiness alone that I have long dreamed of sharing with you. It will be a lonely life, but it is the only one left for me. Never once in all these years have I loved another woman, although I surrounded myself with many. Not once have I betrayed you, although you have seen me with Mildred. My thoughts have always been of you. My dreams have been filled with the joy of loving you.

"Although I am leaving Dallas, I want you to know that the hours we spent locked in each other's arms last night and this morning were the happiest I have ever experienced. For the first time since falling in love with you, I actually held you without Tillings, my charade, or fate coming between us. Unfortunately, those moments were all too fleeting. As I leave you, I know that you have Tillings. You love the company and your father's memory far more than you could ever love me. I will have to settle for my memories of those few wonderful hours. It will be enough for me to know that I came close to having all I ever wanted. Happiness lay at the ends of my fingertips, just beyond my grasp, but I could not get a firm grip on it.

"As for Mildred, before I leave Dallas I will pay one last call on her to make it clear that her involvement with me and Tillings Industries is over, finished as of the opening bell on Wall Street on Monday. She wanted to ruin Tillings and you, because of what she felt you and the company had done to her. I have stopped her from ever being able to harm you again. The enclosed copy of my letter to my stockbroker will explain everything. On the day 'Sarah' was announced, she asked me to go away with her. She must hear directly from me that the possibility of any relationship developing between us is impossible.

"I had planned to give Tillings to you as a wedding present, dear Sarah, but now I will leave it as a parting gift and as a sign of my undying love and devotion. Good bye, my dearest Sarah, and all happiness be yours. Forever, Bryan."

A cold numbness filled her heart as she perused the second sheet addressed to Bilking and Taylor of Dallas, Texas. It was addressed to Sherwood Michael and read: "On my authority, you are to sell as many shares of my stocks in Myrna Incorporated as is necessary for you to purchase all outstanding stock in Tillings Industries. Said stocks along with all of my holdings in Tillings Industries will be transferred to Sarah Tillings by the close of business on Monday. Bryan Carson."

Sarah could hardly believe her eyes as she reread his letters. Bryan had sold controlling interest in one of his most lucrative companies to buy all of the outstanding shares in Tillings Industries. He had stopped the panic Mildred had orchestrated. He had saved Tillings and given it all to her. She owned controlling interest in her father's company once again and this time no one could take it away from her.

Tillings was safe forever!

Yet in her happiness, a nagging voice called out Bryan's name. Yes, she owned all of Tillings—but at what price? Bryan was gone. Her adversary, friend, and supporter had left Dallas and her life forever. She would never again share promotional ideas with him. He would never sit opposite her in the board room again. She would never again hold him in her arms or push the lock of hair from his forehead. Her lips would never again feel the warmth of his kisses.

Sitting stunned in her chair, Sarah knew that she should be happy. She had worked hard these past five years to save Tillings, only to find the financial obstacles too great for any one person to overcome. She had unwillingly accepted Bryan's take-over of her company because she needed his money to give Tillings Industries a new start. Yet, she had always planned to show him that she did not need him. She had succeeded with "Sarah." The perfume had been targeted to meet the needs of every woman. It would fill the financial ledgers with enough black ink to erase forever the rivers of red she had inherited from her father. Already orders filled the marketing department. Sarah had restored the glory of Tillings by herself. And then Mildred, in all her anger and hatred, had started a panic designed to topple Tillings Industries for once and for all. Again, Bryan had saved her. This time, he had made Tillings hers in a way that no one could ever undo. Even her father had not been able to give Tillings to her.

Sarah rose from her chair and walked to stand in front of her father's portrait. Her knees were weak and her mind was numb. "Daddy," she whispered, "Tillings is safe. It's mine. Never again will an outsider hold the strings. Can you hear me, Daddy? Bryan saw to it that Tillings would be safe forever. He gave me your company. . . . But, Daddy, the strange thing is that I'm not as happy as I thought I would be. I just realized something about myself. Tillings isn't enough after all. I love Bryan . . . more than I love Tillings—and now he's gone!"

She buried her face in her hands and wept. The sobs racked her thin shoulders. This time there would be no strong arms to enfold her. There would be no passionate kisses to stop the stream of tears and wipe away their tracks. Bryan was gone and Sarah was alone.

Suddenly, something in his letter jerked her from her misery. He was going to Mildred's one last time. If she hurried, Sarah could catch him there. She would tell him how much she loved him and needed him. She would make him understand that Tillings Industries would never be enough for her now that she had known his love. A company could never compare to the warmth and fire of a man like Bryan. Tillings could never make her toes curl with desire as he did. Tillings could never caress her and make her reserve fall away. Tillings could never make her cry out in desire and beg for more. Bryan did all that and more.

Sarah threw open her office door and darted toward the hall. She ran past Holly and Frank, who were returning from dinner. Her eyes blazed with determination. Her heels beat a hasty tattoo on the polished pine floor.

"Hey, wait! I have your salad. Where are you going in such a hurry?" Holly called after her.

"I'm not hungry . . . for salad. Read the letter on my desk. It will explain everything," Sarah shouted through the closing elevator door.

Holly and Frank looked at each other in stunned disbelief. Sarah did not see them as she bolted into the elevator and pressed the button. As the high-speed express elevator reached the lobby floor, Sarah began the run of her life. Somewhere out there in the warm Dallas night was the man who made her feel complete . . . the man who held the key to her happiness. She had been wrong all these years in thinking that the company was all she needed and wanted in her life. Tillings could never make her as happy as he did and could never need her as much as he did. She knew that, in the next few hours, she would work harder to keep Bryan than she had ever worked to save Tillings. Bryan was leaving, and she wanted him back. Nothing would stop her from getting him. Nothing.

Chapter Fifteen

Sarah called Mildred's house from her car phone but received no answer. She pushed the pedal of her tiny red sports car down and accelerated. Bryan was probably there with Mildred right now. Speeding through the warm night, she thought of her months with him and wondered how she could have made it without him. Without realizing it, she had come to depend on having him near her. She thought of him every morning when she awoke and every night at bedtime. She spent all the hours in between wondering how he had spent his day. Everything she did, she wanted to share with him. Every thought she had, she wanted him to know. Bryan had become part of Sarah's life, even as she tried to keep him out.

She chuckled, remembering the thrill of the press conference announcing "Sarah," the new flagship perfume. Sarah reflected on the excitement of that day as the wind blew through her dark brown hair. Her gold eyes were sparkling slits against the breeze as she steered around yet another curve on her way to Mildred's. The birth of "Sarah" was exhilarating, yet having

Bryan there had made it even more so. She had been aware of his quiet presence behind her as she delivered her announcement and fielded questions. She had felt his eyes on her as she spoke. She had sensed his pride in her ability to handle a room full of seasoned reporters.

From the first day she met him, Sarah had sought Bryan's approval without knowing it. She had thought she was trying to prove something to him, to prove that she was capable of managing Tillings without him, despite its shaky financial picture. In her mind, she had schemed to show him how unimportant he was to her success. She had done everything she could to impress him with her ability. Again, Sarah chuckled. Her understanding of herself had been so small, so narrow. It was not until now that she realized that she had not been driven by a sense of revenge but by a need to win the admiration and respect of this strong, silent man. It took all this time for her to know that everything she did was done to please him. She loved him and needed him as a woman only dreams of loving and needing a man who loves and needs her in return. Her entire body and mind called out for him. She longed for his touch, for the feel of his hands on her body, for the taste of his kisses and the pressure of his lips on hers, and for the pleasure they gave each other as their bodies fused into one at the moment of release.

"You silly fool!" Sarah said to herself. "All this time I thought I wanted revenge on Bryan for his part in the take-over of Tillings Industries. What I really wanted was him. Way to go, girl! Almost lost the man being silly, stubborn, and just plain evil. When I think of the way I treated him . . . It'll be a miracle if he'll even speak to me. I've got to set this right, anyway I can."

Sarah pulled her car through the wide double gates of Mildred's estate and drove down the long driveway to the house. All of the lights were on, as usual, but there was no sign of Bryan's car. Hopping from the car, she straightened her skirt and marched up to the door. The set of her shoulders said that she was a soldier going into battle. She rang the doorbell with warrior-like determination.

An eternity passed as Sarah waited. To her surprise, Mildred opened the door herself. She looked tired and worn. Taking a sip from her drink, she tapped her long red nails impatiently on the glass. She oozed poison like a cartoon witch. Standing with her hand on her hip, Mildred's black hair tumbled onto her black lounging pajamas. Black backless slippers encased her slender pedicured feet. Black pearls adorned her ears and roped around her throat. All she needed was a crow perched on her shoulder to complete the look.

"Yes, what do you want? Haven't you done enough? Why do you bother me at this hour?" she asked tartly, angrily clutching a gin and tonic in her trembling manicured fingers.

"Let me in. We need to talk. Where's Bryan?" Sarah demanded, pushing past her into the marble foyer. A large vase of flowers stood on a table in the center. Beside them rested an opened letter. Sarah glanced at it long enough to see Bryan's letterhead. She turned to face her stepmother and enemy.

"I don't know and, quite frankly, I don't care. He stormed in and out of here a few minutes ago. Said he had some unfinished business before catching the red eye back to Houston. Good riddance. Dallas will be better off without that man. He certainly was a disappointment," Mildred replied, pouring herself another drink from the bar in the living room.

Sarah could tell that Mildred was very upset. Her perfectly coifed hair rested in tangled curls on her shoulders. Tears streaked her makeup. Her shoulders drooped. She no longer looked young and arrogant; she looked her age and older. . . . somehow defeated and tired. She had also consumed many stiff drinks judging from the way she was walking.

"Why, Mildred? Could it be that he did not want you and would not help you to ruin me and Tillings? Is that why you have no use for him? You couldn't manipulate him the way you did Sherwood Michael. Is that it? Now, where is he?'' Sarah almost snarled the words. If she had not been so desperate to find Bryan before he left town, Sarah might have felt pity for the defeated adversary standing before her. But for the moment, all she wanted was to run from this house into his arms.

Mildred turned so quickly her slippered feet became tangled up under her. She had to catch to keep from falling on the floor in her drunkenness. Some of her drink splashed onto the white carpet. For a moment, her expression was one of pure hatred. Even cornered and drunk, Mildred managed to steady herself. As Mildred glared at her, Sarah watched her composure return and her shoulders straighten.

''Something like that,'' Mildred replied tartly with a dry chuckle. ''Anyway, it doesn't matter now. He's gone, returned to where he belongs. He never quite fit in here, never became one of us. He always stood on the outside. He muttered something about needing peace and quiet. The fool! He could have had all of Dallas at his feet, if he'd joined forces with me. I was all set to ruin you once and for all. With his help, I could have paid you and your father back for the pain you caused me. I could have put an end to your precious Tillings Industries. But not Bryan Carson, mister goody-goody. He had to charge in here where he wasn't wanted and make everything better.

''Still, I've never seen a more attractive man. Even your father was nothing compared to Bryan Carson. Looks, money, poise. Oh, well, it's his loss. I gave him the chance, but he turned me down flat. Fool. He could have had it all and me, too. At least he made me a very wealthy woman. The idiot bought out all of my shares of Tillings stock. Can you believe the stupidity of the man? Doesn't he know that it won't be worth a dime by the close of business on Monday? He'll be ruined, destroyed, broke. It serves him right. He could have had it all. No use thinking about him anymore. He's history.

''And you, you little twit. You can drown in a vat of perfume

for all I care. I'm free of Tillings Industries and you, forever.
I'm taking the first plane out of here tomorrow morning. Paris,
London, Rome, Athens. I'm closing the house and going as far
away from here as I can get.''

''Did Bryan say when he would leave Dallas? I have to talk
with him. Do you know where he is?'' Sarah asked impatiently
as she grew tired of her stepmother's feigned glee. She knew
that Mildred was seething inside and was very disappointed
that her plans had been foiled. Money meant nothing to her.
She wanted revenge. She hated not getting get her way.

Shrugging her shoulders, Mildred replied, ''No, and I really
don't care. You and Bryan Carson bore me to tears. The fool
says he did all this for love of you. Stupid man. He prefers
you, a sniveling nothing just like your father, to a woman like
me. He's all yours. I wash my hands of both of you. You two
deserve each other. You can probably catch him at that club
of his. You know the one where all the men gather to talk
business. Gossip is more like it, if you ask me. Your father
spent time there during our marriage. Bryan's probably packing
right now. Look: it's late. You can find your way out, can't
you? I'm going to bed. Big day tomorrow. The world calls.''

Sarah watched Mildred toddle up the long circular flight of
stairs to the second floor. She walked with difficulty from the
effects of drink and the emotional outpouring of the evening.
Flecks of gray hair mixed with the black and sparkled in the
light of the chandelier. For the first time, Sarah saw Mildred
as she was . . . an aging, frightened beauty who had fought
hard and lost everything. Suddenly Sarah realized that she had
finished with Mildred for good this time. There would be nothing more than polite, casual conversation between them ever
again. From now on, Mildred would be no more than an unpleas-
ant memory.

Bryan . . . her mind screamed his name, urging her to hurry.
Sarah ran from the house and jumped into her car. She pressed
the gas petal to the floor and roared around curve after curve.

Downtown Dallas had never seemed so far away. Her red sports car cut through the night air, tires screeching at every turn. She had to reach the club before he left. She had to stop Bryan if it was the last thing she ever did. She could not let him go, not now when she knew just how much she needed him.

Suddenly, Mildred's words echoed in her memory. She had said that Bryan loved her, had risked ruin and bankruptcy for her. If only she were with him now, Sarah would show Bryan how much he meant to her, and how much she loved him, too. She could feel her arms encircle his strong chest and her hands press against his muscular back. The memory of the touch of his lips and the warmth of his breath was real against her own. Her body ached for the touch of his hands, knowing how slowly and deliberately he explored every nerve and pleasure point. She longed for him to pull her under him and take her, to enfold her in his strength, to make her forget everything except the wonder of their love.

Screeching the car to a stop, Sarah pulled up in front of Bryan's club and hastily threw the keys to the waiting attendant. She ran up the stairs two at a time, barely stopping to greet the doorman, who quickly stepped aside. Women were a new addition to the membership of the old establishment and even now they seldom visited the Executive Club unescorted.

Sarah had never joined this elite group, although many had asked her when she became president of Tillings Industries. She remembered that her father became the first black member when the club was integrated years ago. She had always found it to be stuffy and pretentious. She hated the feeling of being watched and constantly assessed. Tillings Industries belonged and often entertained clients there. The company maintained a suite for out-of-town visitors, too. Bryan had occupied it since moving to Dallas, until he could find a more permanent place to live. In his mind, that meant a home he shared with Sarah.

Bryan, however, had no problems with the behavior of the old guard of Dallas and planned to join as soon as he became a resident of the town. During his time living in the suite Tillings rented, he had liked to sip brandy and listen to the latest business gossip. He found it helpful to know the workings of the minds of the major financial players of the city. Since he had not as yet bought a house in Dallas, he made his residence in one of the lavishly appointed suites on the upper floors.

Rushing up to the mahogany reception desk, Sarah asked breathlessly, "Would you telephone Bryan Carson's suite, please? Tell him that Sarah Tillings would like to speak with him. I'll be waiting in the parlor."

"I'm very sorry, Miss Tillings, but Mr. Carson vacated his suite an hour ago. He said he would be returning to Houston tonight. He asked that I forward all of his messages to his home there," replied the clerk.

"Did he leave a message for me?"

"No, Miss Tillings, Mr. Carson left nothing for you. May I be of any assistance?"

"Sorry, but no, thank you. I'll get in touch with him in Houston. Do you think I could take a quick look at the suite? I've never been upstairs, although I authorize payment of the rental fee," Sarah responded with great effort. Her lips curled into an automatic smile as her insides churned with the pain of his leaving.

"I think that can be arranged," he pretended not to notice the pinched look around her eyes. She was a beautiful woman. It pained him to see her in distress.

Following the bell boy, Sarah found herself in the rooms that had until recently been Bryan's home here in Dallas. Pressing a bill into his palm, she closed and locked the door. She wanted to be alone with her thoughts. She needed time to plan her next move. Maybe by looking around where Bryan had lived, she would find some clue as to his frame of mind when he left.

Returning her attention to the suite's living room, Sarah saw that Bryan had not left even a newspaper. The room was immaculately clean and in order. She looked at the dark blue tapestry sofa with the hunt scene design stitched into its fabric. The interior decorator had matched the green of the leaves and grass to the wing chairs that sat opposite it. Throw pillows in the same color as the fox completed the look and gave the room a rather masculine appearance. Sarah could easily see how Bryan could enjoy coming here after work. The mahogany furniture and the heavy gold drapes were somehow comforting and inviting. She could almost envision a gentleman lighting his pipe and resting his feet on the ottoman while reading his newspaper. Everything he could possibly want was within fingertip reach. A well-stocked bar stood against one wall, and the entertainment center was in another. The kitchen was located only steps away.

Turning to the bedroom, Sarah again found no signs of Bryan's stay in this elegant suite. The queen size bed had been remade by an efficient chambermaid. The trash cans had been emptied. A fresh burgundy terry cloth robe monogrammed in gleaming gold threads with the club's circle H lay across the bed waiting for the next occupant. The toilet top was down and covered with one of those discreet notes saying that it had been sterilized. Not even a toothpaste splat on the mirror remained to say that Bryan had once lived here.

The kitchen was equally secretive. No food remnants or dirty dishes lingered anywhere. The refrigerator contained only an unopened jar of the best caviar and a bottle of expensive champagne. The cabinets were bare except for a single box of crackers, Wedgwood bone china, and Waterford crystal.

Nothing remained to tell her how Bryan had lived or how he had felt when he left. Not even a forgotten sock marred the perfection of the suite. The rooms looked as if Bryan had never existed.

But Sarah knew he had not been a handsome figment of her imagination. The pain in her heart told her all too well that he had been very real. Now he was gone, and she was totally at a loss as to how to bring him back.

Standing with her hand on the door knob, Sarah took one last look around the suite's living room. Not even a misplaced pillow marred the view. "What am I to do, Bryan? I've certainly made a mess of things this time, and you're not here to catch me when I fall," she said to the silent room. Like the identity of its inhabitants, kept so well by the impersonal suite, her pain would never be divulged. She switched off the light and closed the door behind her.

"Good night, Miss Tillings," the clerk called as she emerged from the elevator.

"Have a good evening," Sarah called over her shoulder as she walked across the expanse of lobby with her shoulders straight and her head held high. No one must suspect that Bryan's departure was a surprise to her or caused her any pain. She had been Sarah Tillings, president of Tillings Industries, before he came to Dallas. Now that he was gone, she would go on with her life with the same dignity with which she faced every heartbreak or setback that came her way. With her head high, she stepped out into the Dallas night. She muttered good evening to the doorman and accepted her keys from the parking attendant.

As she eased her red sports car into the traffic, Sarah heard the clerk's words over and over in her head. "He vacated his suite an hour ago. . . . returning to Houston tonight . . . forward all messages . . . nothing for you." Bryan was gone and her heart was dead. She felt empty as she turned her car in the direction of her condo and accelerated. For a moment, she thought of following him. It would have been so easy to turn onto the interstate and follow the signs. Maybe if she told him how wrong she had been, he would forgive her and come back to Dallas and to her. No, he would only think she was weak if she went to him. Weakness of any kind was not something that either of them could tolerate.

Sarah's condo was dark and cool. At the touch of a switch, the lights came up, lighting the floral pattern of her sofa. She reached around and turned the dimmer switch. She wanted only as much light as was necessary to see how to walk around the two story condo. The darkness of night suited her mood much better than the brightness of the lights.

She threw herself down on the sofa and rested her head against its back. Bryan was gone. He had returned to Houston. The conversation she had had with him in her office suddenly became even more important. It was the last time they would ever be together.

Sarah rubbed her temples, where a throbbing headache bloomed. The sight of his worn face and the sound of his tired voice would not leave her memory. Their last parting had been painful for both of them. She never would have let him go it if she had known the true nature of his relationship with Mildred. His leaving was all her fault. If she had not doubted his love for her, none of this would have happened. She questioned his intentions, would not accept him, could not trust him, and did not believe his honesty. Now, Bryan was gone forever. He had returned to Houston, leaving her to sit forlorn and alone in Dallas.

She should have believed that he loved her. No man could have made love so tenderly without feeling it very deeply. She remembered the way he had stroked her hair and shoulders, allowed his fingers to linger at her collar bone and then drift slowly down her back to come to rest at the curve of her spine. She could feel the touch of his lips on her nipples, making them hardened into twin points of pleasure. His movements had been slow but deliberate, designed to bring the utmost in pleasure. He had wanted the experience to be pleasurable for her. His own desires were secondary.

Her response had been impatient, urgent. She wanted him to hold her, for them to join together, for the moment of release to begin. She wrapped her legs around his waist and pulled him toward her until they united as one. She breathed deeply as her memory replayed the moment of their union. She grew warm from the flame of her desire for him. She ached to hold him once again.

Sarah covered her face and cried. This time they were not the tears of frustration at being outsmarted by a rival. They were tears of pain that came from her very soul, her inner being. She had loved Tillings Industries too much and believed in Bryan too little. Too late, she had discovered the truth buried deep inside herself. Too late, she had heard the voice that called his name over and over. No one could make her laugh the way he did or make her as happy as he could. Bryan Carson . . . the name had once made her seethe with anger. Now it filled her with pain, knowing she would never see him again.

Sunday came and went in a cloud of agony and confusion. Sarah walked from one room of her condo to the other, thinking and planning. Yet each time she thought she had worked out a way to get Bryan back, she found another flaw and discarded it. She paced the floral Oriental rugs and thought, but hardly ever sat, and never ate.

Her first thought had been to circulate the rumor that she had suffered a nervous breakdown as the result of Mildred's treachery. Almost as quickly as the plan surfaced, she discarded it. She could not afford another run on Tillings stock. The already nervous stockholders would certainly panic when they heard that. Anyway, no one would believe it. Everyone in Dallas knew that there was no love between them.

She could do nothing to frighten the investors, so a minor car accident was out of the question, too. She could not even afford the luxury of a rumored broken heart and a period of seclusion to mend it. She had to be at the helm of Tillings Industries at all times.

Every time the telephone rang, her heart pounded against her ribs with enough force to break them. Her hands shook so badly that she repeatedly dropped the receiver. Sarah could not hide the disappointment in her voice when the caller turned out to be Holly or Frank checking up on her. She appreciated their love and devotion, but they were not Bryan. Too late, she knew that she could find no comfort in anyone except him.

Every room in the condo called his name. His presence filled every corner. His laughter rang through every room. Sometimes her imagination played mean tricks on her, making Sarah think she saw him in the living room, leaning against the mantle with a glass of champagne in his hand. She had to bite back her words to keep from calling out to him.

Sarah felt Bryan's presence most in the bedroom. The smell of his cologne lingered on the pillow where he had slept only two nights ago. She held and caressed it often during the day. That night as she lay sleepless, she wrapped her arms around it and pulled it to her chest. The ache in her heart was too much to bear. With every sigh, she could feel the strength of his fingers as he explored her willing body and drew from her a passion she had never known she possessed for anything other than work and Tillings Industries.

As she struggled to find sleep in her lonely queen-sized bed, she felt the ghost of his body next to hers. She could almost see his sleeping face with the lock of hair across the forehead. The memory of his smile on first waking and finding her next to him filled her with the agony of loneliness. She held his pillow closer and imagined that it was his back as she lovingly stroked it and whispered his name into the silent night. She felt his kisses tease her nipples into hard points of pleasure and draw her womanly warmth from her in rivers of passion. Involuntarily, her body arched for him as she hungered for release from the pain of wanting him. Not finding him over her waiting to enter her moist recesses, she cried and turned her face to the window holding the pillow tightly against her aching body. The pain of loneliness and despair slowly replaced the agony of the unsatisfied passion that burned between her legs.

As the moonlight shone across her bed, Sarah finally drifted into a troubled sleep. Her dreams were filled with Bryan. Together, they sailed the Mediterranean and walked along the islands of Greece. They cruised the Nile and strolled through the Valley of the Kings. They picnicked in Central Park and lunched in the Russian Tea room. They shopped for silver jewelry among the vendors' stalls in Cancun and swam in the Gulf of Mexico. They bartered with the merchants in Istanbul and drank Turkish coffee in a quiet taverna. They frolicked in the waves at Oahu. They danced the night away in Monaco and made love under the stars. She woke up calling his name. When she realized that he was not lying beside her, Sarah hid her face in his pillow and cried herself back to sleep.

On Monday morning, Sarah awoke to the sun streaming through her bedroom window. A new day broke, bright and hopeful. With it came a new determination. She showered and dressed with her usual care, deliberately selecting an apricot-colored water silk suit. Bryan would have loved it, especially the cross-over deep double-breasted effect that accentuated her full breasts and voluptuous hips. With a sigh, she thought he would especially enjoy tearing it from her body before plunging his face against her soft skin hidden underneath. She applied her makeup skillfully to cover any puffiness under her eyes. She coifed her hair carefully. She wanted to show everyone that she was in charge of Tillings and herself. She longed for Bryan, but she had made up her mind that the world would never see her pain. After all, she was Martin Tillings's daughter and the president of Tillings Industries.

The elevator was filled to capacity as she stepped aboard. She smiled and cheerily said "Good morning!" to everyone. Her eyes sparkled a bright gold. She called a happy greeting to the doorman as he helped her into her red convertible sports car. She smiled up at the sunny day as she drove to Tillings Tower. Pretending to be happy actually made Sarah feel better and dulled some of the pain of losing Bryan. Beneath the smile, she ached for him, for the love they had shared and the feel of his body on hers.

She pushed the button for the express elevator to the penthouse floor. People passed by on their way to the coffee shop and newspaper stand in the lobby. They lined up in front of the other elevators to wait for their rides. Everyone seemed happy on this sunny Monday morning in Dallas.

As Sarah rode to the top floor alone, she smiled peacefully. The opening bell on Wall Street had not as yet sounded; no one knew about Mildred's involvement in the stock deal or Bryan's efforts to divert any possible disaster. Before Mildred's actions could cause a stampede, Bryan had taken steps to stop the panic. She smiled softly at the thought that he had done so much for her and for Tillings Industries. With a sad sigh, she wished she could throw her arms around him and thank him. She longed to hold him in her arms and to tell him how much she needed him.

Stepping from the elevator, Sarah straightened her shoulders and walked bravely to her office. Today would truly be a test of her strength. No one must know how much she had lost. No one would ever guess that Bryan took her heart with him when he left.

"Good morning, Holly," Sarah chirped as she entered the outer office where Holly sat scanning the appointment book. Their secretary had not, as yet, arrived.

"Morning, Sarah. You're certainly chipper, considering all you've been through. I thought you'd drag in here this morning looking like something the dog left behind. I know I would have if I'd had your weekend. You're one brave woman," Holly commented. She carefully studied Sarah's face. She was a bit too upbeat after the fiasco of Friday's stock sale and after Bryan's departure on Saturday. Holly had been friends with Sarah for a long time and knew that she often put on a happy face when she was deeply distressed. She would wait a while and then ask her friend for details if she did not volunteer them.

"Why shouldn't I be happy? It's Monday morning and there's work to be done. Bryan may have left us but Tillings Industries is still my company. Mildred tried hard to take it away from me, but Bryan stopped her. By the way, is the board meeting still scheduled for ten o'clock? I need to brief everyone," Sarah replied with careful composure. She would not let even her old friend see her cry. Besides, she was afraid that if she let the tears fall, she would not be able to stop them. She had to keep up the front.

"Sure is. Everyone has called to confirm. They are all quite anxious for news. Is there anything you need for the meeting?"

"No, thanks, Holly. There's nothing anyone can do until Wall Street has been open for a while. I hope Bryan's plan works."

Sarah's office was awash with sunlight. A broad beam fell on her father's portrait. His soft gold eyes seemed to glow as they followed her across the room. She eased into her seat and, for the first time since leaving her condo, allowed her shoulders to droop. It was early, and already she was tired. There was so much work to do . . . a board meeting this morning and a press conference this afternoon, her third in the last week. All this on almost no sleep. She needed the half hour before the meeting to compose herself.

"Sarah," Holly's voice broke the silence of the office. "Turn on the television. A special business report is on. You don't want to miss it."

"Thanks," she answered, reaching for the remote control on her desk. The cabinet door opened and the television appeared. A newscaster spoke, "At the opening bell this morning, large sales transactions of thousands of shares of Tillings Industries stock rocked Wall Street. As you know, Tillings is the black-owned cosmetics empire founded by Martin Tillings. At his death, his daughter, Sarah Tillings, became its president. In recent months, the cosmetics giant has undergone a take-over by Bryan Carson, a high-powered black entrepreneur who specializes in buying companies in trouble, restoring them to health, and selling them off at a sizable profit.

Last week, Tillings announced a new fragrance, named "Sarah," after its president. In the wake of this new success, a major stockholder sold a number of lots, causing speculators to assume that the company was once more in trouble.

This morning as panic selling began, a buyer bought all outstanding shares of the stock. It has been discovered that the buy order was given by Bryan Carson, who has purchased the stocks in the name of Sarah Tillings. Ms. Tillings is now the principal owner of Tillings Industries, holding all but approximately ten percent of the stock. She joins the ranks of the wealthiest women in the country.''

Sarah turned down the volume and settled back into her chair. She allowed the newscaster's words to echo in her mind. . . . ''Ms. Tillings is now the principal owner of Tillings, holding all but approximately ten percent of the stock . . .'' She owned Tillings. The company was all hers, free and clear. This was a dream come true. Bryan's plan had worked.

But it was not enough. For the first time in Sarah's life, she felt lonely and alone. She had always enjoyed being alone, with time to think, knowing that friends were only a phone call away. Now, in her aloneness, she felt lonely. Bryan's arms and love had taught her that something was missing in her life; someone special should be there to share the news . . . someone other than Holly, her devoted friend and confidant.

Yet, no one was there for her, at least not the someone she wanted. Now that every gold-digger and gigolo knew her net worth, there would be plenty of available men knocking on her door. She wanted nothing to do with any of them. They had not been in her life when Tillings Industries was in trouble. They had not helped her to rebuild the company to the glory it had once known, when her father and mother were alive. They had never been there to catch her when she fell. She did not want them in her life now.

Sarah knew who she wanted, and he was in Houston. Bryan had saved Tillings for her when she faced bankruptcy. Now, he had given Tillings to her, and rendered her stepmother harmless, unable to hurt her, ever again. But he was not here with her. She had hurt Bryan by not accepting his love. She had repeatedly pushed him away when he had reached out to her. Now she was alone, and very lonely.

"Oh, Bryan! What a fool I've been! Why did I turn my back on you? Why was I too stubborn to see that you were only trying to help me? Why couldn't I understand that everything you did was because you loved me? I'm so lonely. I need you so. Now you're gone, and I can never get you back. There's nothing I can do to stop the hurt I've done to you. Even if I were to throw myself at your feet, I could never undo the wrongs I've done," Sarah whispered to herself.

Straightening her shoulders, Sarah sighed heavily as she walked to the portrait of her father that hung over the mantle in her office. She felt warm as she looked into his smiling eyes. They were so much like her, or so everyone told her. She was Martin Tillings's daughter, all right . . . same eyes, mouth, and stubborn pride. Her portrait hung beside his. It had been painted during those wonderful months of sharing Tillings Industries with Bryan. The eyes laughed brightly, reflecting a feeling that was gone from her now.

"Sarah, it's ten o'clock. The board members are waiting," Holly's voice pierced the silence.

"I'll be right there," Sarah replied, smoothing her skirt and hair. She walked to her office door and took one last look at her father's portrait. Then she said, "Well, Daddy, I'm off to my first board meeting as the controlling owner of Tillings. It's a new beginning for us. I'm going to make you proud of me, you'll see."

As she closed her door, Sarah heard her father's voice in the recesses of her mind. It said, "I already am."

Chapter Sixteen

Thunderous applause greeted Sarah as she walked into the board room. Holly stood to her right with tears streaming down her cheeks. She was so proud of her best friend that she could almost burst. Jason Parson, her father's banker and long-time friend, dabbed at the tears that dotted his cheeks. He had been waiting a long time for control of Tillings to return to a Tillings from Mildred and assorted other stockholders. Now it had, and he could finally rest. John Fraser, the Senior Vice President for Finance, wiped the tears from his glasses. Patrick Alexander, legal counsel, cheered wildly. The heads of marketing and research and development, Marion Minor and Forest Woodson, raised their cups of coffee in toasts of honor.

Sarah felt her soft pecan cheeks grow warm with embarrassment and emotion. Her eyes glowed amber with the happiness their love gave her. The members of the operating board had stood beside her through the bad times when it looked as if Tillings Industries would close at any minute. They cheered her now that Tillings was on the right path once again.

She took her place at the head of the table with Holly at her side. It was just like the old college days with Sarah and Holly leading the clubs and organizations. She did not know what she would have done without Holly, these last five years. She had been more than an assistant; she had been a source of strength and advice.

She looked around the long mahogany table. Everyone was there except the one person who had made it all possible . . . Bryan Carson. He had given Tillings to her, after disarming her arch-enemy, but he had been deposed himself—removed from her life by her own foolish pride.

As the cheering stopped and all the members of her senior staff took their places, Holly pressed a button signaling for the delivery of the usual board-room food of coffee and donuts. To Sarah's surprise, a cake appeared, instead. It was shaped like Tillings Tower and frosted in apricot-colored icing. Written across the base were the words, "Tillings Tumbles Never More."

The meeting was as sweet as the apricot-flavored icing. All reports were good. Jason Parson made it clear that Tillings Industries would continue to be a valued client. He said that he was sure funds would be made available for any future expansion. To Sarah's surprise, she found out that, before Bryan left for Houston, he had paid off all outstanding loans. Marion Minor stated that orders for "Sarah" had been flooding the marketing department. All morning she had worried that there might not be enough sales support to take all the orders. However, she was happy to have such a problem after the lean years. John Fraser reported that accounts receivable flowed black ink thanks to "Sarah" and Sarah.

At the very end of the board meeting, the members of the operating staff paused for a brief unveiling ceremony as they hung Sarah's portrait on the mahogany-paneled wall next to her father's. The resemblance was uncanny. The same gold eyes sparkled with determination.

Jason Parson hung back when the others had left. He had known Sarah since was a baby. He knew her every facial expression and could read her well-controlled face like a book. He knew that something was bothering her. This morning, of all mornings, she should be happier than she had ever been in her life. Tillings Industries belonged to her. Bryan Carson had saved it for her from the circling vultures, and then delivered it to her, free and clear. And now he was gone. Bryan had been an irritant to Sarah, but now she would no longer be bothered. She should be very happy.

Yet, Jason had seen something spark between Bryan and Sarah. Every Monday at the board meeting, Bryan had sat opposite her at this table. She had tried hard to keep the tension out of her voice and off her face, but Jason had seen it, even if the other senior management staff had not.

At first he thought her tight lips and stiff shoulders covered an animosity she felt toward Bryan for taking over controlling interest in Tillings and infusing it with lifesaving money. She had wanted to be the one to rescue her father's company from his neglect. He had watched her ignore his presence as often as she could. She hardly ever looked in his direction. She acted as if Bryan were invisible.

As the great show of indifference continued, Jason wondered if it did not cover up something other than animosity. He began to suspect that affection was growing in Sarah's heart for Bryan, and that she was fighting against its increasing strength. Watching her at the last meeting when Bryan sat next to her, Jason was convinced that the emotion had grown into love. He had seen her move as far away from Bryan as possible when he pulled the extra seat up next to her. He had also seen the color spread over her cheeks every time he spoke or his hand touched hers. Several times, Sarah's voice had barely been audible from the strain.

Now, on a day when she should be her happiest, with Tillings safe and both of her enemies vanquished, Sarah wore a hangdog expression. Behind her skillfully applied makeup, Jason could see the bags and shadows from lack of sleep that were under her eyes. He stayed behind after the meeting to find out the cause.

"Sarah," he began, "is anything the matter? I thought you'd be jumping for joy with Tillings safe and Mildred and Bryan out of your hair. Is there anything I can do to help?"

She studied his kind face for only the briefest of moments before blurting out, through a torrent of tears, "I love Bryan and now I've lost him. I didn't show him how much I cared because I couldn't trust him. I found him with Mildred and I thought he cared for her and not me. It seems she was trying to use him, to convince him to team up with her against me. He wanted nothing to do with her, but I misunderstood. I turned him away by never giving him a chance to show me how kind and generous he really is.

"Oh, Uncle Jason, I feel so awful. I don't know what to do. I have to get him back but I don't know how. I've spent the last five years of my life being the head of a corporation. I've forgotten how to love, how to be a woman.

"Bryan has left Dallas, and I can't think of a way to get him back. All of my schemes have huge holes in them. I feel so helpless."

Jason could not help but smile at the little girl Sarah who dissolved into his arms just as she had done years ago when something had broken her heart. When she was little, a cup of hot chocolate or a candy had made everything better. He did not think the old remedies would work now that she was all grown up and the president of a major cosmetics company.

Gently patting her back, Jason whispered, "You know, Sarah, everything has a way of working itself out if you give it a chance. I wouldn't be surprised if Bryan isn't as far away as you think. Something tells me he would feel as lost without you as you do without him. Just give him time. He'll be back.

Sometimes a man needs a little space when his pride has been wounded by the woman he loves.''

Jason's voice was so reassuring that Sarah's tears and sobs stopped immediately. She looked up at him through bloodshot eyes and asked, ''Uncle Jason, do you really think he'll be back? I treated him so terribly.''

She had not called him that since she was a little girl. Jason's heart almost burst with love for his old friend's daughter. Quietly he replied, ''I know he will, Sarah. Something tells me he hasn't gone far. Here, take my handkerchief and dry your face. You know, we make a pretty darn good product here. Not a bit of mascara has streaked.''

Sarah took the offered white handkerchief and smiled at his comment about their product. The stainless cloth showed her that he was right about the mascara. Maybe he would be right about Bryan, too.

''Thanks, Uncle Jason,'' she said, ''I don't know what I would have done without you all these years. I'm okay now. I think I'll stay here a little longer before returning to my office.''

Kissing her lightly on the forehead, Jason collected his things and left Sarah alone in her board room. With a smile, he thought that she had grown up rather nicely. Something told him everything would work out for this brave daughter of Martin Tillings.

Alone in the room with her memories, Sarah sat and thought about the happenings of the last few days. She had almost lost Tillings again, only to be saved by the one man in the world she had ever loved, other than her father. Yet, like her father, he was no longer a part of her life. He had left her, too.

In the quiet of the late morning, she sat licking the cake icing from a perfectly manicured finger. The meeting had been a great success, except for one missing element. Bryan Carson no longer sat across the mahogany table from her. He had walked into her life, into that very room, only a few months ago, and now he was gone. She had barely been able to tolerate him when he first arrived, but slowly she had found herself falling in love with him. She could still feel his arms around her. His breath still fluttered on her cheeks from his last kiss. When she closed her eyes, he stood before her with his arms outstretched to pull her close. She wished to cover herself with his body, to sink into the protection of his shoulders and to feel the heat of his flesh. She longed to cover his body in kisses and to feel him cover hers in his warmth.

Even now, Bryan's voice filled her mind with words of encouragement. Sarah knew he would be proud of her—proud that she could stand on her own two feet when in pain, and not dissolve into a puddle of tears. She had seen his pride in the conference room last week as she announced the arrival of "Sarah." Even though he was not with her, Sarah could feel the look of approval as she sat staring at the two portraits. Yes, she was Martin Tillings's daughter, but, at this moment, her heart did not belong to daddy. It belonged hopelessly to Bryan Carson.

Sarah resolved that she would do something to win Bryan's love again. She could not allow him to fade from her life forever, not now that she knew how totally she loved him. She had to have him with her. But how? That was the question.

She considered again the possibility of following Bryan to Houston. She would throw herself at his feet. She would wrap her arms around him and cover his face with kisses. She would beg him to forgive her spoiled, childish actions and misdirected behavior. She envisioned the expression on his face as he opened his door. She knew that at first it would register surprise. But that would change all too quickly. She could see the expression change from the pride of the flattered male ego to sympathy, pity, and hatred. Bryan would not respect and certainly could not love a woman who thought so little of herself as to debase herself by following him. No, that was out of the question. She could not throw herself at him. She would lose him forever if she did.

She paced the room, walking back and forth in front of the twin pairs of watching gold eyes. Her own shone amber from the effort of concentrating. She could have Holly phone him to say that she was ill and calling for him. She could arrange to check into the presidential suite in the hospital. After all, she had contributed heavily to the hospital's capital funds. She was sure the administrator would play along with her charade. When Bryan arrived, he would find her lying in bed, looking very pale and worn. He would fall on the bed and beg her to take him back.

But what would she do when he found out that he had been tricked and that she was in perfect health? How would he react? She did not ponder these questions for long, because Sarah knew that Bryan would leave her again. He would simply say good bye and board the next plane out of Dallas for Houston. She would never see him again. There would be no way of winning his respect after that. No, she could not do that, either.

Pacing, Sarah spoke out loud, "I could send him a simple floral arrangement, something with apricot-colored roses. They would remind him of me. If he still loved me, they would make him want to be near me. I could enclose a note saying 'Thinking of you. Love, Sarah.' He would have to respond out of good manners, probably call to thank me. I would find a way during the conversation to tell him that I love him and miss him terribly."

She stopped pacing as a thought filtered through the web of fatigue. "But what if I can't turn the conversation. He might control it so that the right time to tell him that I love him never comes up. I would hang up feeling even more frustrated than ever. I couldn't stand the thought of hearing his voice and leaving the words unspoken. Worse still, he might speak to me as if I were a love-sick child, someone barely worth the effort, and there might be pity in his voice. I could never bear that.

Worse still, he might not even call. He might send a detached, formal thank-you note in his long looping handwriting. No, something that impersonal would be too painful to bear after our evening and morning of lovemaking.''

Chewing absent-mindedly on the end of her pencil, she knew that sending flowers was out of the question. Too much could go wrong.

Sadly, she slumped into her chair again. Turning her back to the board room door, she allowed the tears to flood her face. The realization was all too real. There was nothing she could do to win him back. Bryan had saved Tillings Industries and given it to her as a gift, a sign of his love and devotion for her. But Sarah had been blinded by her need to rebuild Tillings and had not understood that she had all she really needed in his love. Without him, having Tillings was the same as having a brightly wrapped but empty package. Without Bryan to share the joys of her successes, she had nothing.

Mildred had been right all along. There was something about the Tillings family that caused them to close out everyone and devote all attention to the company. She remembered overhearing her mother and father talking for hours about their plans for Tillings. Sarah had known even then that she had not really been an only child. Tillings had been her sibling. No wonder Mildred had been jealous of both of them. There was no way a stepmother could compete for the father's affection when he so totally loved his ''daughters.''

Bryan knew about her father's devotion to Sarah and Tillings. He often said he admired her father's work ethic. She wondered if Bryan felt paternal about the companies he bought and restored. If he did, selling his shares in Myrna, Incorporated, to save Tillings must have been especially painful for him. Still, he had not hesitated to sell one of his ''children'' to help her. He had loved her that much. Maybe he still did.

Sarah straightened her back and wiped away the tears that streaked her face. Crying would do no good. She had a press conference to run in thirty minutes and she needed all her wits about her. For the moment, she would force her need for Bryan out of her mind and concentrate on giving the performance of her life before the waiting press.

On her way to the press conference, Sarah stopped by Bryan's office. His secretary's head was bent over her computer in concentration as she entered long columns of figures. She barely looked up as Sarah entered the room. The door to his assistant's office was closed. She wondered if Crystal had followed him to Houston. She was very devoted and doted on his every whim.

"Hi, Gayle. Mind if I stick my head into his office for a minute?" Sarah asked, not waiting for an answer. When Bryan occupied the office, she had always been welcome and had always entered unannounced. She did not stop to think that anything should be different, now that he had left.

"Oh, hi, Sarah. Sure, help yourself. It's a bit messy right now. Papers everywhere from the hectic weekend. Can I help you find anything?" she replied a bit nervously. Sarah did not notice. She was too preoccupied with her own thoughts. She did not see Gayle reach under her desk, either, to press the button that sounded a little bell in Bryan's office.

"No thanks. I'm not looking for anything in particular."

"Okay. Give a shout if you need me," Gayle answered, returning to her numbers. From the corner of her eye, she watched Sarah enter Bryan's office. She hoped she had sounded the alarm in time.

Sarah only briefly wondered what Gayle was working on as she opened the door and stepped inside Bryan's office. The fragrance of his aftershave still lingered in the air, as if he had only just stepped out. They had laughingly called this new experimental fragrance "Bryan." He had said that, if she could have a perfume named for her, he should have one that carried his name.

She inhaled deeply of the essence of "Bryan." Its spicy, pungent aroma made her heart skip a beat as she remembered holding him to her and breathing deeply of him. The same smell lingered on his pillow. What had started as a personal joke between them made infinite sense to her now; the aftershave should be named for him. This rich, masculine aroma was Bryan and always would be to her.

Looking around his office, she saw that everything remained in exactly the same place as it had been on Friday. He had packed up nothing. She shook her head sadly. It was obvious that when Bryan Carson was through, he took no memories with him to tie him to the past. Even the publicity photograph of them still sat on the corner of his desk, just as it had last week and the weeks before. The room looked as if at any moment Bryan would return.

Yet Sarah knew that he was gone. She was sure that he would never come back. She had kept him at arm's length, without giving him the encouragement he needed. She had denied her need for him even as she gave herself to him. She had not trusted him completely, although he had proven himself over and over again. The old doubt had always lain between them.

She ran her fingers over the back of the glove-soft blue leather chair. It felt warm under her touch, almost as if he had just gotten up. His desk was strewn with papers. His favorite silver Montblanc pen lay across them. A coffee cup with half drunk cold black coffee sat within reach to the right. He had left everything behind in his haste to be finished with her, Dallas, and Tillings Industries.

A single tear dropped from the end of Sarah's nose onto the pile of papers. It made a puddle in the middle of the top sheet. She brushed it away and hastily left the room without saying good bye to Gayle. She did not want her to see the sadness in her face.

Chapter Seventeen

As Sarah walked into the auditorium, the din of voices grew quiet. Then the pounding of palm on palm as the correspondents and journalists greeted her entry with wild applause replaced the silence. Sarah waved and smiled to acknowledge their tribute. Then she took her place at the podium. "Ladies and gentlemen of the press and members of the cosmetics industry, you have come here today not to bury Tillings Industries but to praise it, to borrow a phrase from Shakespeare's *Julius Caesar*. Yet, you pay homage to the wrong person. I did nothing to save my company. There were no resources available to me. The praise goes to Bryan Carson, who raised the funds at the expense of deflating his personal portfolio. He sold his shares in other companies to buy Tillings stocks as they became available. He then turned over ownership of the shares to me. I did nothing but accept the gift of a dear friend. To Bryan I give my undying love and respect. I will forever be in his debt.

"You may wonder what's in store for Tillings Industries now that I own the vast majority of her shares. Let me assure you that our course is set on success, on building a stronger Tillings, and on restoring her to the glory of my father and mother's days.

"Over the next few months, we will introduce new fragrances that will knock your socks off. Some will be exclusively for women, others for men. One will carry Bryan Carson's name as a token of my gratitude and as a lasting tribute to him. We have also planned a fragrance that is gender blind and smells fabulous on either one. Already some of you have begun to order the new line without ever sampling it. Your confidence in Tillings Industries and in my leadership is greatly appreciated.

"Rest assured that Tillings Industries has returned to its former position as a forerunner in the cosmetics industry. We are a force to be reckoned with. We are here to stay."

As the sound of Sarah's voice echoed through the auditorium, the applause began to build until it reached a pitch greater than the day "Sarah" was born. Sarah stepped away from the microphone and waved. Expecting to see Bryan standing behind her, she looked over her shoulder at the open door. This time Bryan's broad shoulders and smiling face did not fill the emptiness in the doorway or her heart.

Sarah mingled with the reporters and buyers before returning to her office. They all said they were thrilled that Sarah was securely in command of Tillings Industries. She repeatedly checked the door, half expecting to see Bryan leaning against the door jamb watching her. She was somewhat surprised that not a single person asked about him or wondered why he did not stand beside her. Perhaps the gossip vine already carried the story of his departure from Tillings. She appreciated their polite omission. She doubted that she could have answered their questions without crying.

As the press conference broke up, Sarah returned to her office. Opening the door, she found Holly and Frank deep in conversation. They stopped talking immediately when she entered.

"Am I disturbing anything?" she asked, sensing that something important had just been going on behind the closed door.

Frank answered, "No, nothing really. How was the press conference?"

"Everything went just great. The press was supportive, as always. Look, I know something's happening here, but I don't know what it is. Fill me in," she said, looking from one to the other.

"We didn't want to tell you just yet, knowing about Bryan's leaving and all, but I guess you should hear it from us before someone else spills the beans," Holly began. "Frank and I are getting married next month. We're not doing anything big or elaborate. Just a few close friends. We really want to keep it low key."

"Married! That's great. You are just perfect for one another. I couldn't be happier for my two dearest friends," Sarah said as she hugged both of them. Her gold eyes sparkled with true happiness for the first time that day.

She loved them both as siblings, and wished them all the best. She was happy that Frank was finally over his infatuation with her. The way he held and comforted her Saturday night when she was distressed about finding Bryan with Mildred told her that his feelings for her had become quite fraternal. She never could have loved him the way he deserved to be loved, and he had finally accepted it and found someone who would.

Holly would be good for Frank. She was so kind and gentle, yet quite level-headed. She possessed everything Frank needed in a woman. She was warm and responsive to his needs, caring and respectful of his decisions, yet capable of stating her mind and contributing to their relationship on an equal footing.

Frank was perfect for Holly, too. He wanted desperately to lavish a woman with affection and care. He had always married career-oriented, driven, independent women just like Sarah, and found that they did not have the time or desire for the closeness he wanted to give. He had tried to recreate the life his parents gave him, only to find that his wives did not want the same things. He had felt unloved and unnecessary. With Holly, Frank had made a perfect match. When her parents had died, she had missed the stability that came from the togetherness of family, and had looked for it in the men she dated. For the first time, with Frank, she had found it. She already seemed to thrive under his constant care.

As happy as she was for them, Sarah could not help but feel a bit envious of their good fortune. She longed for the closeness they shared, and missed Bryan even more. She knew she would cry at their wedding, not from happiness for her dear friends, but for her own loneliness and her need for him.

The hours passed in happy chatter about wedding and reception plans. Although Frank and Holly had wanted to keep the affair intimate, Sarah insisted on hosting the festivities at the club at which she and Frank were both members. She wanted everyone who was anyone in Dallas to share in the happiness, although she did not plan to invite Mildred to the intimate gathering. She doubted that anyone would notice. Frank and Holly willingly allowed her to make all the plans she wanted. They were glad to see her find happiness in their good fortune. They never spoke about Bryan, but they could see that he was always on her mind. They could tell by the way she constantly checked the door and stopped to listen for footsteps in the hall that she was watching for him.

After they left for the evening, Sarah gathered her things together for the lonely trip home. She had tried to stay at work as long as possible, but, for the moment, there was really nothing else to do. All the department heads had gone home for the night. Besides, she was not in the business of meddling in the day-to-day operation of Tillings Industries. She left that to the highly professional staff she had hired. She was better at crisis management. Thankfully, for the moment, all was calm.

She gazed out the window at the lovely Dallas night. The

view from the penthouse floor of Tillings Tower lifted her spirits. She loved standing high over the city and looking down on it. The lights from the buildings, homes, and cars below twinkled like fireflies in the darkness. She watched the red slug trails of the car tail lights as they whizzed along.

Finally, Sarah pulled herself away from the window. Before she turned out the light, she took one last look at the pair of portraits hanging over the mantle. The gold eyes sparkled gaily. Father and daughter were two peas in a pod. They had both sacrificed everything for the good of Tillings Industries.

On the way to the express elevator, Sarah made a detour to the board room. Passing Bryan's old office, she found the lights out and the door locked. Gayle, his secretary, had long ago left for the day. She could envision him bent over his telephone discussing some element of money management with an investor.

In her mind, he would look up and smile at her when she entered the room. Quickly ending the call, he would hang up the phone, walk to her, and take her in his arms. Kissing first one eye and then the other, he would caress every angle and hollow of her face before giving his undivided attention to her neck and the mound of her ample breasts. Holding her with one hand and unbuttoning her suit with the other, he would soon expose her soft skin to further kisses. His tongue would tease her nipples through the thin fabric of her bra until they were hard painful buds of pleasure. She would moan and pull him still closer.

His free hand would release her breasts from their confinement as she clung to him. As one hand continued to caress them, the other would ease under her skirt to pull away the bikini panties and panty hose. She would moan and sigh as his hard manhood pressed into her thigh, as his fingers played between her open legs.

Her own hands would greedily open his belt and trousers to set his throbbing manhood free of its prison as he flung them away. Her fingers would play around the glans until he moaned into her neck and his knees felt limp. She would rejoice as he finally carried her to the leather sofa on the far wall. As he tossed off his jacket and shirt, she would remove the last of her clothing. She could hear him mutter, ''Sarah, I love you,'' as he eased himself into her. Their rhythm would match and climax in total unity and mutual release. For a long time they would lie half asleep in each other's arms until a renewed hunger drove them to seek the fulfillment of their pleasure once again.

Standing alone and lonely in the deserted hall, Sarah shook off the visions, and the need that gripped her groin and continued her walk to the quiet, deserted board room. Only the hum of the air in the ducts disturbed the stillness. Sarah was not sure why, but she always derived comfort from coming here. Maybe it was the memories of attending meetings with her father and sitting on his lap or at his right. As a little girl, she had loved to watch him conduct business. The sight of him at the helm of Tillings had made her feel secure. Now, she was the captain. Bryan had cleared the way for her to steer a straight course.

She switched on the lights and sat in her usual chair at the head of the table. Bryan's empty seat stood directly across from her. She could almost see him sitting there, nodding approval for her proposals and sipping one more cup of black coffee.

Sarah missed him so terribly. Where her heart once was, there now lay a hole the size of all of Texas. She hurt to think about him. She hurt when she did not think about him. She just hurt all the time. Not even the deaths of her parents had caused her so much pain.

She settled back in the chair and remembered the first time she had sat here waiting for Bryan to saunter in for a meeting. That morning, she had been angry, resentful, and impatient to get on with a relationship she did not want. He was late. The meeting had been scheduled for ten o'clock. It was fifteen minutes past the hour and Bryan had not as yet arrived. She was about to adjourn the meeting and thank everyone for coming when he made his appearance. She remembered the size of him as he filled the doorway. She recalled the sound of him as his voice boomed his greeting. She recalled the arrogance of him as he walked toward her without even a word of apology for keeping her waiting, his outstretched hand a dagger of friendship aimed at her heart.

Sarah remembered the look of him . . . the broad shoulders encased in the black suit, the muscular thighs straining against the trousers, the arms bulging against the fabric, the mahogany skin gleaming with health. Mostly, she remembered the lock of hair that rested on his forehead. He was bold, confident, and self-assured.

She remembered her anger, too. Anger at the thought that Bryan Carson, an associate of her father's that she did not remember and had only read about in the business and society sections of the paper, was all set to ride in on his white horse and rescue her and her company. She loathed the thought of the man. The need for someone like him to undo the mess her father had made of Tillings Industries infuriated her. She fought against her hostile feelings toward her father for being too busy with Mildred to pay sufficient attention to the operation of the company. The idea of being obligated to someone like Bryan Carson, a professional saver of companies, had made her temper flare.

Sarah relived all of her feelings from that day and every day she had spent with Bryan. The memory of the heat and the tension in the elevator when he took her in his arms and kissed her flooded her heart and made tears well in her eyes. The taste of their first lunch at Duke's lingered on her tongue. The fragrance of the roses he gave her to make amends still teased her nose. The sound of the quartet that played at her picnic still sounded in her ears.

And she remembered the sight of Mildred in his arms. She

had seen the green-eyed monster called jealousy for the first time in her life, and she had not liked what she saw and how she felt. Unbelievable pain had torn through her body as she drove away from Mildred's mansion. The drive back to town had been unbearably long. At every turn she had hoped that Bryan would come speeding down the road to catch up with her. Instead, she had arrived at the Tillings Industries Tower alone and confused.

When she saw him with Mildred at the hospital gala and at her mansion and overheard his conversation, she had been convinced that he and Mildred had been planning to ruin her and Tillings. She could still feel the relief that flowed through her body when he told her what had really happened.

The pain of his last letter to her was still fresh in her memory, too. He had loved her so completely and she had treated him so shamefully. She should have shown him how much she loved him. She should have shared her world and her thoughts with him on any number of occasions when they had been together. Instead, she had held back. Even after they had made love, she still did not totally trust him.

Her own inability to reach out for him stung her like a swarm of hostile bees. She would not let the conquering hero take her as a spoil of war. Even after he spoke of his love for her, she would not turn to him. She thought of all the time she had wasted. Her heart screamed in pain for all the missed opportunity to spend her life in his arms, to hold him, and to love him. Now he was gone, and she was all alone in the cold paneled board room of her company.

Sarah sat with her arms folded tightly across her chest. She was too tired from the events of the last few days to cry any more tears. She was emotionally drained. She had not been hurt by Mildred's treachery, since they had never been friends. Betrayal by Mildred was to be expected. It was Bryan's departure after saving Tillings Industries one more time that had ravaged her soul and left her broken into a thousand pieces.

Sarah did not hear the door behind her open as she sat listening to the air blowing in the vent. Her thoughts, as always, revolved around Bryan. She did not hear the tiny creaks of the mahogany floor as someone entered the room. She did not see the man with the lock of black curly hair resting on his forehead take his place beside the fireplace. She did not see him stand under the portraits of Sarah and Martin Tillings that hung over the mantle. She missed the expression of anxiety that tugged at the corners of his usually confident mouth.

"Oh, Bryan, I've been such a fool," she cried to the empty board room. "I should have trusted you. I should have proven to you that I loved you. I should have done anything to keep you from leaving me. Now it's too late. I'll never see you again. All I have is Tillings Industries to keep me warm and that's not enough any more."

"It's never too late, Sarah," his deep voice broke the silence from the direction of the fireplace behind her.

"Bryan! You're still here. Uncle Jason *said* you were still close by," she whispered, hardly daring to hope that he was standing behind her.

Sarah burst from her chair and threw herself against his chest. His arms were strong and comforting as they pulled her closer and closer until the space between them disappeared. Her tears mingled with his as they kissed and clung to each other as drowning people do to life lines.

"I couldn't leave you, Sarah. You're my life. I'd have nothing without you," Bryan whispered into her ear. "I've been here all the time. I've waited for you too long to let you push me away now. Believe me, I tried to go. I got as far as the city limits, but I turned around when I saw the empty vista spreading before me."

"But I didn't see you. Where were you? I expected you to be standing in the doorway during the press conference, but you weren't there. I looked for you all afternoon. I looked in your office earlier, but you weren't there."

"I was afraid to come to the press conference. I didn't think you would want me there and I didn't trust myself not to take you into my arms. I know you stopped by my office because I almost didn't get out in time. You almost caught me. Gayle had just enough advance notice to press the alarm buzzer before you opened the door. I hid in my closet, hoping that you wouldn't look there too. I forgot all about my coffee cup. I left that on the desk half filled with warm coffee."

"You forgot about your after shave, too, but I thought the fragrance was simply lingering after you had left. I never suspected that you were still here. I guess I should have realized something was up, since your office was such a mess and Gayle was so hard at work on figures for you. And Uncle Jason had a strange twinkle in his eye. Why did you stay? I all but forced you to leave."

"I got to thinking about the years of waiting for you to grow up ... the years of watching your every move from afar. I don't want to be away from you ever again. I can't stand the thought of watching you run Tillings Industries without being here with you. I want to be part of your life, part of Tillings. Now that the company is all yours, maybe you'll be able to trust me and let me share the good times and the bad with you. I want to go to sleep with you at night and wake up with you in the morning for the rest of my life."

"Bryan, of course I trusted you—only I was too stubborn and childish to admit it at first. I didn't like you very much in the beginning but, deep inside, I knew you only wanted what was best for Tillings. You saved the company for me. You gave my father's company a rebirth and a new vitality. I took your kindness and love and acted like a spoiled child who couldn't have her way. I even accused you of wanting Mildred and of working with her to ruin Tillings and me. Ridiculous, I know, but that's what insecurity will do to a person.

"The funny thing is that I had to fight against myself and my feelings as hard as I fought against you. I've loved you and needed you for so long, but my pride wouldn't let me show it. The time in the board room when I all but fell into your arms, I almost admitted how I felt about you then. Later, in the elevator, I almost gave in to my feelings again. If I hadn't been so determined to prove that I could run Tillings, I would have come to you sooner. By the time I felt comfortable with loving you after our night together, I found Mildred in your arms. I was shattered and didn't know what to believe. I thought I'd made a mistake in trusting you. I know better now.

"I don't know how to ever repay you for all you've done. My father's memory will live on forever, now that Tillings is safe."

"I know how you can replay me. I've watched from the sidelines of your life for so long, knowing that one day you would be ready to accept and trust me. Now it's time for us to make a future together. Will you marry me, Sarah? I love you and need you in my life."

"You want me after all the trouble I've been and after all the pain I've caused you? Well, you certainly do believe in lost causes. Yes, Bryan, I'll marry you. I'd love nothing better than to be Sarah Tillings-Carson."

Bryan gently pulled her into his arms and sealed their verbal contract with a kiss that conveyed more than words ever could. His hands explored her body with a gentleness that told her that he loved and cherished her. Sarah breathed a sigh of contentment and relaxed against his strength. For the first time since her father's death, she felt at home and totally safe. The portraits hanging over the mantle smiled down on them.

Hand-in-hand, they walked over to the big windows overlooking the Dallas night. They watched the lights below winking up at them. Each silently imagined the people down below, watching television, playing with their children, making love . . . living happy lives together. Soon they would join them and become twinkling lights in the Dallas sky.

When they looked at the portrait of her father over the fireplace, Martin Tillings smiled a look of complete approval. He easily could have been saying that he could not have picked a better son-in-law if he had tried. Sarah knew that he was giving them his blessing.

Sarah's portrait reflected her own happiness. The eyes in the painting sparkled golden, but not as brightly as Sarah's as she looked up at Bryan. Gently, she pushed the lock of hair from his forehead and pulled his face down to hers for a kiss. They melted together as their arms wrapped around each other, preventing the other from slipping away. She eased her arm through his and led him out of the board room. The grandfather clock chimed ten o'clock. The night was still young. There was a lot of living and loving to be done in the hours before morning. Sarah knew that their evening would start as soon as they reached her condo.

ABOUT THE AUTHOR

Born in Washington, D.C. in 1950, Courtni C. Wright graduated from Trinity College (D.C.) in 1972, with an undergraduate degree in English and a minor in History. In 1980, she earned a Master of Education degree from Johns Hopkins University in Baltimore, Maryland. She teaches high school English at the National Cathedral School in Washington, D.C. She was a Council for Basic Education National Endowment for the Humanities Fellow in 1990. She lives in Maryland with her husband, Stephen, and their son, Ashley. Her children's books including JUMPING THE BROOM (1994), selected for the Society of School Librarian's International list of Best Books of 1994; JOURNEY TO FREEDOM (1994), named a Teacher's Choice book by the International Reading Association; and WAGON TRAIN (1995) were published by Holiday House, and her scholarly work on Shakespeare, entitled THE WOMEN OF SHAKESPEARE'S PLAYS was published by University Press of America. She has served as consultant on National Geographic Society educational films on the practice and history of Kwanzaa, the history of the black cowboys, the story of Harriet Tubman, and the African American heritage in the West.

Look for these upcoming Arabesque titles:

October 1997

THE NICEST GUY IN AMERICA by Angela Benson
AFTER DARK by Bette Ford
PROMISE ME by Robyn Amos
MIDNIGHT BLUE by Monica Jackson

November 1997

ETERNALLY YOURS by Brenda Jackson
MOST OF ALL by Loure Bussey
DEFENSELESS by Adrienne Byrd
PLAYING WITH FIRE by Dianne Mayhew

December 1997

VOWS by Rochelle Alers
TENDER TOUCH by Lynn Emery
MIDNIGHT SKIES by Crystal Barouche
TEMPTATION by Donna Hill

TIMELESS LOVE

Look for these historical romances in the Arabesque line:

BLACK PEARL by Francine Craft (0236-0, $4.99)

CLARA'S PROMISE by Shirley Hailstock (0147-X, $4.99)

MIDNIGHT MOON by Mildred Riley (0200-X; $4.99)

SUNSHINE AND SHADOWS by Roberta Gayle (0136-4, $4.99)